The Gardener's Wife

A Novel

By

Edeana Malcolm

TimeSagas Publishing
Victoria, BC
2013
~~

Discover other titles in *The Compleat Gardener Series*
by Edeana Malcolm

Book 1: The Serpentine Garden Path
Book 2: The Gardener's Wife
Book 3: Letters from the Gardener
Book 4: A Garden in the Wilderness

Available at edeana.com

Covers: Photographs of the ruins and garden of Ellon
Castle, Ellon, Scotland, taken by the author in 2000

For my mother, Gladys Olive Dean Malcolm, with love

Table of Contents

Chapter 1

London, Spring, 1780

Susan gasped with the sudden sharp pain. She held her breath to hide it from her children, but Ellie stared at her, eyes wide with fear, and James scrambled up on the bed beside her.

"The children should not be in the room with you, madam." The midwife's voice was sharp and certain.

Susan glared at her. They were too young to be left alone. Where was her husband John? He should have arrived by now. Mary had been sent to fetch him hours before. The midwife already knew this, so Susan said nothing, trying instead to concentrate on managing the slippery ache inside of her.

"Have you no other servants?"

Susan shook her head, incapable of speech while in the pain's tight grip.

Ellie began to cry.

The midwife lifted James from the bed, placed him on her hip, and then scooped up Ellie with one hand. "I shall find a servant at your neighbour's to mind them." She walked out of the room with a child on each of her ample hips. They stared over the midwife's shoulders at their mother but did not even have time to open their mouths to cry before they were gone.

Susan was momentarily relieved to be alone with her pain. Then that feeling too abandoned her and panic arrived to take its place. Where was John? His work was but a half-hour's distance by foot and yet Mary had been gone for hours already. For a brief, unwelcome moment, she imagined that her husband was dead, and that she and the children were left a charge on the parish. That is what happened to a mother without means. Her children went to the workhouse, and there they would likely die of too much work and too little food. In the midst of this horrid vision, another pain gripped her, this time building to an intensity that she almost welcomed to divert her mind from her fears.

As she wrestled with this agony, lying almost senseless, and sweating from the effects of labour in the afternoon heat, she heard the midwife's cool voice again. "It will not be long now, madam."

"The children?" she whispered.

"The surly maid upstairs is minding them, but you will have to pay her when this is done. Have you enough money, madam?"

As quickly as it had clutched her, the pain let go and Susan was annoyed. She did not want to be reminded of the demands of trade at a time like this. Besides, John always paid their debts. "Yes, yes, of course."

But if John did not return, there would be no money and no means to pay even the midwife. What would she do?

She would go to her parents and beg them to take her back in. Perhaps they would relent and forgive her, or at least provide for her children. They had a great deal of money, so much that she had never even understood its necessity when she was growing up. In her ignorance, she had willfully married her father's gardener against her parents' wishes, and they had disowned her. Now money was the only thing that she could think about some days.

Another pain seized her.

"They are very close together now. Let me look." The midwife lifted Susan's chemise and peered between her legs. "I can see the crown."

As if this were the permission she had been waiting for, Susan surrendered to the ineluctable force of nature and began to push and bear down. Yet it was still another quarter of an hour before, at last, the baby's head emerged fully, and then the rest of its tiny body slid out like a slippery fish.

The midwife placed the newborn on her chest where it squirmed, thrashing its tiny arms and legs about and squishing its tiny face. An animal sound like a bleating lamb emerged weakly from between its quivering lips.

"'Tis a boy."

"That it is," Susan said as she examined all of his parts and counted his fingers and toes.

The midwife finished cleaning up the afterbirth and collected it in a chamber pot to be buried in the garden later.

The baby was beginning to discover his voice and his bleating was growing in volume. "Let me wash and swaddle him now." The midwife took him from her.

Susan lay back on the bed exhausted. The thought of the chores still to be done rose in front of her seemingly insurmountable. When the midwife left, she would need to feed the baby and retrieve her children from the neighbour's servant. Where was John? She wanted him to help her. And Mary. Would she ever see them again? Or was she alone? She did not want to think these thoughts. She would have the midwife bring the children to distract her before she left.

"Can you fetch the children for me now?"

"Not yet, madam. First you must be washed and dressed too."

Susan thought of her own mother, always perfectly groomed and presentable, never in disarray, and a desire to hold her baby overcame her.

"Let me hold him," she demanded.

The midwife ignored her and continued her swaddling.

The memory of her mother's coldness to her when she was a child always filled her with such anxiety that she wanted to smother her own children with love.

Finally the midwife finished wrapping the baby and handed him to Susan. Only his squished little face was visible now, but at least he looked contented.

"Would you go and fetch James and Ellie now?" Susan asked.

"You are not dressed yet."

"I will dress while you are gone," she said without the least intention. Instead, while the midwife went to the neighbour's to retrieve the other children, she lay in the bed, memorizing the baby's face and cooing at him. He stared back in silent fascination.

Sometime later, James and Eleanor toddled in, their faces solemn, and James again climbed on the bed with her. "Mama," he said and grabbed at her breast.

The midwife clucked her disapproval. "I told you that you ought to be dressed first."

James was staring at the bundle on his mother's lap.

Susan showed him the baby. "This is your little brother."

"Baby?"

"Yes, he must have a name, mustn't he?" John was not here to help her decide. They had thought of a dozen or more names, spoken them aloud, tried them out, settled on a few. There was only one name in her mind right now, and it was not one that they had considered. "John," she said. "Just like Papa. His name is John."

"John," his older brother repeated.

Eleanor, still hanging on to Susan's chemise, tried to mouth the name too. "Don, Don," she repeated, encouraged by her mother.

"I shall go now," the midwife announced. "You know where to reach me for the bill."

"Good-bye," Susan said, glad to see the last of her. Then she laid the baby beside her and turned to Ellie. "Do you want to come on board?" Ellie nodded, so she pulled her up on the bed. "Let us pretend that we are on a ship," she said to them, "and we are sailing to somewhere safe."

~~*

At Vauxhall Gardens, a light breeze blew between the orderly lines of plane trees, stirring the gardener's hair and touching his cheek like a soft kiss. John Dean uncurled his back slowly and stood up. He felt a sharp spasm in his lower back. He had been bent too long, pulling weeds in the shrubbery. As he stretched out to lessen the pain, his eyes skimmed over the fashionable people in their boxes in the amphitheatre eating their sweetmeats. By their number, he calculated that it was getting late in the day, almost time to go home to his family, he noted happily.

One of the ladies among the bon ton, wearing a gown so absurdly wide that it would not be contained on one chair, was attempting to sit between two gentlemen. She began to giggle and the ship on the top of her high hair rocked as if a storm had risen suddenly. A shipwreck seemed imminent, but the lady grabbed the ocean on her head and sat down, merrily displacing the gentlemen on either side of her.

John scowled and thought of Susan. He imagined that she too might have dressed so ridiculously had he not married her and rescued her from the gentry. He would not have given a second glance to such a silly creature. As he dismissed the vision from his mind and turned to resume his weeding, he caught sight of their servant Mary coming up the Grand Walk, searching for him in the shrubbery. Immediately, he knew that it must be time for Susan to give birth again. He hallooed her and she ran to meet him, her face so strained and anxious that he was suddenly concerned. Perhaps this third birth was not proving as easy as the first two had been.

"Is there aught the matter, Mary? Is Mrs. Dean not well?"

"No, no. She is fine although she is in childbirth."

"Then what is amiss?"

"Oh, sir..." She was unable to finish her statement, overcome by tears.

John was at a loss what to do. He pulled a handkerchief from his pocket and handed it to her, looking away. He could not bear to see young ladies cry. Fortunately, Susan seldom did so. "Try to compose yourself, Mary, and resume your speech."

"Thank you, sir." She wiped her eyes and blew her nose before beginning again. "You cannot imagine what an ordeal I have come through. There was a great mob close by the Palace of Westminster and even more crowds coming across the Westminster Bridge towards the Palace. It was nearly impossible to move against the tide of people. I was terrified at every moment of being knocked over and trampled to death."

"A mob! What was their business?"

"I do not know, sir, but they wore blue cockades and carried a banner that read 'No Popery.'"

John had almost forgotten that there was to be a rally today. If it were not for the necessity of making a living and caring for his family, he would have been a part of that "mob" as Mary called it. On Sunday, the preacher had condemned the Catholic Relief Act and urged his parishioners to aid Lord George Gordon, president of the Scottish Protestant Association, in delivering a petition to Parliament. John wanted as much as anyone to see the repeal of an Act that was intended to relax the restrictions against Catholics in the kingdom. As far as he was concerned, it was naught but an excuse to gather more soldiers from among the Catholics in Ireland and the highlanders of Scotland in order to fight the war in America. It pleased him to hear that Gordon's call to action had found enough support to be considered a "mob," although he suspected that Mary's distress had caused her to exaggerate.

"I am sure that I do not want popery any more than the next person," she continued. "But to have my life come so close to being ended because of the pope! I had no notion that he was even in London!"

John smiled inwardly at his servant's ignorance. "He is not, Mary. 'Tis naught but a rally to make sure that the pope's influence never again predominates in the British Isles."

She looked somewhat relieved at his comments, and he suggested they attempt a return trip. "It will not be such a difficult journey in going back. We will at least be traveling in the same direction as the petitioners," he assured her.

So, when Mary was sufficiently recovered, they set out and joined the throng of people still crossing the Westminster Bridge. John soon learned that Mary had not exaggerated in the least in her description of the mob. While perhaps 20,000 people had been hoped for at the rally, he reckoned that there were tens of thousands more than that number, a seething tide of mankind stretching out for miles, farther than the eye could see, sweltering in the heat of the late afternoon. John immediately sensed the danger: there was an undercurrent of restlessness and enough ruffians in the crowd to provoke violence. Indeed, he could see that some violence had already been done. Several carriages were lying like vacant boxes on the ground, their wheels removed and their windows smashed. He tried to escort Mary around the shards of glass scattered on the road, wondering as he did so what had become of the carriage occupants. For once, he was glad to be on foot.

His principal thought was to remove himself and Mary to safety at once, but it was difficult to make their way through the shuffling bodies of shouting men. The crowd was thickest as they neared the Palace of Westminster where Parliament was sitting.

One of the scoundrels called out to him, "Where's your cockade?"

John wanted to upbraid the man for his rude manner, but in his situation, protecting Mary and trying to get home to his pregnant wife, he did not dare.

"I am for your cause, sir," he said to placate the man, "but unfortunately a pressing personal matter makes it impossible for me to join you."

The man looked taken aback at John's Scottish accent, but let him pass with only a sneer.

These were not Christian men at all, John thought. Their behaviour was decidedly heathen. He was embarrassed and ashamed by the words, ill dress, and unruliness of the crowd, and he was heartily relieved that his own concerns had prevented him from joining their number. He took Mary's hand in order to keep her secure and tried to hurry on, wishing that he had a blue cockade himself to make his way more safely through the mob.

By the time they reached home, his third child was already born. John smiled fondly at his wife and child, and Susan burst into tears. He removed the baby delicately from his wife's arms and held him close.

"What kept you so long?" Susan asked. "I was so afraid that I would never see you again that I named him 'John'."

"What? You hae named him without my consent?" In spite of his words, he was pleased.

The baby gave him a good strong kick in the ribs with the heel of his foot, knocking loose his swaddling clothes as he did so, and John smiled at his namesake. My name, he thought, but his mother's spirit, and the bairn, as if to prove it, began to cry lustily.

"You have not answered my question," she said.

Before John could reply, Mary began describing in great detail the tumult they had witnessed. John could see that Susan was only half attending, being worn out by her own ordeal, so he interrupted the maid and handed her the baby, asking her to take him from the room to give his wife a respite.

When they were alone, Susan asked him. "Was it really as bad as she described, John?"

"Aye, 'twas as bad and worse. I should not think it safe to go out of the house until the mob is dispersed."

"Truly? Are there that many people in the streets?"

John shook his head soberly. "I pray God that the civil war in the colonies has not found its way to our doorstep." She looked at him with such frightened eyes that he was almost sorry he had mentioned it. Long ago, before he had met her, before he had even come to England, he had considered emigrating to America where his older brothers had gone. He was grateful that the path of his life had led him away from that land, where war was being waged, and he often prayed for the lives of his two brothers. Still, he had not entirely abandoned his dream. He had read the Declaration of Independence and it had moved him, rekindling his passionate yearning for a society where a man would be judged by his work alone and not by his social class or religion. When the war was over, if his own situation did not improve, he would consider emigration once again. But he said nothing of this to Susan lest he alarm her.

The rioting, which had begun on Friday, June 2, abated somewhat on Saturday, but on Sunday, which was the King's birthday, it began again in earnest, confirming John's opinion that this was no Christian crowd. He did not venture out to work on Monday, fearful of the mob that was roaming the streets, looting and rioting. Mary helped him fashion a banner from a bedroom sheet with the words 'No Popery' painted in blue. This they placed in the window of their home in order to discourage vandals. On Tuesday night, the family watched from that same window the fires that were burning on Holgate and Ludgate Hills to the north of Westminster.

In spite of the violence raging out of doors, a cozy kind of peace reigned in the Dean household. John enjoyed the time he spent with Susan, alleviating her of some of the burden of caring for the three children. Finally, on Wednesday, martial law was declared and on Thursday, the King sent out the militia to crush the rebellion. On Friday, a week after the rally, John walked back to work at Vauxhall Gardens. When he passed by the Palace of Westminster, he was relieved by the sight of a regiment of Horse Guards patrolling its perimeter. The cobblestones rang with the clip-clop of the hooves and, in the cool morning air, the horses seemed to breathe fire. The sight of the mounted soldiers was fierce enough to quell the heart of any would-be rioter.

When John arrived at the Gardens, his employer threatened to dismiss him for his long absence. Apparently the riots had not made a whit of difference to the *bon ton*. They had continued to patronize the Gardens while London was besieged. In the end, he persuaded his employer only to dock his wages for the time lost, even though it was an expense the young family could ill afford.

John soon forgot that he had ever been attracted to the cause that had precipitated the riot and was relieved when he learned that Lord George Gordon had been arrested for his part in disrupting the peace of London life.

London, Summer, 1782

John walked through the Ladies flower garden and scrutinized the flowers, searching for those which pleased the palate of scent as well as the palette of colour. The first odor to strike him was the pungent perfume of phlox, but he knew that Susan preferred a subtler bouquet. The sweet smell of stocks called to him, but he did not tarry over them either because the carnations' bright colours and cinnamon scents demanded his attention. They would last a long time once cut, he thought. Although such a consideration suited his practical temperament, this was a gift for Susan. So, his decision finally came to rest with the sweet peas, whose aroma and pastel colours he knew she favoured.

She would have a nosegay of sweet peas then. He set about to cut a variety of colourful blooms, choosing those with the longest stems. He hoped the delicate flowers would withstand the hour-long walk home in the sweltering heat. Last year the family had moved from their apartment in Westminster and taken less expensive lodgings in the City. Westminster had always been beyond John's means, but it had had three assets to recommend it: first, it had been within easy walking distance of his workplace in Vauxhall just across the Westminster Bridge; second, it had not been far from the Presbyterian Church in Covent Garden; and third, but most importantly, it had been a more elegant address for Susan, who had been raised to expect a higher position in life.

However, the birth of their third child, and its attendant expenses had finally convinced them that they could no longer afford to affect a position in society which they did not hold, and so they removed to the cheap, but still respectable address of Fetter Lane. John had to walk an hour or longer to his work at the Vauxhall Gardens, and a somewhat shorter distance to his church on Sunday, but he did not complain. He felt acutely the embarrassment of seeing Susan descend even further in the world's assessment, but it would have been wrong to complain. Of greater value than wealth, God had blessed them with health, which gift John daily improved with his increased perambulation.

~~*

Susan was standing at the looking glass tying a ribbon around her neck when she saw his reflection in the glass. He looked tired. The three toddlers at her feet squealed with delight and jumped up. "Papa," James cried, putting his arms out to greet his father. John did not pick him up as he usually did, so James wrapped his arms around his father's leg.

Then Ellie let go of her mother's skirt and clutched his other leg.

"Do you know what day it is today?" Susan asked him.

John pulled some flowers from behind his back, and she smiled at the cascading sweet peas.

"You remembered my birthday."

As he was unable to walk with a child attached to each leg, she went to him and took the flowers. Johnny, the youngest, toddled beside her, and pushed his sister so that he could take her place at his father's leg. Ellie screeched, and John bent down to pick her up, planting a kiss on her fat cheek.

"They are beautiful," Susan said, burying her nose in the blooms.

John was going through his evening ritual of kissing the children, and Susan waited her turn patiently. When he had put down the last child, he kissed her lightly on the cheek as well.

"I hope you will do better than that later," she smiled at him coquettishly.

"I promise I will." He returned her smile. "Let me put the flowers in water." He took the nosegay from her and left the room with the children toddling after.

Susan returned to her image in the looking glass, frowning at the reflection. It had been five years since she had met him, and her face seemed to show every one of those years. She looked as weary as he did. She tried a smile and different creases formed.

John returned, this time alone. She looked at him, replacing the smile on her face with a pretty pout. "Where is my proper birthday kiss?"

"You seem a little peevish today," he responded. "Is anything the matter?"

It was not the response she had hoped for, so she tried a different tack. "Do you know how old I am?"

He did not answer immediately and seemed to be counting mentally the years from the time he had met her. "I am twenty-one," she said, impatient with him. "I am twenty-one," she repeated, hoping he would realize the significance of the number, but he said nothing. "You do not remember." She was disappointed.

Five years before they had gone together to her parents and professed their love for each other. Her father had immediately dismissed him from his employment as the head gardener on the Kirke estate. Then, he had asked her to wait for him until she was twenty-one, that being the age of consent in England. She had thought this to be an eternity, especially when her parents had arranged her marriage with a man she disliked. Then she had run away to John, arriving at his doorstep in the middle of the night. He had had no choice but to elope with her to Scotland in order to save her reputation. She had gotten what she wanted, but she could not have imagined the result. Her parents had not only disowned her, but even worse, had placed John on a black list so that he was unable to find employment as a gardener on any estate of consequence in England. He was considered to be a common thief who had stolen a rich man's property.

"Aye," he said. "I remember."

"You do not look happy about the memory."

"On the contrary, I am glad we didna wait. I cannot imagine a life without James and Eleanor and little Johnny. I cannot imagine coming home from work every day and not meeting you at the door with your sweet smile."

"You do not lie very well, John."

"That is because I do not lie, Susan. I do not regret a moment of the last five years. Do you?"

"I love you, John, and I love our children, but you were right when you said that I was silly and impetuous. We had three children in the first three years! I am exhausted, and we are impoverished! How can I not regret it? How can you not regret it! You are lying to me, I know you are."

He shook his head. "I am not. Our children are a bountiful harvest from our maker and they are all the riches I will ever need. I dinna blame you; indeed, I love you as you are, even your silliness." He added, smiling.

She was not impervious to this smile, but she pressed on. "Perhaps you do not blame me, but you must surely blame my parents. Even though we named our first two children after them, they have neither forgiven us nor even acknowledged our existence."

"That is their loss. I pray that they may change their mind one day, but I dinna require their approval for my happiness. Do you?"

Susan said nothing. She wished for it of course. As long as her father blacklisted her husband, he would not be able to make enough money to support his family. How could she not blame her parents for their intransigence? It was their grandchildren who suffered for it.

John tried to show her that he did not blame her by giving her the kiss she had asked for, and Susan finally succumbed to his charms.

London, Autumn, 1783

The streets south of the Thames still held traces of the countryside, though the old mansions here and there were being torn down and the former fields were rapidly becoming building sites for housing developments. John admired the small two-story clapboard houses that were being erected and wished that he had the means to purchase one for his growing family. As he walked towards London Bridge, he came to the older and more densely populated area of Southwark. There he crossed the Bridge and entered the business section of the City. Here the narrow, cobble-stoned streets were quiet now, the bankers and other businessmen having long since made their way home. At his lodgings, he usually opened the door to a happy chaos, but today was different.

The children were sitting on the floor crying at the frightening sounds emanating from the bedroom. He realized immediately that Susan must be in labour.

Mary greeted him. "You have arrived in time for the birth this time," she said smiling. "The midwife is in with the mistress, and all seems to be going as it should."

"God be praised!" He removed his cap and jacket and hung them on the rack. "Would you let Mrs. Dean know that I have arrived and that I shall mind the children." Mary nodded and went in to the bedroom to impart the comforting news.

"Come, my bairns," John cried, feeling somewhat like Jesus suffering the children to come unto him. "Dinna fash. Your Mama is in the capable hands of God. Let us pray together that He will care for and protect her."

He sat down with them, making a little circle, and showed them how to put their hands together and close their eyes to pray. Though he did this every evening, this was the first time that they all obeyed without fidgetting. The cries of their mother must have put the fear of God into them, he thought and wondered what would affect the same change in her. They had been together for six years and, by his standards, she was a heathen yet, but he loved her and would love her till the day he died. So he prayed for her, earnestly, lovingly, remembering how she had given up everything for him, and how she had given everything to him: these three beautiful bairns seated beside him, and another one whose cries he could hear just now coming from the other room.

"Let us thank God for the gift of new life, children."

~~*

Susan was sitting up in bed, and Mary stood beside it with a bowl of soup.

"You have to eat so the baby will have milk, madam."

She could sense that Mary had no more patience with her. Susan could not explain her lack of will. A kind of lassitude had invaded her spirit and it felt too much effort to raise her limbs, never mind to get up and move about.

"There will be more food for the rest of you if I do not eat," she said, aware of, but unable to curb, the petulance in her voice.

"What about the baby? Do you want Sweet William to die?"

Sweet William. That was Susan's name for him. It was the name of a flower and a line from a song that she had sung a long time ago, or so it seemed to her, when she had once been in love. "Sweet William died of love for me, and I will die of sorrow." Such melodrama, she thought, but she could not keep herself from wallowing in it.

"Eat your soup, madam."

Susan could hear the anger in Mary's voice now. Perhaps she had gone too far.

"Fetch me my bairn," she said.

In spite of her anger, Mary smiled then. "Your bonny wee bairn?" She affected a Scottish accent like John's.

"Aye. Fetch him." Then Mary left Susan with her soup and her misery. Sweet William would have his supper soon. She started to sing that sad and sugary song because it suited her mood so well and perhaps it would purge her.

~~*

Something had to be done. There was another mouth to feed from a fund that did not provide for the opened mouths already sucking from it. It was impossible to let Mary go: Susan was already unable to cope with the burdens that mothering and housekeeping demanded of her, and the children were still too young to help. Besides, it would not be possible to find someone else willing to do so much for so little. John could think of no other economies he could make that he had not already put into practice.

So he went through a list in his mind of the people he might turn to for assistance in this time of need. He would not ask for money. He wanted only a more remunerative employment. It was no use applying to Susan's parents: they had returned all of his previous letters unopened. His own family in Scotland had no connections. There was only one person he could think to appeal to, and that person was Herbert Fitzwilliam, a distant cousin of Susan's on her mother's side. He was the man that Susan had been engaged to marry at the time of their elopement.

One might be surprised that John should consider this jilted suitor as someone who would aid them now, unless one already knew the gentleman, for it was he who had given John the funds required to undertake the elopement with Susan, a fact that John had never divulged to her. He had also never told her that through all these years he had been setting aside a tiny sum from his wages every month in order to repay Fitzwilliam for his uncommon generosity.

As great as his need had been, John would not visit Fitzwilliam to ask for his assistance until he was able to repay him. After six years of effort, he had at last amassed the sum required, and, before the temptation to spend it on his family became overwhelming, he went directly to the gentleman's London house and enquired after him. Fortunately, he was in town.

Fitzwilliam greeted John with an enthusiastic and uncomfortable hug.

"Dean! It is so good to see you again at last! Have a seat. Stay a while. Where have you been hiding? I have been so hurt that you have not come to visit me before this. How long has it been? Five years at least, I'd say."

"Six years, sir."

Fitzwilliam seemed not to have heard and continued. "And how is your good wife, the former Miss Kirke?"

"Mrs. Dean is well."

"I am so glad to hear it. Have you any children that I might enquire after their health as well?"

"Aye, sir. We have three sons and a daughter."

"Three sons! Upon my word! Three sons and a daughter! That is amazing, Dean. But you were always such a prodigious gardener that I ought not to be surprised by your procreative abilities."

"I thankee, sir," John said, though he was not sure that the remark was meant as a compliment. He began to wonder if he should ever be asked to state the purpose of his visit.

Fitzwilliam finished chuckling and ordered his footman to fetch them some sherry. "We must drink a toast to your productivity, my good friend. It has been a long time since I have laughed so heartily, sir. Five… or did you say? six years, at least. I am so pleased that you have come to enliven my day. I was about to leave for Parliament. Can you imagine anything more dull? No, I suppose you cannot. Not in your life with your beautiful wife and all of your babies about you. When I think what a fate you have saved me from, I must thank heaven. I have to ask, how do you tolerate it, Dean?"

"I must protest, sir..." John was about to say when the footman arrived with a decanter of sherry and two beakers on a tray, and Fitzwilliam interrupted him.

"No, no, Dean. I know that you are some kind of dissenter, and probably an abstainer at that, but I must insist you drink a toast with me. It is most probably a lack of alcohol that has made you such a prodigious sire. Perhaps you ought to drink more as an antidote, my good man. Have you considered that?"

Fitzwilliam poured the sherry into the cups and passed one to John. Then he took his glass and raised it. "To the health and well being of the family of John Dean, gardener."

John could never have refused to drink to such a toast. "I shall drink with you, sir," he said.

"Good man."

John raised his glass and swallowed the sherry quickly. It burned his throat, sending pleasant fumes through his nostrils and leaving a sweet and cloying taste on his tongue. He replaced the glass on the tray and began to speak before Fitzwilliam could resume. "The health and well being of my family is the very subject I have come to discuss with you."

"Then, what can I do to assist you, Dean? Name it and it shall be done."

"You are most kind. I dinna ken if you are aware, but since my marriage I am blacklisted by Susan's father and hae found myself unable to obtain work suitable to my abilities and with sufficient wages to support my family. I am hopeful that you might be in need of a gardener perhaps?" Dean felt himself demeaned by the necessity of his plea.

"I should not wish my father dead, of course, but until that unhappy occasion, I am not in possession of an estate worthy of your talent. I cannot offer you employment on my father's behalf as he remains on good terms with Mr. Kirke in spite of our failed engagement, for which he blames me."

"Surely he does not know of your involvement in our elopement?"

"No, but it springs naturally to his mind to consider me as the guilty party as I have already so many failed engagements to my credit."

"Perhaps you might know of someone among your acquaintances who is in need of a gardener."

"Now, there I may be able to aid you. I have some friends among the peers and gentry at Parliament. I shall make enquiries and mayhap find some gentleman who will act like one and rescue your family from penury. I am only sorry that you did not consider me enough of a friend to come for assistance before this."

"I confess the reason that I did not visit you earlier was my shame that I could not repay the money you had lent me. Now that I have managed to amass the sum required, I feel that I can come before you as an honest man." Then John took a small bag heavy with coins from his pocket and handed it to the gentleman.

Fitzwilliam would not take it, waving his hands so that John could not place the bag in them. "No, no, sir. I know from your own admission that you cannot afford such an expense. Besides, I am afraid that you mistook my meaning at the time I gave you the money. I intended it as a wedding gift for you and Mrs. Dean. I will not take it back."

"There was no mistake, I assure you. If you had given it under any other pretext than as a loan, I would not have accepted it. I maun insist that you receive it. If it is any consolation to your generous spirit, I hae not paid you any interest."

Fitzwilliam laughed heartily. "You do amuse me, Dean." He said, taking the bag at last.

John continued to sit, looking as though there was still something on his mind.

"Is there anything else I may do for you?"

"There is, sir," he finally said. "I would be much obliged to you if you could give me any news of my wife's family. She seldom speaks of her parents, but I ken they are often in her thoughts."

"I am afraid that my family has had few dealings with the Kirkes since the engagement was broken off, as you can well imagine. All the information that I have is at second and third hand, so you must not value it as very reliable."

"I shall keep that in mind, but I would still appreciate any information that you might have."

"Because of my particular interest in the Kirke family, I have heard much gossip on their account. It is said that Mr. Kirke drinks a good deal, even more than he did before. It is further said that Mr. Kirke's inebriated state blinds him to the fact that his butler has moved in to his wife's apartment. But I cannot vouch for the truth of this slander to the lady's reputation. The world takes pleasure in a cuckold, and it could indeed be pure invention. How can anyone know for sure, especially since the Kirkes do not often come to London? Of course, the Kirke Hall Gardens were on the tour of the *bon ton* for a few years, but they have recently fallen into disrepair without your expert hand, and without Mr. Kirke's will, to keep them up. I believe the man is heart-broken, and not on account of his inconstant wife either, though I rather suspect it is she and the butler who keep him from visiting his daughter."

John was so disheartened by this news that he decided not to repeat it to his wife. He knew it would only upset her, but an idea began to form in his mind that he might ask Fitzwilliam to be an intermediary once again, as he had been in the days of his engagement to Susan. "You have been so kind that I hesitate to impose on you further."

"Ask anyway, Dean. I can scarcely refuse you."

"Perhaps you would be able to arrange a meeting between Mr. Kirke and Susan and his grandchildren, without the ken of Mrs. Kirke and the butler, of course."

Fitzwilliam looked thoughtful a moment. "You do present me with an interesting and challenging assignment. It would be most amusing for me to consider this scheme. Just let me know the time and place of the assignation, and I shall endeavor to bring the old fool there."

"Aye. I shall need some time to prepare Susan before such an event. I will let you know. In the meantime, you may devise the means of implementing such a scheme."

~~*

As Susan sat in the rocking chair nursing Sweet William, there was a rap at the door. Mary was upstairs washing baby clothes. Susan called to her, but the maid did not hear. Disturbed from his meal by her raised voice, William started crying. Then the children came out of their room and little Johnny ran to answer the door before Susan could stop him.

She could see the outline of a man indistinctly through the open door to the anteroom. Though the baby was still screaming, she placed him in his cradle and arranged her gown to cover her breast. Then she commanded the other two children to stay and went to the door.

The man was squatting in order to talk to Johnny face to face.

"May I help you?" she said, and he stood up.

"Good morning, Mrs. Dean," he said, and Susan almost fainted from the unexpected shock of seeing Fitzwilliam after all these years.

He saw her distress, deftly stepped around the boy and caught her arm. "I see that you recognize me," he said smiling. "I do not often have such an effect on women, I can assure you. Here, let me escort you to your seat."

He led her back to the parlour where James and Ellie, having stayed at their mother's command, now seemed entranced at the sight of this strange man who was not their father holding their mother's arm. Johnny came running back into the room. At the rocking chair, Fitzwilliam released Susan and said, "Have a seat."

"Thank you, sir, but I am fine. I must see to the baby." William was kicking and screaming in the cradle.

"Allow me." Fitzwilliam went to the cradle, picked up the baby as if it were a delicate figurine in danger of being smashed, and handed it to her. She took him and sat down. Immediately that he was in her arms, the baby started groping for the breast again. She did not wish to resume feeding him in front of Fitzwilliam. Fortunately, at that moment, Mary arrived and stopped at the bottom of the stairs.

"Mr. Fitzwilliam!" she cried, as astonished as Susan had been.

"Mary!" He responded equally enthusiastically. He went to shake her hand. "It is good to see you. I am glad you are gainfully employed again."

Mary blushed, unaccustomed to so much attention from a gentleman. After a moment, she came to Susan's aid, roused by the baby's renewed crying. "Let me take the infant, madam. Ellie, James, Johnny, come with me. It is time for your nap." She herded the little ones effectively and they trotted reluctantly to the nursery, looking back over their shoulders one last time at the strange man.

"Extraordinary!" he said as the door closed behind them. "And all of these marvelous creatures are issue from your body, madam?" He shook his head. "It is simply extraordinary."

"I rather think that such a feat is all too ordinary," she replied.

"Not in my experience, madam." Fitzwilliam was still shaking his head as he took a chair and pulled it next to hers.

"I would offer you some refreshment, sir, but Mary is our only servant, and she is otherwise engaged at the moment."

Fitzwilliam shook his head vigorously again. "Not my purpose in coming, madam. I can get refreshments at any coffeehouse in London where I will not be so thoroughly entertained as I am by your company."

She blushed, unused to hearing such nonsense now that she was no longer part of society. She was suddenly conscious of the thought that John would not approve of her entertaining Fitzwilliam alone. "I am afraid that my husband is not here, sir, if that is your purpose in coming."

"I know that he is not, madam. I have timed my visit to coincide with his absence so that I may speak with you alone."

Again she blushed. "You have placed me in a compromising position of which Mr. Dean would not approve."

"I am sure he would not, but be assured I have not come to dishonour you in any way. Let me explain. Some days ago your husband visited me in order to return a sum of money that I had given him before your marriage."

"Is that true?" she was astonished.

"I see by your reaction that you were unaware of that transaction."

"I knew you had given us several items, all of which were most useful in our escape to Scotland; however, I was not aware of any sum of money."

"An elopement to Scotland was an expense that Mr. Dean could ill afford. At that time, you were ignorant of the cost involved in such an adventure. Perhaps you have since learned the value of money?" He looked at her slyly.

She nodded, blushing again at the thought that she had placed her husband in a position of indebtedness to a man he despised.

"Mrs. Dean." Fitzwilliam looked directly in her eyes, so that she could see his sincerity. "I want you to know that I always intended that money as a wedding gift for you and your husband. It was Mr. Dean's mistake to consider it a loan."

He paused for a moment, but she did not know how to respond to him. He continued.

"You know your husband better than I, I am sure, but I know him well enough to realize he is too proud to accept money from me no matter how sincerely I offer it as a gift. So, I have come to you in the hope that you will receive it in the spirit in which it was given, and for the sake of your children, if for no other reason." Fitzwilliam revealed the bag of coins which her husband had given him.

How could he have kept that money from them? She thought of the days when they had eaten little more than bread. But here it was now returning to them.

Before she could extend her hand to take it, Fitzwilliam continued, "I know you will scruple to take it behind your husband's back."

She felt a little ashamed that she had not, but with small children and an overriding concern to keep them alive, she could ill afford such scruples.

"But consider that Mr. Dean did not tell you about this loan. Consider that all this time, he has been keeping from you and your children, a sum of money with which to repay me, a sum of money which must have been greatly needed at home. Pride is such a terribly expensive commodity, is it not?"

"I do agree," she said.

"I trust you will not tell Mr. Dean."

She nodded and Fitzwilliam handed her the bag.

She took it. "I will be as secretive about the money's return as he was about its disbursement."

"And about my visit as well?"

"You can rely on my discretion, Mr. Fitzwilliam."

"I thank you, madam."

"I owe you a debt of gratitude, sir. Indeed, I am so overwhelmed by your generosity that I am at a loss to comprehend it."

"I know your opinion of me is coloured by your husband's. He is an extremely moral man who sees the behaviour of others only in black and white. In his eyes, because of my peculiar sexual appetite, I am purely black. But I believe you can see other colours in people. You see that I am capable of good as well as evil. I am a liar, that is true, but society has forced me to perfect that particular skill. In fact, most people are liars. Even Mr. Dean himself, though in many aspects a paragon of virtue, has lied to you by omission, and you would do no worse to keep this truth from him."

She wondered what Fitzwilliam meant by his "peculiar sexual appetite." He had never shown any odd sexual desire for her or anyone else that she could ever remember. When he was gone she would ask Mary about it. In her experience, servants usually knew about such things. Besides, she would need to take Mary into her confidence in order to keep the meeting a secret, and Mary should be the one to spend the money. Susan suddenly realized that the money was probably owed to Mary at any rate, because her wages had too often been cut short in the past.

She saw that Fitzwilliam was preparing to leave and she still had something to ask him. "Sir, have you any news of my parents?"

He stopped his preparations and looked her straight in the eye. "I am sorry, Mrs. Dean. I have none, other than to say they are both in health. As you can imagine, our families no longer keep in touch."

She could not deny the truth of such an excuse. She did not know if the rest was a prevarication, but it was the sort of thing a person might lie about to spare another from grief.

"They are alive then?"

"Yes, madam. I can assure you of that fact. I should not tell you this because you have enough secrets to keep from Mr. Dean already, but he has charged me to arrange a meeting for you and your children with your father."

She must have shown her pleasure because he immediately said, "Now, do not hope for too much. It may not be possible but I shall try what I can do."

She started to cry, unable to adequately convey the joy he had given her. "Oh, thank you, sir."

He stood up, kissed her hand, and said, "I am at your service, madam." Then he turned away. "Now, do not rise. I shall show myself out. Good day."

He departed quickly after that, and Susan sat in her rocker a long time, crying softly. She thought of how much she had hated Fitzwilliam in the past, while all this time, unbeknownst to her, he had been her greatest benefactor and friend. She had never understood him. What was this sexual peculiarity that he spoke of?

Then suddenly she recalled the last time she had seen him. It was at a masquerade, and he had been attired as a bride wearing her wedding gown. Surrounded by a coterie of men, he had fluttered his eyelashes coquettishly. Silly as the scene was, he had looked extremely happy, happier than she had ever seen him, and a realization came to her. Perhaps Fitzwilliam had wished all his life to be a woman! She had never heard of such a thing, except perhaps among the ancient Greeks, and yet it explained what he had meant when he said that society had taught him well to be a liar. If he had always wanted to be a woman, then he would have always had to lie about himself. A feeling of profound sadness came over her. How unfortunate that nature had trapped such a compassionate and feminine nature in the awkward body of a man, and how sad it was that only now had she recognized what a truly good friend he had been to her.

London, Winter, 1783

John was eating his breakfast and contemplating what his chores would be that day considering the dullness of the sky and the possibility of rain, when Mary announced the arrival of a letter by the post. His curiosity excited by the unusual event, he hurried to the door, where the postman was waiting for his penny.

John was tempted to say, "Indeed I have not any," like Simple Simon of the nursery rhyme, but his desire to know the contents of the unexpected letter compelled him instead to ask Mary if she had the money.

She nodded and reached deep into the pocket of her pinafore, extracting a copper coin which she gave to the postman. He handed her the letter and made his departure.

John's surprise at her hidden wealth was overshadowed by his curiosity, so he said only, "Thank you, Mary. I will repay you."

She nodded again, but did not leave. He considered sending her away so he could read the letter in private but decided her penny had bought her the right to know. So, he unfolded it, noticing as he did so that the fine quality paper bore a coat of arms and the handwriting was immaculately formed. John read the letter aloud.

"My Dear Mister Dean:

We request your presence at our London residence at Bloomsbury on January 28, 1784 at three o'clock.

You will no doubt be surprised to receive such a summons from such an eminence most certainly unknown to you. The explanation lies with the fact that we have lately been apprised by a mutual acquaintance, his honour Mr. Herbert Fitzwilliam, that you are seeking employment as a gardener. As it happens, we are also in need of a gardener. If you would please come to the above-mentioned location at the appointed time, your suitability for this position will be ascertained by us.

Your humble and sincere patron,

George Gordon,

Lord of Haddo,

Third Earl of Aberdeen."

The signature, though not as neatly penned as the rest of the letter, was nonetheless legible. John read it again. "George Gordon, Lord of Haddo." Could it be the same Lord George Gordon who had precipitated the riots just a few short years ago, upsetting the city of London and the peace of his own family? He hoped it was not, because he did not think he would like to work for such a man.

Well, John argued with himself, but the riot was not really Gordon's fault. He may have initiated the rally but it had been for a good cause. Indeed, John himself had been supportive of it, before the tumult began. He could not have known beforehand how large the mob would become and how unruly it would behave. Besides, the King himself had acquitted Gordon of treason. Who was John then to judge him so harshly?

"Mary," John said. "Do not say a word of this letter to Susan in case nothing comes of it. I do not wish to give her false hopes." But his own heart sang with hope and he said a silent prayer of gratitude, asking God to have mercy on the immortal soul of Herbert Fitzwilliam. Then he went with trepidation to his appointment with Lord George Gordon at the appointed time.

John was ushered into a great hall where the Earl met him. He was an attractive man of middle age, wearing a fine embroidered jacket unbuttoned to reveal a vest so tight that the buttons were strained almost to bursting. His graying and thinning hair gave him a distinguished appearance, and he carried himself in a self-assured, almost haughty, manner that befit his rank.

John inclined his head politely. "My lord."

"Mr. Dean." The Earl stood aside to reveal two ornate chairs. "Have a seat."

"Thank you, my lord."

John sat, but the Earl continued standing, strutting about the room and orating as if he were addressing the House of Lords. "Us wish you to know, at the very outset, that us is not the same Lord George Gordon who started the anti-Catholic riots some years ago. Were you in London at that time of tumult, Mr. Dean?"

"I was, sir."

"Yes, well, then you remember what a terrible time it was. So, us wants to assure you that, although we share the same name, us is not he."

John was taken aback at the Earl's peculiar manner of speaking.

The Earl continued. "No. That Lord Gordon is our cousin, the brother of the Earl of Gordon, whose intercession saved his life. A grave injustice was thus done.

Us believes that the king should have hanged the scoundrel for the treason he committed. Then there would have been an end to this confusion of names."

"I am relieved to hear that your lordship is not that Lord George Gordon."

"Aye. That Lord Gordon is now in Amsterdam, fomenting more treason, no doubt. Us has our faults to be sure, but religious fanaticism is not one of them." The Earl laughed heartily.

When he had finished, John said, "'Tis true that we all have our faults, my lord. In my own case, you may be aware that I am married to the daughter of a gentleman, which is considered to be a kind of thievery in England, though not quite a hanging offence. Instead, my punishment is to be kept on a black list, which has prevented me from obtaining employment equal to my abilities."

"Pshaw," the Earl made some such utterance of dismissal. "The English! What do they know of love? They have no heart for such an emotion! A man cannot choose whom he loves, and love breaks the bonds of class. Love does not recognize class." The Earl approached him. "Us will not hold your love against you. Us is only interested in your gardening ability." He leaned forward, holding the back of his chair and looked John directly in the eye. "Can you make a pleasure-garden from a wilderness? That is all us wants to know."

John's heart was beating loudly in his chest. "You may place a wager upon it that I can."

"Good man, good man." He patted John on the back vigorously and then resumed his pacing. "You have no objection to moving to Scotland, presumably, being a Scot yourself?"

John hesitated before answering.

The Earl stopped and faced him again. "Do you have such an objection?"

"I dinna have such an objection, sir. I am only considering my wife's opinion on the matter since she is English."

The Earl waved his hand dismissively. "She can have no objection, sir. A wife goes where her husband goes. Surely love will bid her follow you."

What could he say? "Of course, my lord."

"Then it is settled. Us has purchased a property in Ellon just north of Aberdeen and not far from our home estate of Haddo. Until this year it has been uninhabited but now us has finished restoring the castle and now the garden must be attended to. A pleasure garden will make a splendid decorative addition to a castle, do you not agree?"

John smiled. It sounded even more splendid than Kirke Hall. "I canna wait to see it, sir."

"Nor will you have to. Us shall arrange a private coach to transport your family this fortnight. Can you be ready?"

John nodded.

"How many be in your family?"

"Six, sir. Including my wife and our four bairns."

"Will there be a servant to accompany you as well?"

"I dinna ken if our maid will make the journey. Since she is English, she may not wish to be uprooted to Scotland."

"Probably not. The English think Scotland a wild, untamed place, and she has not the inducement of love to lure her there. If she will not go, us shall arrange a servant to accompany you."

"Thankee, my lord."

"Come, let us settle the bargain with a bumper of Scotch whiskey."

And so they did.

~~*

Susan was pregnant again with their fifth child. It was early enough so that she was still sick in the morning, indeed, sometimes sick the whole day.

John came home from work early. That was her first intimation that something was amiss. He greeted her at the door with the smell of whiskey on his breath, and his kiss almost turned her stomach. The second intimation. His face was beaming. She was going to say third, but truly this had her baffled.

"What is amiss, John?"

"Amiss, Susan! Why should anything be amiss?"

"You are home too early. Have you lost your employment?"

"I hae given my notice."

She looked at him then. This was clearly the third intimation. Her heart was beating so irregularly that she feared for the life of her unborn baby.

"Sit down." John took her by the arm and led her to a chair. "You are looking ill, my dear." She sat down. "You have no reason to fear," he said. "I have good news for you."

He stood there with his hat in his hand not saying anything. How could this be good news then? The maid was in the room now, seeming to know that something was amiss. "Mary, take his hat please." Its movement was distracting her.

"Yes, madam." She took it and hung it on the coat rack.

"Well?" Susan said. "Out with it. If it is good news, let me hear it."

"I have found employment on a nobleman's estate."

Now, this was good news. She smiled, put her hands on each of the arms of the chair and lifted herself up and into John's arms. He hugged her and kissed her and danced her around the room. As she twirled by, she could see that Mary was smiling.

"Stop! Stop!" she cried, getting dizzy and fearing she would soon need to run to her dressing room to look for a basin. "Tell me the rest. Who is the nobleman? Where is his estate?"

"The nobleman is Lord George Gordon, the third Earl of Aberdeen, and the estate is near Aberdeen in Scotland."

Her heart felt as if it had stopped beating. For the longest time she stood as if waiting for it to start again.

"Say something, Susan."

"When are we to leave?"

"In a fortnight. The Earl will have a carriage for us."

She remembered the trip that they had made to Dundee to be wed, days and days of coach travel. It had been grueling then when she had been young, alone and healthy. What would it be like with four small children? "I cannot imagine," she said, "how I can manage such a journey in my present condition. Is Aberdeen closer than Dundee?" she asked innocently.

"Considerably farther. Several days farther."

"I am not sure that I will make it, John."

"Of course you will," he said lamely.

Mary came to stand beside her, and Susan saw tears streaming down her cheeks. Why was she weeping? "Surely you will come with us, Mary?"

"To Scotland, madam!?" She said it in such a way that Susan knew she would not. She could not blame her and began to cry as well.

"If Mary willna come, the laird has promised to employ a servant to accompany us," John said.

She and Mary were too busy weeping to respond. Mary might have been her servant, but she was the only friend she had, and the oldest friend she had left from the time before, when Susan was someone besides a wife and a mother.

For several years now, Susan had been grateful for her loyalty while at the same time being sorry for it as well. Mary could have obtained a better position elsewhere with far less work to do and greater remuneration. Or she could have married and had her own babies. She would have made someone a far better wife and mother than Susan did because she knew how to cook and keep household accounts. In the face of such competency, Susan felt useless. So now, though she should have been happy for Mary, she felt selfishly sad because she would miss her so much and because she could not imagine how she would manage without her advice and assistance.

Later, when they were alone in their bedchamber, John and Susan talked of the matter.

"We willna gang," he said, "if you dinna wish it."

"But you have already told the Earl that we will, John."

"'Tis no great matter to tell him that I willna. He will hire another man. That is all."

"But you cannot continue to work at Vauxhall Gardens where you do not make enough money to support us! It is not an option that we can afford, John. We have no choice. We must go."

"But there is another choice, Susan. Now that a peace treaty has been signed with America and the war is over, we can emigrate there, as I have so long wished to do."

Susan had been expecting John to make this suggestion for several months, ever since September when the treaty had been signed. She had been preparing an argument against such a possibility; she saw it now as an argument to be used in favour of moving to Scotland. "If I am reluctant to move so far as Scotland, how can you think that I would be willing to go to the other side of the world? I am not. However, I will agree to go with you back to your homeland."

"You are willing to do so even though it means you maun leave your family and friends behind you?"

"What family is that, John? Where have my family been in the last six years? We have sent an announcement at each child's birth, and never once have my parents come to see any of the children. There will be no forgiveness from them should we wait another six years. Besides, you have family in Scotland, and your family shall be my family, as it should be, as your blessed Bible always says it should be."

Then he could not help but quote chapter and verse, for that was his nature and the way he had been raised. "Intreat me not to leave thee, or to return from following after thee: for whither thou goest, I will go; and where thou lodgest, I will lodge: thy people shall be my people, and thy God my God; from the Book of Ruth."

It was a beautiful piece of scripture, and Susan felt her life was bound by it, then and now, always, whatever her will.

"And what about your friends?" he asked.

Without thinking she answered, "It is pitiful when the only friend one has is a servant."

He gave her such a look then, and she remembered that he was, in truth, a servant too.

"I would rather be a doorkeeper in the house of my God, than to dwell in the tents of wickedness; from the Psalms," he continued quoting to assuage his anger.

"Better to reign in hell than serve in heaven," she added for good measure.

"Who said that?" John asked, surprised by her erudition.

"Satan said it," she answered, "in Milton's Paradise Lost."

"So, you did have a good governess once. I wish that I had met her."

"The pair of you would have got on famously!" Then they laughed, and the terrible thought of her future travail, the journey back to the wilds of Scotland, seemed to slip from her consciousness, though it was always there, in the back of her mind, another trial to be endured.

~~*

As they were making the arrangements for their trip to Scotland, John sent a letter to Fitzwilliam advising him of their imminent departure. Fitzwilliam replied by return post that he would do his best to accomplish his assigned task. Then John finally broke the news to his wife, unaware that she was already apprised. In anticipation of the meeting, the family remained at home as much as possible during this period, nervously awaiting a knock at the door. On the weekend before the Deans were to leave, the visitors arrived.

Mary started at the sound of the knocker. Then, smoothing the front of her gown, she walked to the door to answer it as a proper butler would have done, closing the anteroom door behind her.

Susan, sitting in the rocker with the baby on her knee, and John, interrupted in his romp with the three older children, could hear only a muffled cry from the anteroom. A few moments later, their suspense was ended and the door opened.

Mary announced the visitors. "Mr. Fitzwilliam and Mr. Kirke," she said, and then stepped aside.

Fitzwilliam, grinning from ear to ear, entered the room and nodded at both John and Susan. "I have the honour to present your father Mr. Kirke." Then he stepped aside, revealing a man much reduced in stature since Susan had last seen him. When he saw the family, he tottered a little, and Mary took his arm to support him.

Susan placed the baby on the floor and skipped to embrace her father, holding him tightly in her arms. When she finally let go and stepped back, he was weeping, copiously and unashamedly.

"Have a seat, Father." She led him to the chair she had just vacated.

"Papa, why is the old man crying?" little Johnny asked.

Ellie began to cry in sympathy, and John picked her up to comfort her.

Susan was trying desperately, but with little success, to hold back her own tears.

Her father began to rock himself in the chair, muttering over and over, "Oh my! Oh my!"

"Are you all right, Father?" Susan asked.

He did not answer, but kept on muttering and rocking as if he had not heard.

"Is he right in the head?" John asked Fitzwilliam.

"Well, he seemed right enough on the way here. He was quite excited when I told him where we were going. I expect it is just the shock of seeing you that has put him in this state."

Mary said, "Do you think some smelling salts will bring him round to his right mind?"

"Why not?" Fitzwilliam said, and Mary made a move to fetch them.

Kirke spoke up suddenly. "I would prefer gin, Mary, if you don't mind."

"Are you sure that is wise, sir?" Fitzwilliam asked.

"I am not a very wise man," Kirke stated unequivocally.

"At any rate, there is not a drop of gin to be found in the house," John said, shifting Ellie, who no longer cried but still had the snuffles.

"What do you have, Dean? Whiskey?"

"The house is dry, sir, save for a little ale."

Kirke made a face. "Not even brandy?"

"No, sir."

"Ale will do then."

Mary nodded and went to fetch the ale instead of the smelling salts.

"You have not changed, Father," Susan said, her eyes now as dry as the house.

"'Tis not true, Susan. I am not the same man any more. I am all filled up with regret now. But enough of that. I do not expect your forgiveness. Just introduce me to my grandchildren. How many are there?" He looked about him. His eyes lighted on the baby sitting at his feet looking up at him. "Who is this, then?"

"This is the youngest, William. But you must meet them in the correct order. John, bring the children to meet their grandfather."

John pushed the boys gently forward. "This is the eldest, your namesake, James." He nudged his son's shoulder. "Go and shake your grandfather's hand, lad."

James, looking very solemn, did as he was bid. The old man shook the offered hand and then kissed the palm that the youngster had touched. His whole body began to tremble and he burst into tears again.

The introductions were thankfully interrupted as Mary arrived at that moment with the glass of beer. Susan was almost sorry that they did not have stronger liquor in the house to assist her father through his ordeal.

When Kirke had recovered himself enough, he took the glass in his two hands and shakily brought it to his lips, finishing it off in one gulp. "Thankee," he said, returning it to Mary. "Now, who is this?" He looked at the cocky young boy who was glaring at him.

"The correct order," Susan stated simply. She would not have her daughter passed over.

John understood immediately, setting Ellie down in spite of her protests. He gave her a warning look and she stopped struggling. "Next we have Eleanor. Go and see your grandfather, Ellie."

She shook her head stubbornly.

"I can see she is as eager to approach me as her grandmother, for whom she is named," Kirke commented.

Susan ignored her father's remarks and took her daughter's hand, leading her forward. "This is my papa, Ellie. He is your grandfather. Give him your hand."

Ellie put out her hand tentatively and Kirke took it. "How do you do, my dear." He bent his head to kiss her hand, but she snatched it away and ran back to her father's arms. John caught her up and gave her a hug.

Mr. Kirke straightened himself and stood for a moment watching father and daughter, his eyes shining and his face wet with tears. Then he looked down at the third child. "Now, might I meet the young soldier who is shooting at me with his eyes?"

Susan laughed. "You may. This is young John, named for his father. We call him 'Johnny.'" She did not need to encourage him as she had Ellie. He stepped forward on his own and shook the old man's hand vigorously.

"Good afternoon, sir," Johnny said.

"Good afternoon to you." Kirke smiled when the young man's shaking finally ended. "How old are you, boy?"

"I am free," he lisped.

His grandfather laughed and the youngster glared at him again.

"And now the baby," Susan said, hoping to defuse her young son's anger. She picked him up from his seat on the floor. "Would you like to hold William?"

"Well." Kirke looked hesitant. "It has been a very long time since I have held a baby. You were that baby yourself, Susan." He smiled.

"'Tis not something you forget how to do." Susan handed William to him, and he began rocking again, although now he was crooning at the child, who continued to stare.

"Father, have you dined yet?"

The old man, rapt in his attention to the baby, did not respond, so Fitzwilliam, who until now had held himself in the background, stepped forward. "No, he has not. We came here directly from Kirke Hall this morning." Fitzwilliam's eyes were rimmed with red and he held a moist, crumpled handkerchief limply in one hand.

Susan smiled at his sentimentality. "Will you dine with us also, Fitzwilliam?" she asked.

"I would be delighted to be included in such a party."

"Amen to that," Mr. Kirke commented from his rocking chair.

While they waited for Mary to prepare the dinner, Susan asked after her mother and others of her acquaintance in the vicinity of Kirke Hall. Her father was not very informative in his brief responses.

"What I would like to know," he asked, "is if I might come to visit you again. I should like to come often, if I may."

Susan and John exchanged glances.

"Then you have not told him, Fitzwilliam?" John asked.

Fitzwilliam shook his head.

"Told me what?"

"I could not," Fitzwilliam said.

"I ask you again, Dean. Told me what?"

"We asked Fitzwilliam to bring you here not only to meet your grandchildren but also so that we might say good bye to you, sir. We are moving to Scotland next month. I have found employment on an estate there."

A strange ungodly sound erupted from Kirke, and all the children turned to look at him. Susan took the baby from him before one of them began to wail.

They all waited until he recovered his power of speech. "Could you not have found any employment closer to home, Dean?" Kirke asked his son-in-law accusingly.

"I could not, sir, as you well know, since it was you yourself who put me on a black list because I married your daughter." John spoke coldly.

The same strange noise emanated from the old man again. There was a wild look in his eye. "What have I done?" he muttered.

Susan wanted to say something to relieve his obvious suffering but could think of nothing.

Fortunately, Mary arrived at that moment to announce that dinner was ready.

The group found their places at the dining room table and sat down. It was not the sumptuous suppers of Susan's youth when far more food had been placed in front of the Kirkes than three people could ever eat at one sitting. It was instead the kind of simple meal the family had become accustomed to: a hearty soup with some bread and butter.

Usually, the children would have been fed before the others, but since the visitors were hungry, not having dined on their long journey, the company was quite content to eat at the same time. With only one servant and one table, they were obliged to dine in one place as well, which had they not, old Mr. Kirke would have insisted upon at any rate. William was put in his cradle beside the table, although he was already at an age when he would rather have been included with the company at the table. Mary was constantly interrupted in her serving duties to attend to him.

Kirke gradually regained his equanimity, not wanting to waste a moment of the brief time that remained of the only visit he would ever have with his grandchildren. He began to propose a toast to each of them in turn, not forgetting his daughter and husband.

The health of each member of the family was drunk to, and the children happily lifted their tumblers of milk to join in.

"I would like to make another toast, but we have no more ale."

William, whose health had just been toasted, cried even more lustily to be picked up.

"Go and fetch the ale, Mary, and I will take the baby," Susan said, picking up William and sitting him on her knee so that Mary could fill her father's glass.

Kirke raised his beaker.

"Who is left to toast?" Fitzwilliam said, laughing.

"Saving your kind self, sir," Kirke spoke sincerely. "I wish to raise a glass to Mary Turnbull, a loyal servant, unjustly dismissed from my household, who is doing the duty of several servants at once at this fine feast. Mary Turnbull!" he exclaimed, lifting the tumbler that she had just filled.

The maid blushed prettily, unused to being singled out, especially by her ex-employer.

After putting down his glass, John said, "If I may be so bold as to speak, I would like to ask a favour of you, sir. Mary will not be going to Scotland with us. As you can well imagine, she does not wish to travel so far from her native country to leave her family and friends behind. But as you say, she has always been loyal and hard-working, so if either of you gentlemen could provide her with a position here in England, we would be most grateful to you."

"I will make it my first priority to find her a place as a lady's maid, a position that she so richly deserves after the devotion she has shown to your family," Fitzwilliam said.

"And I will provide a testimonial of her service," Kirke added.

"Thank you, sirs," John responded.

Mary wiped a tear from her eye with the corner of her pinafore.

Kirke held his glass for Mary to fill it. He raised it to toast again. "I give you Fitzwilliam, a true gentleman."

Again the children lifted their glasses, and Susan thought to herself they had never drunk so much milk at one sitting and perhaps the proposal of toasts might be a good tradition to continue at meal times.

Kirke and Fitzwilliam left reluctantly some time later. The next day a parcel arrived from Kirke Hall containing a set of silverware engraved with the letter "K", a pair of brass candlesticks, and a glass finger bowl. There was a brief note included.

"My dearest children,

Forgive me. I know these gifts are pitifully little, and that they do not make up for all that you have lost at my hands, but I saw your need of such items at table yesterday. I hope they will bring you fond memories of your childhood, Susan. I am certain that they will not be missed in this house. It is my hope that we may correspond by way of Fitzwilliam in the future. God be with you on your journey to Scotland.

Your loving but negligent father,
James Kirke."

Chapter 2

En route to Scotland, Spring, 1784

"James! Stop teasing your sister! Eleanor, sit still as a young lady should."

The children were restless after three hours in the coach. Maude Ashcroft, the young girl that the Earl had supplied as their servant, was not up to the challenge of amusing three children for such a long time in such a confined space. The youngest child was not faring any better than the others. Poor Susan sat there bouncing him on her very crowded knee as the youngster blubbered and whined.

"Maude, take William from your mistress, will you? She maun hae a rest from the children while we are at the inn."

Maude, showing her displeasure, reached for the child, who took one look at her sour face and began to bawl. John was almost afraid to leave him in her care, but he had no choice. Susan needed a respite. "And mind you watch the other wee'uns as well. I willna have them running about and getting in the way of other travelers at the inn." Not at all confident that she could control them, he turned to the children, hopeful that they would mind him. "Children, obey your nanny and behave yourselves. I shall hae a full report when we resume our travel, and if I hear ill of any of you, you will receive a whipping when we arrive at our destination tonight."

As they entered the inn, John asked, "Do you remember this place, Susan?" In response, he saw on her face a look of happiness that proved she recognized the inn in Leicester where they had stayed on their elopement to Dundee seven years before.

"Yes," she said. "This was the inn where the sergeant was recruiting soldiers for the war. I recall that when he approached you, you informed him you had two brothers in America and you did not wish to be staring down the barrel of a gun at one of them one day. He left you alone right enough after that. Thank God that horrible war is over! But John, this was where we spent our first night, and we are only arrived here for dinner! How can that be?"

"We set out on our journey later in the day this time, and we maun travel more slowly with all of the bairns. They canna sit still for such long stages. Thank God and the Earl that we have our own private coach and may travel at a pace we can manage. How are you doing, my dear?"

She sighed. "Very well, John."

"You look tired."

"I am that. But the slow pace of our travel will suit me as well, although unfortunately, it will be a longer voyage."

"When we reach Dundee, you will have your reward. You may stay behind with my mother there and rest until you are delivered. It will do you good to have family with you, and my mother is anxious to meet her grand-bairns for the first time. Then when your health is sufficiently recovered, you and the children may rejoin me in Ellon."

The smile came back to her face, ever so faintly, but at least it was there. For the next leg of the journey, John took young James with him on the top of the coach. It made the boy feel like a young man, and then there were only three bairns for Maude to govern. He had charged Eleanor with the care of her younger brothers, hoping she would rise to the occasion and her mother would be able to stretch out a little and take a nap. If all went well, but when did it ever?

~~*

Eleanor slapped her brother Johnny, and he started to howl. Maude yelled at him to be quiet, and William woke up and added to the noise. Susan awoke, tired and irritated. The turbulence of the coach upset her, and the unfamiliar food she had just eaten at the inn churned in her stomach ominously.

"John," she yelled for her husband. His little namesake in the coach looked at her with wide, frightened eyes as if he thought she was scolding him. "Mr. Dean," she amended, "please stop the coach."

It took a moment for the message to be relayed and the horses to be brought to a standstill. Susan struggled to retain the contents of her dinner as she opened the carriage door and jumped down, not waiting for her husband to assist her. She had no time for such niceties, and besides, she had traveled this road as a man before and could look after herself if she needed to.

Moments later, she was retching in the grass.

Little Eleanor, watching from the window of the coach, asked, "Why are you throwing up, Mama?"

Susan heard her but could not respond as she was otherwise engaged. "She's feeling sick," Maude said, stating the obvious.

John was soon at his wife's side, trying to comfort her. "You are usually over the morning sickness by this time," he said, his brow furrowed with worry.

She used his arm as a support to stand up, and said, "'Tis only the movement of the coach and the food I et at the inn that have upset me."

He helped her back in to the carriage and the journey resumed.

~~*

Several long tedious days later, when they finally reached Edinburgh, the passengers in the coach were in full revolt. Not Maude's feeble entreaties, nor their mother's exhortations, nor even their father's commands, had any effect on the rebellious children any longer. Indeed, Maude herself had become one of them, a large petulant child.

Susan looked near to expiring, and John felt compelled to find a solution. So, against his own inclinations, he decided to go to Forrest's Coffeehouse and book passage for the family on a ship bound for Dundee. The last time he had done so, seven years before, he had been kidnapped by a press gang. He shivered at the recollection, remembering how frightened he had been imprisoned in the cargo hold of a ship that would soon leave for America and wondering if he would ever see Susan again. Perhaps fate had played him a cruel joke, sending him where he had once dreamed of going when he no longer wanted to go there. He had thought himself done for, when Susan, dressed as a man, had rescued him. How could he not have married such a woman? And how could he not overcome his own trepidation and rescue his wife from her present tedious fate? Besides, the war was over and the chances of being impressed again were few.

So he bravely set out for Forrest's to book a ship on which the children could exercise their cramped muscles and amuse their curious minds, and then sent the coachman on alone to Dundee where he would meet them later.

It proved to be a good decision from the children's point of view. John had been mistaken about his wife's enjoyment of the sea cruise, however. She spent the better part of the voyage with her head hung over a basin, throwing up. When she looked up from the basin, the tears streaming down her cheeks and the expression on her face showed him that his company was not much appreciated. He decided it best to absent himself and spend his time supervising the young ones on the upper deck and making sure that they did not come to any harm, since Maude was unequal to the task.

When they at last debarked at Dundee, Susan smiled as her feet touched the solid ground. No one but Maude complained when John suggested they walk the short distance to his family home since they were not burdened with baggage. The Earl's coach would shortly arrive with most of their belongings, if indeed it had not already. Taking the ship had not been a means to shorten their voyage, only to diversify it.

It was a pleasure to look upon his mother's smiling face and outstretched arms once again. He could see that she was overwhelmed with happiness at the sight of her beautiful grandchildren. Most of her own children were abroad: the two oldest boys, Andrew and Adam, in America; Esther, her only daughter, lately married and moved away to Glasgow; and John, formerly in London and now on his way to Ellon; only her youngest sons William and Charles were still in the neighbourhood.

She beamed while the children swarmed about her. Over their heads, Susan handed her the youngest, little William, who, after days of confinement, had joyfully practiced his sea legs on the deck of the ship. He kicked out at his grandmother, wanting to be released among the other children at her feet. Understanding immediately, she put him down, and the little one teetered about as though the dry land was rocking like a ship on water. After two reeling steps, he landed hard on his behind, and everyone laughed to his mortification. He opened his mouth to howl at this insult, and the incompetent Maude, rather than comfort him, put her fingers to her ears.

After rescuing Sweet William, John made the introductions to his mother, who went swiftly to Susan's side the moment she saw how exhausted she was.

"Come and sit down, my dear. I'll get Cook to make ye some parritch. Ye'll be needing aught to stick to yer ribs," she said.

Knowing how little Susan liked parritch, John was about to object, but Susan gave him a look and thanked her mother-in-law for her hospitality. "Will you see to the young ones with Maude?" she asked him as she went with her mother-in-law.

He nodded, and took all his young family to show them the rooms where they would stay.

Susan was weary beyond the words to describe her weariness. She wanted to lie down and sleep for a hundred years. But that was not yet to be. First, she would require some sustenance to feed this unborn baby. If she did not eat, then he would die, and she could not live with the death of a child on her conscience.

Still, she had no appetite. If John's mother had offered her strawberries, she would not have wanted them any more than she wanted the parritch that was so graciously offered. She thought, when eating is done by rote, without savour or enjoyment, it may as well be parritch as syllabub. So she spooned the glutinous substance into her mouth and swallowed it, trying not to make a face, willing her churning stomach to settle and accept what it must. When she had finished a small bowl of the horrid stuff, Margaret, John's mother, brought her a cup of steaming tea. Never had anything ever tasted so good. She sipped it, dreaming that this moment of repose, on land which did not move beneath her, would last forever.

~~*

Before John boarded the coach to continue his voyage alone, he tried to console his crying children. James, at six years old, was begging to be allowed to go on with his father. He had cherished their moments together on the top of the coach, and considered himself enough of a man now to travel without his mother.

"You will gang to school now," John said to him. "You can gang to the school here at Dundee. The next time I see you, you will ken how to read and write. Then you will be a young man capable of helping me with my work at Ellon Castle. Would you like that, do you think?"

James could scarcely contain his excitement at the prospect.

"I can hardly wait for your arrival, but I need an assistant who is able to read and write," John continued, though he had already convinced James.

John then tried to placate little Eleanor as well. He charged her with the important task of looking after her younger brothers. "Your grandmother will be busy taking care of your mother," he told her, "and Nanny canna do the work alone. I am sure that you can help her. What do you say?"

"Aye, Papa," she said. "That I can." She also seemed to relish the responsibility her father imposed upon her.

With the other two bairns, Johnny and Will, he was not so successful. "Ye maunna behave like rascals," he abjured them. "Ye maun gie your mama some peace." At his words, the lads proceeded to jump up and down like rascals, not giving anyone a moment of peace.

His mother laughed. "Dinna fash, John. I'll see to the lads," she promised him as he climbed in the carriage.

Susan was not at his leave-taking. He had said good-bye to her earlier in private where she could weep unseen.

Now he was to travel on alone in the Earl's coach until he reached Ellon Castle. Sorry as he was to watch his family recede into the distance, he was also happy to anticipate his new life as a gardener on an Earl's estate. He sat back in the carriage, relishing the peace and quiet in which to contemplate his good fortune at finally having an employment he could be proud of again.

~~*

The taciturn coach driver, who had scarcely spoken ten words to John since they had left London many days since, became unusually animated as they approached his home town of Ellon. As they forded a river, whose sparkling fresh waters held promise of days of fishing to come, he began to speak.

"This is the river Ythan," he said. "Folks come every year all the way from Aberdeen to fish in its water. Look yonder." He pointed at some distance to the right where John could see several gentlemen casting their lines.

"Salmon?"

"Aye," the coach driver nodded. "The river is teeming with salmon. And mussel pearls. The brightest jewel in the Scottish crown is a pearl that was found in this river and gi'en to James VI."

John was more impressed by the length of the coach driver's sentence than by the beauty of a pearl he had never seen.

A few minutes later they passed a large church. "This here's the Ellon Parish Church, erected only six years ago."

"Its appearance is somewhat older," John said dubiously.

"That's on account of they used the original stone. Part of the foundation of this here wall is the original structure."

"It's very picturesque," John offered as encouragement.

"Aye," he said. "'Tis."

"This here's the Castle Road. Lookee. Ye'll be seeing the castle anon. To the right there."

An imposing four-storey edifice with a tall slender tower came into view. As they approached, John could see above the entrance, an armorial stone displaying a shield with a key and a sword on it and a helmet above them.

Below was the inscription: "Jo Kenedy Constable of Aberdeen Isobel Cheyne his lady 1653."

"The present owner, the Earl, has much enlarged the original building," the driver explained.

As they dismounted, John noticed the garden stretching out for many acres, on the other side of the driveway.

"The Earl has also planted all them trees," the man said proudly.

"You like the Earl, then?" John said to encourage him.

"Aye. Dinna listen to the gossips who will call him all manner of names. He has doun many a good thing for Ellon, for a' that."

"For a' what?" John asked, but the driver's taciturnity had returned, and he busied himself unbridling the horses and did not respond.

At the door to the castle, John was met by a woman who introduced herself as the housekeeper, Lavinia Henry.

"My husband Matthew wanted to greet you as well," she said amiably. "He is the steward, but in the absence of a head gardener, he has found himself occupied with the outdoor chores these days." She chuckled good-naturedly. "He will be most happy to greet you I am sure when he comes in for his supper."

"Thank you," John said. He was disposed to like the woman and wished to extend the same opinion to her husband when he should appear.

"I was led to believe that you would arrive with rather a large family. Pardon my inquiry, but have you mislaid them?"

He laughed. "Aye, that I have. I have left them with my ain family in Dundee. My wife Susan is pregnant, and, as the travel was very fatiguing, we thought it best that she be confined there until she is delivered."

"How many children do you have, Mr. Dean?"

"There are three boys and one girl at the present, madam."

"God be praised! You have been blessed, Mr. Dean."

John could not help but feel proud at her exclamation. "Have you any children yourself, Mrs. Henry?"

"Aye. Three sons, Alexander, Daniel and Robert, all grown now and gone off to make their fortune in Nova Scotia. They would rather be their ain masters in the New World than servants like their old parents in this one."

"'Tis sad for ye."

"Aye. We miss not having grand-bairns. 'Tis why I looked forward to meeting all of yourn."

"They will be here in a few months time, dinna fash."

"Aye. In the meantime, let me show you to your apartment."

As they walked through the castle to the servants' quarters, he asked Mrs. Henry about the castle's principal occupants.

"Is the Earl in residence, Mrs. Henry?"

"Nae. Ye'll find he is not often here. Sitting in the House of Lords takes him to London at this time of year of course, and when he is in Scotland, his principal residence is Haddo House."

"'Tis a wonder he requires this castle as well."

"No wonder, as you will soon discover."

They arrived at his apartment, so that the answer to this mystery was postponed while Mrs. Henry showed him around the several rooms that had been appointed for his family. He was quite satisfied with the three bedrooms and sitting room which were to be theirs. Mrs. Henry explained they could take their meals in the servants' kitchen or bring them to their sitting room, as they preferred. He was glad that Susan would be relieved of the burden of cooking and housekeeping, and he imagined the children would be enchanted with the idea of living in a castle, playing knights and ladies all day long.

His first day at Ellon Castle seemed to bode well.

His first night in Ellon castle, however, was somewhat more ominous.

John was awakened from a profound sleep by a scream that seemed to reverberate off the old stone walls. In the stupour of his semi-conscious state, he imagined he was hearing a ghost. As his terrified mind struggled to a state of consciousness, he realized that it must be a woman's cries as there was no such thing as a ghost. If he had been more awake, he would never have imagined such nonsense. Such superstitions were not worthy of entertainment.

The wail continued, intermittent but incessant, and he finally sat up and put his slippers on, searching for his robe. Someone was in need of assistance. He must discover who it was and offer whatever assistance he could to the damsel in distress.

He sought the apartment of the only people he had thus far encountered in the castle, the amiable Henrys. He tapped at their door until Matthew Henry admitted him. Mr. Henry was as lean as his wife was stout, and Dean's predisposition to like him had been rewarded by a shy, kindly smile earlier in the evening. Now the good man looked as worried as John felt.

"So, now that you have made the acquaintance of the castle ghost, Mr. Dean, what do you think of her?"

"Castle ghost, Henry! I am surprised at you. How can you believe in such nonsense?"

"You do not, sir?" Henry smiled. "You fancy yourself an enlightened man, then? More's the pity. I do love a good ghost story myself."

"As long as you know they are just stories, sir."

The "ghost" screamed again.

"Now, what is that wail, Mr. Henry?" John asked. "And I want the truth. None of your stories."

"Ye dinna ken the cries of a woman giving birth? I would have thought you had heard the sound often enow."

John could not remember his wife screaming with quite such urgency. "Who is the woman?" he asked.

"'Tis the mistress of Ellon Castle, Penelope Dering. My wife has gone to assist her until the midwife arrives."

"The mistress of the castle?" Dean echoed. He had not said Penelope Gordon, so she could not be the Earl's wife. How could she be the mistress of the castle then? Dean wondered.

"Aye. The mistress." This time Henry said the word in such a manner that there could be no doubt.

Realizing his assistance was not required, John returned to his apartment in such a state of shock that he lay awake long after Penelope Dering's cries ceased. His mind turned over and over this unwelcome discovery that he was now the gardener on the estate of a "kept" woman. How could he stay? And yet, where could he go? He almost wished the screamer had been a ghost instead.

The next morning, exhausted and bleary-eyed, he went to breakfast in the servants' quarters where he found not as much joy as one would have expected after the birth of a bairn.

"The bairn has died," Mrs. Henry whispered to John as she handed him a bowl of parritch.

"Indeed," he said, uncertain how to greet such news.

"Aye. The mistress is not as fortunate as you in the number of her children," Henry explained to him. "But she does have one wee bairn that my wife delights in spoiling, does she not, my dear?"

"Aye. Wee Alexander. Little Sandy, we like to call him. He has just begun to walk, so be careful ye dinna run him over when you meet him about the castle corridors."

"Dinna fash, madam. I have much experience at dodging infants."

They laughed.

After breakfast, Henry showed him around the garden. Before long, he found himself with so much work to occupy himself that he almost forgot about the fact that his new mistress was indeed a mistress. He scarcely had time even to think about the imminent trials and travails of his own wife.

~~*

Due to her indisposition, it was several days before John met the mistress of the castle, Penelope Dering. Through Mrs. Henry, she requested that he come to her sitting room before he went to work in the garden. She was sitting on a well-stuffed chair with a blanket wrapped about her, gazing at her little boy playing on the floor. For a moment, his keen perception deserted him and he had a brief vision of Susan. Then she looked up at him, and he saw that his vision was mistaken. Though she was beautiful, her features were softer and more childlike than Susan's, and her eyes were dark brown and not the sparkling blue of his wife's.

"Mr. Dean," she said extending her hand to him.

He shook it in a business-like manner. "Madam," he said, checking his customary nod.

"I hope your lodging's to your liking."

By her voice he ascertained that she was an Englishwoman, not a Scot, and a commoner, not a gentlewoman. He did not know which of these two facts astonished him more. "'Tis most satisfactory."

"And is the garden up to snuff?"

"Aye."

"Good. His Lordship will be pleased that you like it. I know he's in a pother to get back and discuss it with you. Till then, he's written you a letter with instructions for the garden." The mistress handed him the letter in the manner of a little girl playing at princess.

"Thank you."

"Now, if you need anything, just let Henry know."

"That I will, thank you. May I greet your little boy, madam?"

"Certainly," she said.

John crouched down and extended his hand to the bairn. "Good morning to ye, lad," he said.

The boy smiled at him, that guileless smile of the very young. How John missed his own sons at that moment!

"You have some children yourself I understand, Mr. Dean?"

"Aye. Three sons and one daughter."

"My goodness!" she exclaimed, without a trace of sadness or bitterness in her voice.

John patted her son on the head and said, "Good bye, Alexander." Standing up, he nodded at her. "And good day to you, madam."

"Good day, Mr. Dean." Then she smiled and cocked her head at him in a most beguiling manner, so unnerving him that he felt a sudden irrational desire to run from her presence. He restrained himself lest he should embarrass himself by tripping over his own feet in such a hasty departure. Taking his time, he exited slowly, conscious of his stilted, unnatural gait as he left. The mistress of the castle was a wench to be avoided whenever possible, he concluded.

Dundee, Summer, 1784

As Susan's time of delivery drew nearer, Margaret set her up on a cot in the dining room, from which position she could observe the activities in both the kitchen and the parlour, but still be sufficiently isolated to take some rest if she needed it. Although she was restless and would have liked to participate more in the household routine, this pregnancy was proving more physically challenging than her previous four had been. So she stayed put and observed, attempting by that occupation to learn to be a better wife and mother.

Through the open doorway to the kitchen, Susan could watch Margaret directing the cook, who was also the housekeeper. She wanted to know what foods were served in Scotland and their method of preparation, because she thought she would soon be called upon to know these things and hoped to be able to surprise John with the dishes he remembered from his childhood.

One morning Susan was so engaged, observing the cook prepare a kind of barley soup for dinner when there was a great clamour from the parlour where Maude and the children had just come indoors to escape a rain shower. James and John were tossing Eleanor's doll back and forth above her head and she began to howl when they would not let her have it. Instead of stopping them, Maude was laughing with the boys. Margaret came out of the kitchen to see what the disturbance was.

"What on earth is the matter? Why are you making such a din? You will disturb your mother. Maude, take that doll away from the boys and return it to Eleanor."

Susan felt a familiar twinge in her belly. Oh no, she thought, it's starting.

Maude snatched the doll from Johnny's hands, tearing its skirt. Then she handed it to Eleanor, who resumed howling the moment she saw its tattered gown.

"Come, Ellie," her grandmother said, "Let's go into the kitchen and help the cook, shall we?"

Eleanor took her grandmother's hand and went with her. As they were passing her cot, Susan asked to see the doll. Ellie stopped. A sob escaped her as she tried to master her tears. She wiped her eyes and handed the doll to her mother.

Susan looked into her daughter's wide, hopeful eyes and felt a wave of tenderness toward her such as she had never felt before. She inspected the doll. "Well," she said at last. "If your grandmother will fetch me a needle and thread, I shall stitch up the skirt as good as new." Needlework was one occupation Susan had learned from her own mother.

"I shall fetch them right away," Margaret said.

Ellie sat on the cot beside her and said, "Thank you, Mama."

Ellie had always been her father's pet: she adored him and he reciprocated. Susan had sometimes watched the two of them together and felt jealous. "You miss Papa, don't you, Ellie?"

Ellie nodded. Susan could see she might start to cry again and she hugged her to her breast.

"But I am here for you too, my pet," and all of the jealousy she had ever felt vanished. She understood for the first time how her own mother's jealousy had grown into hatred. And in her warming love for her daughter, she realized that she forgave and even pitied her mother, for her irrational and unnecessary hatred.

Love felt so much better, she thought, as she repaired the doll's skirt with Ellie curled up beside her, watching her every stitch. She had never before enjoyed needlepoint as much. Susan could see now that Eleanor needed a refuge from the stormy sea of boys that surrounded her. She could be that to her, even if it meant teaching her needlework.

In the parlour, the boys were again arguing loudly over which of them had torn Eleanor's doll. Margaret returned to the scene.

"Maude, you maun get the boys to play less roughly when they are in the house. We canna have them breaking furniture."

"I'm sure I don't know any boys' games, madam. I am not a boy, as you can plainly see."

Her manner was so petulant as to be insulting, and Susan wanted to scold her. She began to call out, "Maude…" At that moment she felt another, fiercer twinge of pain. She held on tightly to the doll and waited while it passed.

"Are you all right, Mommy?"

"Yes, dear. Mother, will you take Ellie now."

"What game shall we play now, boys?" Maude asked them.

Margaret took her granddaughter. "There will be no more games in the house. Maude, you will watch the children and keep them quiet while I go upstairs with their mother. She needs peace and quiet now." Margaret directed her remarks to the boys. Then she called her maid. "Fetch the midwife," she ordered. "Let's go upstairs while you're still able, Susan."

Giving birth seemed to Susan the most tedious process in the world. Even though each of these events had been unique in her experience, they had all blended together in her memory so that she could scarcely distinguish one from another. However, there was one that stood out: the birth of little Johnny had been memorable for the great fear that attended it. Once again she was giving birth without the presence (even if it were only in the next room) of her husband. However, his absence was much mitigated by the blessed companionship of his mother and the compassionate midwife she provided.

Still, Susan would not have foregone any of the painful experiences of the births that she had suffered if it meant being deprived of the children that were issue of them. There was no greater pleasure in the world than to lie exhausted after hours of labour with a wee bairn lying on her belly as she counted the fingers and toes and marveled at the perfectly formed little nose and sweet little lips sucking and sucking, seeking sustenance, just as her lovely newborn son lay on her belly now, and she smelled his just-washed pink skin.

With foreknowledge of his absence on this occasion, John and Susan had chosen names for the baby this time. If it were a girl, she was to be named Susan, and if a boy, he was to be named David, which meant "beloved" in the Hebrew tongue. He was the only one of their children not given a family name.

Ellon Castle, Autumn, 1784

The time came at last when Susan was sufficiently recovered to embark with all of her children, five of them now, and their incompetent maid, into the horrid confines of a hot, stuffy coach in order to suffer the hours of excruciating commotion on the days of travel to reach Ellon Castle.

As arduous as the journey would be, she was eager to arrive, as her appetite had been whetted for the experience by her husband's letters. John had written her describing the Castle and their family apartment in it. She did not know whether to be happy or sad that she would not have her own house. On the one hand, she had been studying to be a good housewife. On the other hand, and this was the hand that felt like applauding, there would be others about her to share the burden of the children. She would not have to rely solely on Maude, whose greatest competence it seemed, was in tying Susan's gown in the morning, something she did with more vigour than was strictly necessary.

John's description of the housekeeper Lavinia Henry comforted Susan most. She would miss his mother (they had wept together copiously at their farewell, uncertain whether they would ever see each other again on this earth), but she had hopes that Mrs. Henry would be an adequate substitute grandmother for the children.

His letters were also full of extravagant descriptions of the garden at Ellon Castle. He told her of the trees the Earl had planted and the flowers and shrubs which he himself had selected to complement them. He described the general environs of Ellon so that she felt she knew it before they arrived—the sparkling river, the charming village, the new church and the old school in the Tollbooth that James would attend.

His letters, however, had contained no mention of the principal residents of the castle. Susan did not consider it to be an important matter and was not overly concerned about what such a lack portended. Neither was she particularly impatient to meet the Earl and his family herself when she should arrive at Ellon Castle. She naturally presumed that they were not the people she would spend her time with and so did not waste her time in wondering about them.

In spite of their eagerness at the outset, the coach ride from Dundee to Ellon soon sank them all into a foul mood. First of all, it was bitterly cold. The wind blew fiercely off the German Sea and the fog's icy fingers crept everywhere, obscuring the view of whatever scenery there might have been. Brief glimpses between fog patches did not hold much promise, however. She could see no trees: only miles and miles of wind-blasted moor. Where had John brought them? she wondered. To the edge of Hell?

When the children complained of the cold, she wrapped them in blankets as best she could. Maude soon complained the loudest.

"My fingers have all turned blue. Look, madam. Surely we are not going to continue any further north. Let's return to England. This is madness."

"Hush, Maude," Susan admonished her lest she alarm the children.

Her big brown eyes glared at her mistress above the woolen blanket. "I'm sure I've never met such an imperious gardener's wife," she said, sulking.

Susan wished she could have dismissed the insolent nanny there and then, but she did not know if she would be able to find another servant in Scotland that could speak the King's English so that she could understand.

"Hold your tongue," she said, not intending to be ironic.

The coach turned inland away from the coast, and, as the sun broke through the fog, they found themselves fording a lovely stream with dippers flying fast and low above it. She knew it at once from her husband's description. From the low-lying stream, the carriage went up the hill through the village and towards a castle whose towers could just be seen through the tall trees that surrounded it. A few moments that seemed an eternity later, they found their way to that castle, and John's happy face appeared at the carriage window before the horses had even come to a stop. As he ran alongside the coach, the children exclaimed and clapped their hands, disarranging the blankets as they jumped up to see him. When it finally stopped, he flung the door open and the children tumbled out, one after the other, on top of each other. He managed to sort them out somehow, picking up each one, and kissing them, before replacing them decorously on the gravel driveway.

"Johnny! It's good to see you, lad." Smack. Down.

"Eleanor! Look at you, lass. How you've grown!" Smack. Down.

"Sweet William! I swear you've grown sweeter." Smack. This one refused to be put down and kept his arms wrapped tightly around his father's neck.

John was obliged to continue holding him and so extended his free hand to his oldest son, James, who puffed himself up as proud as possible that he was being treated with respect and not grabbed and kissed unceremoniously.

Scowling Maude descended from the coach next, and John congenially took her hand to assist her. "Good day to you, madam."

Then he looked past her into the dark interior. His eyes, full of love, met Susan's. "And who do we have here?" he asked. "Why 'tis the most beautiful woman in the world and her latest bairn! Let me look at him, madam."

Susan uncovered the baby's face and held him so that he could see. "He has all his fingers and toes, John. I have counted."

"Gude, gude. And he has a bonny wee face at that. What is his name, madam?"

"David, as I wrote to you and as we agreed before you left."

"Wee David Dean of Dundee. 'Tis quite alliterative. Do you think he will be a poet?"

"I should hope not, sir," she said. She had grown so practical in her outlook that she could see naught but trouble for one who practiced a profession so dependent on the good will of noblemen.

John extended his one free arm (he was still holding young William) and helped her debark as best he could. He kissed her gloved hand, wishing for so much more and realizing how much he had missed her. There would be a sweeter reunion later. Then he presented her to all the people who would make up her life for the next few years. First there was Penelope Dering, a young woman with a child the age of William entwined in her sumptuous silk skirt. Thus encumbered, she tottered forward and extended a hand to shake Susan's. Susan noted the fine lace work of the *engageantes*.

"Welcome to Ellon Castle, madam. Let me see your babby? Oh, he is lovely."

The moment she heard her voice, Susan identified her as a servant, most probably the lady's maid, since her gown was so splendid. It was not uncommon for a maid to dress as well as her mistress, especially if she were given her cast-off gowns. Susan was touched by the interest the young woman took in her baby and complimented her young son, who was introduced as Alexander, in return.

Then she met Lavinia Henry, whose stout smiling face suggested a kindly nature, and Matthew Henry, a thin shy man who tugged his forelock as he shook her hand.

"Now, Mrs. Dean," Mrs. Henry said. "Let me show you to your apartment where you and the children can rest and be refreshed. When you are ready, your husband may bring you to the kitchen where I shall have some supper prepared."

"You are most kind, madam," Susan said, and indeed she was, herding the flock of children through the great castle to the servants' quarters, not an easy task, since the boys were so enchanted by the idea of living in a castle and kept wandering off to explore the passageways and stairwells.

Susan was not disappointed by their apartment. There was a lovely wooden cradle in their bed chamber. John told her that the mistress had provided it herself after the recent death of her own bairn had made it available. There was another bedroom for the boys, and one for Eleanor as the only girl. James and John claimed the boys' room and Eleanor willingly agreed to share a room with her little brother William, who still needed extra care. At five years old she was already becoming a little mother.

Susan was able to recuperate from her long voyage because John took care of the children in the sitting room, trying to calm them by asking them about their activities during the months they had been apart, while their mother slept on the bed with the baby in the cradle beside her.

Just before supper he looked in to see if she would come down to the kitchen or if he should bring her a bite to eat. She said that she would go down. She left the baby in the care of Maude, who had her own apartment, so, thankfully, they would be relieved of her company occasionally.

~~*

The enormous joy John felt at the arrival of his family to their new home was a little overshadowed by his anxiety that Susan would shortly discover that her position in the household would be in subordination to a common and disreputable wench. Not knowing how she would react to this fact, he avoided telling her but was still astonished when she exhibited no signs of having discovered it herself. Susan met Miss Penelope Dering with equanimity. She did not flinch even a little when the young girl spoke to her in that execrable and unbecoming accent. Finally, after days of unfeigned lack of comprehension on Susan's part, John examined his conscience regarding the necessity to reveal the truth.

"Susan," he said, one evening after the children had all been bedded and they were seated in their sitting room.

"Yes, John?"

"It strikes me as peculiar that you have not yet remarked on the position of Miss Penelope Dering, the mistress of the castle."

"Is she the mistress of the castle?" She seemed genuinely surprised. "I would not have imagined that. I had assumed that Penelope was one of the servants, perhaps the maid of the Earl's wife. I did not suspect that she was the

Earl's wife herself. He married quite beneath his station, did he not?" She smiled.

"I have no idea," John said, "as I have not met his wife. She resides with her five children about ten miles from here at Haddo House."

"My goodness!" Susan said. "Then what is Penelope's relationship to him?"

"She is the Earl's mistress and the mother of his bastard son." He paused to gauge her reaction, but her expression did not change, so he continued. "I am sorry, my dear, to have brought you and the children into such a reprehensible situation. I am especially sorry that you have been placed in a standing beneath someone who is in every respect your inferior."

She did not respond immediately and the expression on her face was inscrutable. Finally, after a long pause, she said, "Dinna fash, John. I will survive."

John tried to smile at her imitation of the Scottish accent, but if she had intended to lighten his mood, it had not succeeded.

Susan took pains to hide her true feelings because she was aware how much they were at odds with John's. Although she had not been raised with her husband's strict moral principles, she knew that Penelope's deportment was shocking from his point of view. Indeed, his was the perspective shared by polite society in general. However, Susan also recognized that, from Penelope's more practical vantage point, she had made a felicitous match. Society would have confined her to a position as a charwoman or some such menial worker, and yet, here she was, the mistress of a castle with servants like the Henrys and Susan's own husband to wait upon her! Susan was somewhat in awe at how Penelope had managed it, but she kept her expression totally blank so that John would not suspect the admiration that she felt for the hussy.

As for his words that Penelope was her inferior in every respect, she thought not. In fact, from a purely worldly point of view, Susan had fallen from a higher social position to a lower one by following her wayward heart. Whereas, Penelope had led an Earl by his heart and ascended to the heights of social wealth, if not respectability. Having crossed social boundaries herself, Susan felt a kind of sisterhood of experience with Penelope Dering.

~~*

It was November. The sky was overcast and had been overcast for endless days it seemed. Water oozed from the great sponge-like sky, hung in droplets on the trees, and seemed to seep through the castle walls and hang invisible in the air. Dampness hung upon the clothes that they donned in the morning. It hung about Susan's hair, making it frizzle around her head. It lingered on the baby's napkins so that they always seemed in need of changing. It invaded the very sheets they climbed into at night.

The children too seemed to hang about the house like condemned prisoners, except for James who had to trudge off alone to the village school at the Tollbooth. No one wanted to walk with him in this dreadful weather. Even John stayed indoors, but he locked himself in his office, doing whatever gardeners do in the winter months.

Susan watched the children playing their games in the halls of the castle. Johnny was King Arthur (he was always King Arthur, unless his older brother was at home) and Eleanor was Guinevere.

"You are Sir Lancelot," they told Sweet William. He nodded enthusiastically but made no attempt to repeat the awkward name. They were endlessly frustrated by the fact that he wandered off in the middle of their game. When he started to cry, Susan took him to her bedroom to sleep with the baby there. She sang to him, his own song of "Barbry

Allen" in which Sweet William dies of love. It was too maudlin, too sad for a little boy, but it fit this dreary, dreary place.

In the evenings, after supper in the servants' kitchen, the family sat around the table and the usually quiet Matthew Henry would find his voice and tell ghost stories in the flickering light of the fireplace.

"The castle is surrounded by trees, and at nicht, 'e critter covered in black hairs comes oot kerryin' a licht moaning aboot and clawin' and groupen' at anyone aroon' it wi' blood curdlin' screems. Its clives wid be covered in blood and then it wid disappear into the dark castle.

"If ye hear 'e critter at nicht screeming, ye wid ne go oot o' yer beds, bairns, wid ye?"

The children shook their heads emphatically.

Susan listened, rapt in wonder at the sound of his voice, comprehending little at first. Then, after many evenings, she grew slowly able to make out the unfamiliar words and put them together to form a coherent story that was so frightening she wished she had not understood. She was surprised at John, who surely understood from the first, that he allowed the children to listen to such tales before bed time, so she asked him why.

"You can see how they like them. When we put them to bed, they stay there and dinna go wondering about for fear of ''e critter'."

"I am more afraid they will wake us in the middle of the night with their blood-curdlin' screams because of their nightmares."

"'Tis naught but a little harmless enjoyment. They will soon enough ken what is real and what is not."

Susan was surprised. She had not suspected that her practical husband had a fanciful side. "Are you so certain that there are no such things as ghosts? This castle is such an eerie place that sometimes I am afraid of the noises in the night."

"Dinna be daft, woman. Perhaps you are the one who ought not to listen to Henry's tales. You should say your prayers at bedtime, and you'll have no cause to fear the critters that go bump in the nicht," he said.

Ellon Castle, Winter, 1784

There was bound to be an attraction between two lonely young women cooped up in a castle with children, old servants, and the rain outside. At first their paths merely crossed in the hallways occasionally, and they would exchange a few words of greeting. Gradually, as they found a commonality in their situations, they began to talk longer. One day, during such a meeting, Miss Dering remarked on Susan's gentility of speech.

"My father was a gentleman, madam. He had a large estate in Kent. Mr. Dean was the gardener on that estate."

"Oh!" Miss Dering seemed at a loss.

Susan could almost hear the unspoken words in the silence, so she filled them in. "Yes, I married very much beneath my station, but I have not regretted it."

Miss Dering seemed to regain her composure as Susan spoke. "I hope not, missus. Still, you must miss the fine gowns and the fine company."

"We were never much out in fine company. Nor do I miss the gowns so much." Susan could not help herself. She sighed, but then said, "Although I have remarked that your gowns are very fine indeed. Especially the one you are wearing now. That pale green silk accentuates your eyes so well."

"Thankee." Miss Dering curtsied and then blushed prettily.

"As I was saying, it is not the gowns that I miss so much, it is the company of other people of my age. Every moment is taken up with caring for my children, and I scarcely converse with anyone anymore."

Miss Dering laughed, a delightfully sympathetic laugh. "And the only grownups you have to converse with speak English so dreadfully 'you dinna ken a word.'" She laughed again. "I know exactly what you mean."

Susan had not meant exactly that, but Miss Dering's broader interpretation of her words was just and near the mark, encompassing more of the truth than she had admitted to herself.

"Mrs. Dean, we shall have some womanly conversation. You must come to tea with me tomorrow."

Susan shook her head.

"I will not take no for an answer. I too have no one here that I may speak English with except my son Alexander, and though I love him dearly, I do grow tired of his senseless prattle some times. Come tomorrow. You must. What hour is most convenient to you?"

Susan was hesitant. She doubted John would approve. And Maude was still so useless as a nanny that it would be difficult to find the time to break away. Still she felt a sincere regard in Miss Dering's expression and she longed to have a companion to talk with, about fine gowns perhaps, even if she could not wear them. Much as she loved her husband, he was not much interested in topics beyond his garden.

"You will do me a great service, if you will come. You may instruct me in genteel manners, seen as you were raised a gentlewoman and I was not. At what o'clock should tea be properly served?"

"The time varies according to convenience. For example, two o'clock is much too early, but in my situation, it is the hour I shall be best able to attend, as the children will be napping at that time."

"I shall expect you at two o'clock then, Mrs. Dean." Miss Dering swept past, her silk gown rustling in a fashion that stirred fond memories in Susan's heart.

The next day Miss Dering ushered Susan into her luxuriously appointed sitting room.

"Sit down, Mrs. Dean," she said, indicating a finely upholstered chair.

"Thank you, madam."

"How are the children?"

"Fine. How is Alexander?"

"Splendid."

"Is the weather always this awful?"

"Please don't mention the weather. It goes on and on like this until the spring. At least this winter I shall have some company to help me survive it, if you will be so good as to visit me often. You are most welcome to come at any time, except when the Earl is here, of course. When his lordship is in residence, all of my time is occupied." Penelope folded her hands in her lap and pursed her lips as she said this. "By the way, he is coming for Christmas!" Her eyes lit up.

Susan nodded in response. She wondered what kind of man the Earl was to inspire such devotion. "What preparations must be done for the Christmas season?" she asked, to change the subject.

"We celebrate Christmas at Ellon Castle much the same as in England because I insist that we do. Otherwise, the Scots would ignore it altogether. Can you imagine that Christmas is illegal in this godforsaken place?"

"What? No Christmas! The one occasion that might enliven such a dismal season. Why is that?"

"Because of that humorless little man John Knox is why. He declared it to be a papist tradition."

Susan imagined how aghast John would be to hear Miss Dering speak so disparagingly of his hero.

"Well, I show him! I make a great to-do about Christmas just to spite the silly man and all who follow him."

Susan thought her life as a mistress served well enough to spite him, but she did not say so. "So how do you celebrate?"

"We decorate. Your husband will bring in mistletoe, holly and yew. And we'll make a great big Christmas pudding. Lavinia will put together the ingredients soon and then everybody in the house will have a stir and make a wish. And we'll give gifts." Her face dropped of a sudden. "I had forgotten something. The Earl insists that gifts must be given at New Years. He's a Scot, too, unfortunately. Tell me, what would your children like?"

"I am sure that it is not necessary for you to give them gifts."

"Another Scottish tradition. The master gives gifts to the servants on January 3rd."

"Well, it is always so cold here that they are constantly in need of mittens or socks."

"How dreadfully dull. I shall write to the Earl and have him bring a doll for Eleanor at least."

"That is too much, Miss Dering."

"I insist. She is the only girl among all the children here. She must be spoiled a little."

Susan was so pleased by her kindness that she could not speak.

"I'm only sorry we can't exchange gifts at Christmastime, but the Scots make a great to-do about the New Year, you know. They call it some terrible name. What is it? Pigmania?"

"What a horrid name!"

"Well, that is not quite right. But it has something to do with a pig if I recall. We must ask Lavinia what it is. At any rate, since they cannot celebrate Christmas, they release their frustrations at the New Year, make a dreadful racket and keep everyone awake all night."

After this initial meeting, they often found the means to visit. Sometimes Mrs. Henry would watch the children for Susan, and other times, Susan would bring the children with her and Alexander's nanny Mrs. MacPherson would watch them all. They became fast friends and neither one of them gave a care that they were not the same class as they had each transcended class in their personal lives. Susan sometimes wondered why John thought that she should feel superior to Miss Dering. On moral grounds, she supposed she had a right to, but moral grounds had never figured prominently in her education. At any rate, her desire for friendship outweighed any moral compunction she might have had, and her last friend had been a servant, so social class was not a consideration. Social class was, in this situation, ambiguous at any rate.

~~*

The Earl looked at John's plans for the garden plantings and said nothing. At the end of it, he rocked back and forth on his heels and said, "Well, then."

"Is everything to your liking, my lord?"

"The New Jersey tea," he said, shaking his head. "Us don't like it. It is not very pretty, has dull little white flowers. Take it out."

"Certainly, my lord."

"And the turpentine tree. Ghastly specimen. Remove it as well."

"Aye, sir. You do not like botanical collections then, my lord?"

"No. Us likes a good show in the pleasure-garden. Lots of pretty flowers, none of 'em skimpy exotics. If you must have a collection, put it under cover behind the castle somewhere and out of our shrubbery."

"As you wish, my lord." He should have known a man who kept a pretty young mistress would have no interest in science and the study of botany. Big ostentatious flowers it would be in future.

"Well, the rest is acceptable. Carry on." The Earl turned to leave the office."Before you leave, my lord, I would like to ask a favour of you, if I may."

The Earl looked suspicious. "What might that be?"

"Mrs. Dean and I are most dissatisfied with our nanny, Maude Ashcroft. She is quite incapable of dealing with five lively children, and she shirks her duties at every opportunity."

The Earl was glaring at him so severely that John wished he had not said a word in her disfavour.

"Miss Ashcroft is young and must be given much leniency and time to learn. Have you and your wife made every effort to teach her her occupation, remembering it is her first experience in such a position?"

"We have, my lord."

The Earl scowled.

John thought that the young lady must be a favorite of the Earl's.

"Well," he blustered. "Us will look for a position that is less strenuous for such a delicate girl. In the meantime, us would suggest that you try again, remembering to use Christian patience and forbearance."

John bowed deeply to hide the insult he felt at the Earl's hypocritical adjective. "My lord," he said and returned to his labour, wishing his employer to the devil.

~~*

John was in his study when he heard a light tap at his door. At first he wanted to believe it was Susan, but his heart knew such a timid tap would not be hers.

"Come in," he said.

Matthew Henry put his head inside the door. "My apologies for disturbing you at your work, Mr. Dean."

"No apologies are necessary, Henry. Come in." John stood up to welcome him and offer him a chair. "What can I do for you?"

Henry chuckled. "Ye ken 'tis Hogmanay tomorrow?"

John nodded.

"Well," he said. "Before I grew these grey hairs, I was much in favour for first footing." It was a Scottish tradition that if a dark-haired man was the first person to cross one's threshold on New Year's Day (or Ne'ers Day, as it was called), then one would have good luck all year long.

"Some of the neighbours have seen you in the village, Dean, and a great number of them have solicited me to ask you if you wouldna mind to pay them a social call at Hogmanay."

"Me!" John said. Such a thought had not crossed his mind living in England all these years. "Why, of course, I should be delighted."

"Gude. The missus and I will fix you up with all you will need."

"What will I need? Ye ken I hae been in London for many years and scarcely remember the old ways. Besides which, my family never held much truck with them, being strict Presbyterians and all."

"Ye'll need salt, coal, shortbread, black bun, and a wee bit of whisky, if ye dinna mind, Dean."

"Of course I dinna mind."

~~*

Most of the servants went together to the Ne'er's bonfire which was to be lit just before midnight. Maude sulked to be left behind with the baby and wee William, but the older children, James, Johnny and Eleanor, who had had a sleepless nap earlier in the day, were allowed to go to the bonfire and stay up well past their usual bed-time. They were so excited that they chattered and skipped through the snow beside their parents.

"Papa, my feet are cold," Eleanor complained and felt herself lifted high above the heads of the crowd. She watched while the bonfire was lit and as it grew larger, the crowd drew closer warmed by its flames. Eleanor watched fascinated by the laughing faces of the fold, so usually dour and gloomy. The men occasionally drank from bottles and their faces glowed in the firelight.

"'Tis time, Dean," Uncle Matthew said, and her father swung her down through the air and placed her on her feet back in the snow again.

"Papa, my feet are cold."

"'Tis time for you to go back home now, sweetheart. You will have new socks in the morning. Meantime, Papa maun go a-first-footing."

She had no notion of what he was saying, but she watched while Uncle Matthew and Aunt Lavinia gave him two sacks so large she wondered how he could lift them. One of them clanked so she knew it must be filled with bottles. Eleanor had no time to puzzle out this mystery before her brothers took hold of her.

"Ellie, 'tis black nicht out. You ken what that means?"

She shook her head.

"'Tis the hour that Uncle Matthew told us not to be out or we'ud see the critter covered in black hair kerrying a licht."

Eleanor shivered. She looked around at the people all moving away from the fire now, going back to their village homes. She saw Uncle Matthew, the teller of tales laughing with a group of men.

Aunt Lavinia left him there and walked with Ellie's mother. Ellie took her mother's hand as they made their way back to the castle. Her brothers were turning left and right all along the pathway, searching for the "critter." Eleanor kept her eyes fixed on the path in front of her, and began to breathe well again when they had entered the castle. Their mother saw them to their apartment but did not stay with them as Aunt Lavinia asked her to keep her company in the kitchen till the men came home. Besides, Maude was wide awake, glaring at them resentfully from a chair in the sitting room. Mother asked her to see that the children went to bed.

When she left the room, Maude ordered the boys to go to their room and change. Then she grabbed Ellie by the collar and pulled her into her room. Ellie cried out, and then whispered so as not to wake Willie. "You're a critter," she said to her nanny.

"You mind your tongue."

Then Maude started to remove her gown roughly.

"I can do it myself. Go away!"

"I shall then, you ungrateful baggage."

Maude looked in to the boys' room on her way out. "What! Already abed! What mischief are you up to?"

There was no answer.

"Well, never you mind. I shan't care. I am tired of looking after you. I am going to my apartment now. Any mischief you do now is on your own head."

Then she walked out the door. A moment later, Ellie's brothers were in her room.

"Go away," she said. "I am removing my gown."

"Dinna take it off, Ellie. We are going back to find the critter," Johnny said.

"Aye. You'll come with us, Ellie," James told her. It was not a question, but she answered it anyway.

"I think I shall go to bed."

"You're a coward, Ellie. Afraid of a critter!" Johnny laughed.

"Aye, that I am."

"Come on, Ellie," James cajoled her.

Johnny was her younger brother; she could refuse him. But James was the oldest, and Ellie always admired him.

"I shall protect you," he said, and that clenched the bargain. She picked up her blanket and followed her brothers.

The great door of the castle creaked as they opened it. James pulled it slowly, hoping no one would hear, but it only served to lengthen the eerie sound. Once it was open wide enough, they paused a moment to hear if anyone was coming before they slipped through and out into the snow again.

They stayed by the door waiting till their eyes adjusted to the darkness again, watching the dark shapes of the tall trees that bordered the property. It took scarcely any time for their eyes to adjust since the reflection of moonlight on snow brightened the garden till it seemed almost like daylight. They watched the forest waiting for the "critter with the licht, its clives covered in blood."

Eleanor pulled her blanket around her tightly and wished she were back in bed.

~~*

John knocked at the door of the last house of the street and heard the now familiar words: "Are ye black or fair haired? If yur no fair haired yur welcome tae be ma first foot o'er 'iss threshold after 12 o'clock."

John entered to the skirl of a bagpipe and presented what was left of the gifts he had brought: a pinch of salt, a lump of coal; one last piece of shortbread, for which he apologized profusely, seeing as how this was a large family; half a dozen of Mrs. Henry's favoured black buns, which almost made up for the lack of shortbread; and a bottle of the finest single malt highland whiskey, the water of life, which most surely did.

There was a great deal of palavering in the Scots tongue, which amounted to little sense since most of the company had already drunk a great deal of life's water by this late hour. Even John, who had tried to limit his imbibing to careful sips, had become increasingly careless, and his head was spinning by the time he made his way back to the castle.

He carried the two empty gunny sacks now and a lantern to light his path home. The cold air helped to clear his head, but in spite of it, he could sense that he was not as steady on his feet as he usually was. A sense of guilt assailed him. Long ago he had promised Susan that he would never drink to excess. He shook his head hoping to rid himself of the dizzy feeling, and wondered if he should not go to the kitchen and find something to take away the reek of whiskey on his breath before he went to their bed.

At that moment John emerged from the border of trees that surrounded the garden and on to the moonlit lawn in front of the castle. From the doorway he heard ungodly screaming and recognized it immediately as his children. He ran like the devil was after him to find out who was attacking them. As he came closer he saw that the door was open. Someone must have broken in, he thought. The screams continued even louder. He followed them. There was no doubt they seemed to be receding as he advanced.

Lavinia came running from the kitchen. "What on earth is the matter?" Mrs. Henry asked him. He stopped for a moment.

"I dinna ken," he replied.

He continued to follow the cries of the children, running up the stairs two at a time. He could see them just in front of him in the hallway.

"Oh my God, 'tis the critter," Johnny cried, as the three children disappeared into the apartment and slammed the door after them.

John paused. He was breathing hard. When Lavinia caught up to him, he was smiling.

"What is so humourous, sir?" Lavinia asked.

"'Tis Matthew's tales."

"Whatever do you mean?"

"The children believe that I am the critter covered in black hair," he lifted the gunny sacks, "and kerrying a licht." He lifted the lantern, which had gone out in his furious flight.

Lavinia laughed.

"You had best go in and settle them when you have made yourself more respectable. They have been punished enough for their knavery."

~~*

It was New Year's Day, or Ne'ers day as the Scots called it. The younger children, being too young to celebrate the night before, were up at the crack of dawn demanding their mother's attention as usual. Susan turned and looked at her husband. She had no idea what time he had come in the night before. He was snoring and she could smell the peaty odor of Scotch on his breath. She was surprised since he was not a drinking man. She had only seen him drunk once before, after which time he had vowed to her never to drink too much again.

Oh well, she thought. He was too hard on himself. It would do them all some good if he slipped up now and then.

Susan did not disturb him and went to tend to her crying babies. When they were all dressed, she and Eleanor went with Will and Davy to the servants' kitchen for breakfast. There they found that Lavinia Henry was in a little bit of a fuss because the Earl had announced he was leaving that day.

"His lordship has moved Handsel Day forward."

"What is Handsel Day, Mrs. Henry?"

"'Tis the day that the Lord of the house gives gifts to the servants. An occasion celebrated on January 3rd usually, but as I said, the Earl has amended that this year. So we must all meet in the foyer after breakfast this morning to bid him adieu and receive our tokens."

"Goodness. Then I shall have to get my boys up after breakfast. That may be difficult. I am afraid that Mr. Dean celebrated to excess last night."

Mrs. Henry tapped the back of her husband's head. "I am afraid that is the fault of my husband, introducing your good man to the vices of Hogmanay."

Henry flinched and scowled at her, but said nothing.

Susan finished her breakfast and went to their apartment to waken her sons and husband. John was very sore-headed about being disturbed. He muttered at her menacingly. "Bring me the chamber-pot," he said.

She handed it to him. "I shall tell them you are ill, shall I?"

"Aye," he said before he put his head in the pot. She left quickly after that to urge the older boys to hurry in their toilette.

At the foyer all the servants were assembled, many of the males looking somewhat the worse for the previous night's celebration. A kind of early morning sleepiness hung over the damp cold room. Susan shivered and wrapped her shawl tighter, wishing she had dressed the children in their outdoor clothes.

In the middle of the circle of servants stood the Earl, with his mistress at his side, and beside them was a great wicker basket heaped with colourful gifts. It was the first time Susan had ever seen the man, and she thought he looked very handsome in his elegant suit. He was posed with one hand on his hip so that his coat was pulled back to reveal a shapely leg and a beautifully embroidered waistcoat.

He waited until everyone was completely settled, and then he gave a little speech to thank them for their service. Susan noted his unusual manner of speaking, replacing "I", not with "we" as the king did, but with "us". She thought he sounded pompous and affected, and in spite of her best efforts, could not bring herself to like him. She wondered what Miss Dering saw in him that she did not.

Then the Earl, with his mistress at his side to aid him, began to distribute the gifts and tokens to the assembled staff. After almost everyone's names had been called, and Susan noticed the children were near the end of their patience, the Earl finally said, "Mr. Dean."

She stepped forward. "I am sorry, my lord. Mr. Dean is indisposed this morning. I am his wife."

"Good morning, Mrs. Dean. Miss Dering has told us of your friendship. She has urged us to give you a special gift."

"Thank you, my lord." Susan curtseyed.

"But first, here is your husband's gift."

The Earl handed her a sturdy pair of gardening gloves that she was sure John would appreciate. "I thank you on his behalf, my lord."

"For your children, madam." The Earl gave her a pile of mittens. "I have heard you have several."

Susan went back to the children and passed them out. There were four pairs, so she was one pair short, but perhaps the baby was not meant to have any.

Miss Dering spoke. "Have you forgotten that your daughter is to have a special gift?" Then she took from the great basket of presents a doll with a painted porcelain face.

"Oh," Susan said. She retrieved it, looking gratefully at Miss Dering, and brought it to Eleanor, who, almost speechless, repeated the same single word.

Susan remembered her manners and turned back. "Thank you so much," she said, curtseying again.

The Earl smiled condescendingly. "That is not all, madam." He turned to Miss Dering. "Give her her gift."

Miss Dering bent down and brought forth a silk gown, the very one that Susan had so admired at their first tea together. Susan had so long denied her own desire for fine clothes that she was overwhelmed.

"Oh, I could not, madam."

"Of course you shall. It is nothing, only a cast-off. I have already a new gown to replace it, compliments of the Earl." She curtseyed to him, and he beamed, seeming to enjoy his own generosity as much as anyone else.

Susan cringed a little, and almost wished she had the strength of will to refuse it. But she took it and went back to her place among the servants somewhat chastened.

"Is there not a gown in there for another servant as well?" The Earl could scarcely contain his excitement.

"Yes," Miss Dering said. "There is a gown for Miss Ashcroft as well."

The useless nanny bounded from the ranks, full of flutter and squeals of joy. Susan repressed the sneer she felt. She knew it was unkind of her to wish that Maude had not received a gown too, for it somehow cheapened the gift in her eyes even more than Miss Dering's words had done. She resolved to put her gown in the back of her wardrobe at the first opportunity and try to forget about it.

When they returned to the family apartment, the children, full of exuberant and excited energy, burst into their father's bedroom. Susan took the opportunity of the commotion to hang up the dress, but she removed the lace *engageantes* from the sleeves as she did so.

John had arisen at the sound of their voices in the sitting room and was still trying to keep the room steady. He did not have the capacity to deal with so many scrambling, screaming bodies, and yet he could not use his customary authoritarian voice to control the mob. He was afraid the attempt would do even more damage to his sorely injured brain. Instead he merely whispered, "Madam," so that Susan could not fail to hear him.

"Children, children," she chattered at them, wholly ineffectually. "Your papa is sick. You must be quiet."

He wished at this moment that they had a nanny who could control the children. He would speak to the Earl about it before he left. "Please leave the room. All of you," he whispered, hoping someone would hear him.

"They only want to show you their gifts from the Earl, John."

He looked at her, trying to ignore the children's noise. "Gifts from the Earl?"

"Aye, Papa. For Handsel Day," James replied.

John turned to him. "Have I not asked you to leave the room? And as my oldest son, I would expect you to set an example for the others and obey."

James looked so chastened that John almost felt sorry for his words, except that they had the desired effect. James took control of his brothers and sister and hustled them out.

John sat on the bed then, exhausted. Seeing his wife at the door about to leave, he said, "Not you, Susan. I should like a few words."

She looked a little frightened, but turned back. "What is it?"

"What is this nonsense about Handsel Day. Have I really slept for two whole days?"

Susan smiled. "No, dear. The Earl has decided to make his departure today and so has given out the servants' gifts today. Would you like to see yours?"

"Has he left?"

"Yes, or he is on the point of departure. If you look out the casement, you might see his carriage departing. Why does that disturb you? I thought you did not like the man?"

"I do not, and he should be with his own family today, but I wanted to speak to him about dismissing the nanny."

"Oh," Susan said. "That would be good. But I think she is a favourite of the Earl's."

"Why do you say that?"

"It is just a feeling that I have. Would you like to see your gift now?"

"Aye. Have the children come in one at a time, quietly, to show me their gifts, and I will try to restore their good opinion of me if I might. Begin with James."

Susan smiled and curtseyed to him. John laughed at the strange extravagant gesture, but the sound burst like gunfire in his head, and he choked it off quickly.

At first, seeing his own work gloves and James's mittens, John was pleased by the sober practicality of the Earl's presents. But when Eleanor walked in the room with her gaudy doll painted like a harlot, John felt even sicker inside. All of his worst fears were realized. He could say nothing to the little girl, who looked so happy carrying her own baby. But how he wanted to smash the doll's head against the wall, as John Knox would no doubt have done. But he had not the heart to hurt his own child like that, and truth be told, he had not the head to do it either, which fact reminded him of his own freshly committed sin. So he would sit still while the Earl corrupted his family. He smiled the weakest, most hypocritical smile at his darling daughter, Eleanor, vowing to reform his own behaviour in the future.

The bitter taste stayed with him through all the subsequent exhibits of the children's gifts. In the back of his mind he was wondering what his wife had been given, for he suspected that she had been bought as well. When he asked, she showed him the pair of lace *engageantes*.

"They are very pretty, Susan, but totally useless."

She nodded.

He felt a little tenderness toward her because she seemed so sad. "When will you ever have occasion to wear them?"

She shrugged and looked as if she might cry. He put his arm around her, sorry for his bad temper, and too overwhelmed with mixed emotions to know what to say.

Chapter 3

Ellon Castle, spring, 1785

At long last, after the long damp dreary days of winter, the spring arrived. Tiny crocuses, seeming too delicate to brave the cold, poked their heads through the soil between the snowy patches. The first robin was spotted in the garden pluckily attempting to pull a worm from the still hard ground. Slowly, slowly, winter released its talon-like grip on the earth, and its creatures opened their hearts and began to dare once again.

So too, Susan walked out with John one morning at his invitation. He had said it was his purpose to inspect the damage that winter had done to the garden and to see how far the spring had advanced in its rebirth, but she suspected that he wished to show her the beauty of his handiwork and perhaps stir some dormant memories.

After strolling side by side for some time, John bent down in the shrubbery and pulled back the leafy rosettes of a mandrake to reveal violet-coloured flowers. "Look, Susan," he said excitedly. "The Mandragor officinarum is in bloom." She knew that he was teasing her because she had often complained of the ugliness of Latin names for flowers. "And look at the Cheiranthus cheiri sanguineus." He smiled provokingly.

"You mean the red wallflower," she responded. She could sense his happiness and suspected that it was due, at least in part, to his being a true gardener again at last, and not merely a worker in a public exhibition ground. Soon he would transform the Ellon Castle Garden into an Elysian field that all of Scotland would come eagerly to see, just as he had done with her father's garden at Kirke Hall. They continued walking arm in arm along the garden path as they had once done so long ago and far away, and she felt perfectly content, as if paradise had at last been restored to them.

"I am glad that you could accompany me on my walk this morning," he said, as if reading her mind.

"I wish that we could spend more time together like this, but the children keep me occupied. I cannot leave them to Maude's care. Heaven knows what would happen if I did." She imagined them running wild through the castle. It was the stuff of her nightmares.

"The next time the Earl comes I shall speak to him again about replacing her. I will not accept his vague promises as I did at Hogmanay."

"I could speak to Miss Dering about it, if you wish."

Immediately she felt the muscles in his arm tighten and was sorry she had said it.

"I do not wish it." His voice was unnaturally soft. "You spend far too much time with the hussy now." She could hear his repressed anger in the way he hissed the word.

"But she is the mistress of the castle, John." She tried to match his quiet tone.

"She is the mistress of the laird, and that is all." He waved his hand dismissively.

Susan bowed her head. "All right. I will not speak to her of it."

"Nor nothing else neither."

Why could he not compromise? Why must he insist when she was being accommodating? "That is harsh, John. Miss Dering is my friend. We live in the same house and see each other every day. I cannot stop speaking to her."

"There is no reason for you to see her every day. You go out of your way to visit her. If I tell you not to speak to her, as a good wife, you ought to obey me. For it is written in the Bible,…"

Susan interrupted him. "Do not cite scripture to me, John." She removed her arm from his. She did not at all like to be spoken to as if she were an unruly child. Whether he was right or not, she could not abide his lectures. She turned around then, and walked back to the house, her eyes filling with tears, sorry that their tender mood had been spoiled by a quarrel.

All winter long he had locked himself away in his office leaving her to find her own amusement, and now he emerged like a grumpy bear from hibernation to tell her with whom she could or could not speak. If he had given her such a clear injunction at the beginning, perhaps she might have obeyed him. However, now that she had formed a fast friendship with Miss Dering, it would be exceedingly difficult, even heartbreaking, to begin to shun her companion. Not to say that she did not understand his injunction. She knew that his moral principles made him hold the mistress in contempt. She knew that it grated his pride every day to have to work for the woman, but he ought to understand her. She always followed her own heart, which was why they had married in the first place and why they were here now. He should know that she was not about to change.

Or rather, she was about to change, at least in the literal sense. She decided she would put on the gown that Miss Dering had given her. She wanted to make a definitive statement to her husband, to show him that she had a position in this household as Miss Dering's friend, whether he liked it or not. She would wear the gown all day, so that, even if she forgot her anger, she would still make her dissatisfaction clear to him at the end of the day.

~~*

As he always did, John immersed himself in his work to help him forget the feelings of unhappiness engendered by his disagreement with Susan. The garden was a demanding taskmistress in need of much work: he pruned the dead wood of winter, he pulled the pernicious weeds that were always the first greenery to arrive, and he prepared the hard compacted soil to receive the seeds that had lately arrived. At the end of a long day of hard labour in the garden, John inspected his handiwork, imagining how his winter gardening plans would look at the height of summer. Blackbirds sang from the treetops in the fading light of dusk. He looked up and admired what nature had already wrought in the garden without his interference, the variegated hues of the striped hollies -- the golden hedgehog and the silver milkmaid—whose gaiety contrasted with the somber laurels and phillyreas. Lost in his delight, a woman's voice startled him from his reverie.

"Ain't it lovely, Mr. Dean?"

John recognized the uncouth English accent of the woman who had been the subject of his argument with Susan earlier in the day. He turned around, prepared to glower, but instead was shocked into silence by the calm beauty of her person. As a gardener, he possessed a great appreciation for natural beauty, and there was no doubt that Miss Dering was beautiful, especially at this moment. He had not noticed before that she was pregnant, her small, round belly a perfect complement to the freshness of the spring garden. He smiled, in spite of himself.

"It is so seldom that I see you smile, Mr. Dean! I was beginning to wonder how on earth you had managed to captivate a lady like Susan, but now I see why she lost her heart to you."

His illusion was shattered by her imprudent chatter, and, rather than respond to her remark, he looked once more around the garden. This time his mind was fixed on business. He was searching for any tools that he might have left behind. When he was satisfied that there were none, he said, "I maun go, madam."

"No, stay a little. The evening is so lovely, and I am sure you would like some company."

"Aye, that I would, but all the company I desire awaits me in the castle. I havena seen my wife and bairns all day. So, if you will excuse me, madam, I maun go."

He passed beside her on the narrow path, close enough so that his clothing brushed against hers. In that moment he felt a spark of emotion pulse between them. He was so proud of his bloodless triumph over her that he interpreted it as her anger at his scorn.

As he entered the castle, John recalled the tender happy meeting with Susan earlier in the day. His anger at her truculence had left him with the sweat of his labour. Then Miss Dering had presented herself to him as a visible contrast to his wife. He smiled as he entered the family apartment in anticipation. He was not disappointed. He had never seen her looking so beautiful, standing by the table, surrounded by the children, holding the youngest on her hip.

"Good evening, John."

"You look lovely." She did too, but there was something amiss, something about her beauty. It was as fresh as the garden. Her gown! It was not worn and plain. It was a new gown, made of shiny blue silk with lace *engageantes* at the sleeves. He had seen those before. He tried to remember when. At Hogmanay. The Earl had given them to her. "That is a new gown," he stated sternly, daring her to tell him how she had obtained it.

"Yes," she said. "Miss Dering gave it to me when she was finished with it."

She spoke nonchalantly, as if it were nothing, as if she did not know how his blood would boil at the words. She said it to him in front of the children, using them as a kind of screen so that she would not feel his heat. "I will speak to you," he said, almost in a whisper.

"Yes, John. We shall speak later."

"Put down the bairn. We will speak now. In the bedroom." He could see the glint of fear come into her eyes, and his anger loved it, but he did not.

She put down young Davy, smoothed her gown and walked haughtily into the bedroom ahead of him.

He followed and shut the door. "We shall be but a moment," he said to the children, pitching his voice as normally as he could. Then he turned on her. "What do you mean by making your defiance of me into an open declaration that all can see?"

"No one can see any such thing. It is but a gown. Besides, who shall see? The children have seen. Eleanor remarked that it was very pretty. The boys did not notice. Only you have made a fuss."

"Mrs. Henry has no doubt seen. Miss Aschroft and the other servants have no doubt seen. Miss Dering, I have no doubt, is gloating about it even now."

"You have a vivid imagination, John. It is only a gown, of no significance whatsoever."

"Then you will not mind returning it to its rightful owner, who obtained it through her wicked, sluttish ways. I cannot believe that you would have demeaned yourself so much as to have accepted it."

"I cannot return the gift: that would insult the giver, whom I consider to be my friend. However, to show the respect I owe to you as your wife, I shall not wear the gown again. Please acknowledge how much pleasure I am denying myself on your behalf, and do not mention it again." She was dismissing him.

Should he press his advantage further, or should he withdraw? He had not achieved a total victory: she would not return the gown. But at least she promised not to wear it again. It was a compromise. He decided to go back to the sitting room where the children were playing. Before he closed the door, he said to them, "Your mother is dressing for supper now," loudly enough that she would hear.

~~*

There was a happy bedlam in Miss Dering's sitting room one rainy morning as the five children of Susan and Penelope looked for ways to amuse themselves. Finally, unable to hear each other above the din, Susan sent Johnny with Eleanor, William and Alexander, to hunt for "critters" in the castle hallways, so that the two mothers could carry on a conversation.

Davy cried for a few minutes at being left out of the expedition, but he was soon pacified with a sweet biscuit.

"Dear me, Susan! Imagine what a chaos it will be when we add another baby to the fray!" Miss Dering alluded to her pregnancy.

Susan noted with some irritation that Miss Dering had taken to calling her by her first name of late. Of course, she had a perfect right to, given the differences in their stations, but it still felt presumptive to her. After all, were they not friends and, thus, equals? Then Susan remembered that she had always called her maid by her fist name, even after they had become friends, and to her shame, she had never invited Mary to call her "Susan."

"I am become so fat that I have outgrown all my gowns. You must come and take your pick from among them because I cannot abide seeing them unworn. Which, by the by, reminds me that I have never seen you wear the gown I gave you at Christmas, Susan. Do you not like it?"

Even the act of being given a cast-off gown felt demeaning to Susan, but she must not let it show. "I like it very much, Miss Dering. I simply have not found the right occasion to wear it."

"You need not wait for an occasion. You need simply take one. You cannot feel uncomfortable wearing it? I should have thought you would have worn such a gown on many occasions, even every day."

"You are so kind, Miss Dering. But how my situation has changed! With five children to care for, it would be rash to attempt to wear a silk gown every day."

"I think I understand you after all." Penelope sat up and leaned towards Susan. "You feel belittled at having to accept such a gift from me."

"How do you come to think that?"

"It is the way you keep repeating my name, 'Miss Dering', as if to remind us of our different stations. Really, Susan, I insist that you call me 'Penelope' even if we must keep the practice inside this room. We are friends; I am not your mistress and you are not my servant. Call me 'Penelope' and consider the gown a gift between friends."

Susan was somewhat chastened by the offer. "Thank you, Penelope," she said. But in the back of her mind there was another obstacle between them. Dare she mention that Maude Ashcroft had also received a gown? It was too petty of her, so she did not. Nor did she vouchsafe the real reason she would not wear the gown: she had promised her husband that she never would.

Ellon Castle, Summer, 1785

The castle walls encircled a dark silence in the moonlight, seeming to portend the empty ruins that they would one day be. A piercing scream broke the stillness—whether the cry of the living or the dead it was at first impossible to tell at that hour of the night. One thing was certain, however, it fractured the sleep of the living. Susan stirred from deep drowsiness and started up, even before she was fully awake, to go and verify the safety of her children. She could hear her husband moaning on the bed she had just left.

"Where are you going?" he asked her as she reached the door.

She turned and said, "I must go and see if the children are all right."

"'Tis not the children that are screaming."

Susan stopped. "What is it then? Do you know?"

"'Tis the same sound I heard on my first night in the castle when the mistress was in labour."

There was another blood-curdling scream, and Susan realized that it was too early yet for Miss Dering to give birth.

"Oh! Then I must go to her. Will you comfort the children, for I am sure they must be awake?"

"There is no need for you to go. She has a maid and no doubt Mrs. Henry has already sent for the midwife. Go and see to the children yourself."

She could tell by the coldness of his voice that he was angry. He turned over and set his back to her like a wall. When he wanted to, he could be even more stubborn than she was, so she knew there would be no turning him. She would have to comfort the children herself; it was, after all, her first duty. While she went to reassure them, she could hear the screams of her best friend and was afraid for her. She could not recall ever having screamed so much during her labours.

James and John scarcely stirred in their sleep, so she did not waken them when she looked in. However, in the other bedroom, Eleanor was already up and sitting on Will's bed trying to comfort him as he whimpered and David was crying alone in his crib.

"Is it the ghost critter, Mama?" William asked, pitifully.

"No, it is not. Hush now." She picked up Davy baby and gently rocked him.

"Who is it, Mama?" Ellie asked, wide-eyed.

"It is Miss Dering. She is having a baby."

"Like you did, Mama?"

"Yes, precisely."

"Why is she crying so much?"

"Sometimes it hurts a great deal. You know, Will, how you always cry when you fall down and hurt yourself."

He nodded.

"Now, go back to sleep, children."

"May I stay in Will's bed, Mama?"

"Yes, and I shall stay here with you until Davy falls asleep again."

She had to stay half an hour with Davy, nursing him and singing gently until his eyes closed again in spite of the continuing noise. When the children were finally settled, she put a robe over her chemise and walked to Miss Dering's part of the castle. As she grew closer, she could hear that the screams were punctuated by gasps and panting. At the sitting room, Mrs. Henry greeted her.

"Good morning, Mrs. Dean," she said, as if it were not unusual for them to meet in the middle of the night. "There is no need for you to disturb your rest. The midwife is with her now."

"I thought perhaps I might be of help since I have been delivered of so many bairns myself."

"'Twas good of you, but not necessary. 'Tis not the same to attend a birth as to give birth. Best leave it to the midwives who know their own business, I believe."

"Is this usual for Miss Dering, Mrs. Henry?"

"I am afraid the last time was like this. But Alexander's birth went well. Quite peacefully, when I think of it. He was a bonny wee bairn from the beginning. I ought to go and see if the lad is all right with his nanny. Would you come for me if there is any news?" she asked and Susan reassured her. She sat alone, listening to the cries that continued to come from the mistress's bedroom. Sometime later, Mrs. Henry returned with a cup of tea. Susan noticed then that the sun had risen, but she decided not to go back to the children just yet. She would leave John to deal with them.

As if reading her thoughts, Mrs. Henry asked Susan about her children.

"Maude will see to them," she said.

Interpreting Mrs. Henry's look as censure, Susan said, "All right," and got up to leave. Just at that moment, Miss Dering's maid came out of the bed chamber, her eyes moist.

"Is she all right?" Susan asked in a panic.

"Aye, madam. She is fine."

"Then it is the bairn?" Mrs. Henry asked.

The maid nodded and left the room, unable to stem her tears.

The midwife Mrs. MacGregor came out next. "'Twas a girl. Stillborn, like the last one. Madam is fine, though she has lost a great deal of blood. When she is able to take food, give her some broth." She was a dour unsmiling woman whose every word sounded like condemnation.

"I will get Cook to prepare some immediately." Mrs. Henry got up to see to it.

"May I see Miss Dering?" Susan asked.

"If you wish," Mrs. Mac Gregor said as if she could not believe anyone would wish such a thing.

If it were me, Susan thought, I would want my husband there. "Will someone send for the Earl?" she asked. Mrs. Henry had already left in search of broth. The midwife shrugged. Susan went in to see her friend.

She was weeping. When she saw Susan, she opened her mouth to speak but only sobs came out. Susan went to her bedside, sat on the edge and took her hand in hers. Poor Penelope! Her second stillborn baby! She could find no words to comfort her, so Susan gave her silent company until Miss Dering fell asleep. Then she went back to the care of her own family.

The next day, Susan went as usual to visit her friend, who was still lying in her bed chamber. Miss Dering's greeting was not particularly warm, and Susan asked her if she would rather be left alone.

"I am sorry," the mistress said. "I should not chase away the only friend I have in this godforsaken place. But you must understand. When I look at you, I am overcome by a most unkind and unwarranted jealousy."

"What do you mean?"

"How can you not know? You have a loving attentive husband and five healthy children!"

"But you have nothing to complain of. You have a son, an Earl who dotes on you, and a castle filled with servants."

Miss Dering did not respond. "I have a son and a castle filled with servants to be sure, but where is my Earl? Surely he should come at once when I need him, if, as you say, he dotes on me."

"Has he been sent for?"

"I believe so."

"Then, he will soon be here, I am sure."

"I doubt that. It was inconvenient for him to come the last time I miscarried."

Susan sought some other means to console her. "At any rate, I am surely not your only friend. You have your maid and Mrs. Henry at least, and all of the servants treat you well."

Miss Dering looked at her derisively. "Do you think I do not know what you all say behind my back? Only Mrs. MacGregor is unkind enough to say it to my face."

"I am sure I do not know what it is that they say."

"Mrs. MacGregor says that God is punishing me for my sinful life. Though the other servants do not say it, I can see the same belief written clearly in their faces."

"Not in mine, I assure you."

"You do not believe it then?"

"Not at all. Many a righteous woman has lost a baby, and what do the tongues wag then? Hardships come to all of us, whether or not our behaviour is good or evil."

She looked surprised. "Then to what do you attribute my lack of success in child-bearing?"

Susan had never given much thought to such a question before. What could account for the differences in their childbirths? After a long pause, she suggested, "Perhaps it is due to diet. You are overly fond of sweetmeats since you were deprived of them as a child, and I am indifferent to them and rarely eat them since they were always available in my youth. As well, the Scottish climate does not provide you sufficiently with fresh vegetables, which might otherwise counteract the evil of your indulgence in sweets."

Miss Dering laughed. "So you think if I ate less sweets I would have more babies!"

"Perhaps," She said tentatively. "But only God knows the real reason."

"Which brings us right back to the fact that God is punishing me for my sins—only you think that too many bonbons is a worse sin than fornicating."

Susan laughed uneasily. She had not meant anything quite so crude by her remark. Miss Dering made it sound ridiculous, and she found an excuse to escape her presence at her earliest opportunity. She was spared the necessity of another unpleasant visit because the next day the Earl at last responded to his mistress's plea for his presence.

Ellon Castle, Autumn, 1785

Before bed every evening, it was John's habit to pray. He got down on his knees and silently addressed his maker. After his usual thanksgiving and prayers for the health and safety of his family, there was often a complaint to God about his wife Susan. It was in no way a whiny complaint, since it often came after his gratitude and solicitude for her. It was rather an expression of his desire that she should be a little more compliant and recognize his authority, at least in regards to her relationship with the mistress of the castle, whom he was convinced was not her friend. He was thus engaged in his deep communion with God one evening, when the subject of his supplication walked into the room and rather noisily disturbed his prayer.

"John, I need to talk to you... Oh! I am sorry. I did not realize that you were in conference."

He glared at her.

"Forgive me."

He tried to continue his prayer, but she was watching him. He should have asked her to leave but knew that, even if she left, he would not now be able to restore the concentration required to continue. "Amen," he said to his folded hands, then stood up. "What is it you want?"

"It just occurred to me since Eleanor is now six years old that she should begin school at the Tollbooth with her brother James this year."

John smiled. This was exactly what was wrong with the woman. She did not think. She made rash assumptions without any consideration for the natural boundaries and constraints of society. "It just occurred to you, did it?"

"There is no need for you to be facetious, John. I suppose by your sarcasm you mean to tell me that the Scots are no more enlightened than the English where the female sex is concerned, and that girls are not educated at school with their brothers."

John was rather taken aback by her words. He had always considered the Scots far more enlightened than the English. "There are at least schools that we can afford to send our sons to here. In England there are none."

"I suppose that is true. But what of the education of Eleanor? That is the matter I came to speak to you about."

"You are an educated woman, Susan. You may teach her to read and write."

"When shall I do that, John? If only Maude would do some of the work she is meant to, perhaps I might have time."

"Well, you know I have spoken to the Earl regarding her shortcomings and our displeasure, but to no avail. I am at a loss what else to do about it."

"Perhaps I might speak to Miss Dering. It could do no harm."

He clenched his fists and spoke softly. "You know my position on that, and it has not changed."

Susan averted her eyes and he knew he had cowed her, if only a little. It was what he had prayed to do, but each time he was successful, he felt as if a little of himself had died with her decreased spirit. Chastened, he said, "All right. Since the winter is coming and I have less work to do, I shall set aside a portion of my day to teach Eleanor reading, writing and small sums, but you must find the time to teach her needlework."

"She is already well advanced in that regard. The necessity of repairing the clothing of four active boys has made it imperative that she learn to sew."

"I am happy for that," he said.

"She will make someone a far better housewife than I," Susan stated.

He did not think it honest to disagree.

~~*

The next morning while the family was at breakfast, John and Susan told Eleanor the plan.

"Your father will give you lessons in his office every morning, Eleanor."

The little girl smiled demurely at her father.

"Girls don't go to school," her brother James gloated.

"That remark is unnecessary." John spoke sternly.

"But it's true they don't, Papa."

"Unnecessary," he repeated, silencing his oldest son.

"I am a boy. I want to go to school with James!" little Johnny cried.

"It will be your turn next year, Johnny," Susan explained.

"I am big enough now," he cried.

"But you are not old enough to attend school yet," his father explained.

"Then I want to have lessons like Eleanor," he shouted.

Susan looked at her daughter who had not been given an opportunity to say one word due to the clamour of her brothers. She was still smiling contentedly as if an injustice had not just been done to her. Instead, it was Johnny who was whining petulantly. "If you take lessons, then who will play with William?"

"Willie is a baby. He can play with Davy."

"You are behaving like a baby yourself, Johnny. You will learn to read and write at school next year. This year it is Eleanor's turn to learn with her father," Susan said.

Johnny kept up his relentless agitation while placid Eleanor said nothing. To Susan's disappointment, John relented and let his little namesake sit in on the lessons with Eleanor, as long as he was quiet. Susan doubted that he would be, but trusted that John was a strict taskmaster and would keep him in line.

Ellon Castle, Winter, 1785

Because she had spent so much of her adult time in the condition, Susan knew the moment that she was pregnant. There was a sudden sensation of dizziness, as if the solid earth had shifted for a moment under her feet, and a sort of buzz in her head as if a bee had taken up residence. In spite of some reservation, she was elated. They had enough children already, but now that their life was more secure financially than it had been in London, she could afford to enjoy the experience. The joy she was feeling had nothing to do with such practical considerations, however. It was a physical sensation, a love of the state that her body was in. She felt like the fallow earth that John had seeded, bursting with the promise of new life. Even in the midst of the darkest winter here in the wilderness of Scotland, she was carrying within her hope and joy.

She passed Christmas and Hogmanay in this blissful state, and then on a February morning, after John had left their bed early to go to the greenhouse to plant the seeds he had received the day before, she arose and felt a sharp pain in her side. It was not the kick of the infant in her; she knew that feeling. It was not the bairn turning somersaults: she knew that feeling as well. It was not any feeling she had felt before, which was fortunate, for it was more pain than she ever wished to experience again.

She cried out.

Davy, standing up in his crib watching her, grew alarmed at her expression and started to cry. She took a step toward him to comfort him, but doubled up in agony instead.

She did not know how long she stood there taking short shallow breaths, focusing only on the pain and willing it to go away, while Davy howled. Finally, Maude arrived.

"Madam," she said. "Are you all right?"

In spite of the wrenching pain in her belly, she managed to say, "Stupid girl, do I look all right?"

"Well, there is no need to be cross," Maude said, drawing away from her instead of helping. "I'll go fetch Mrs. Henry, shall I?" and she started to back out of the room.

"Take Davy with you," Susan managed to gasp out.

Maude picked up the baby without so much as a word of comfort to him and went out the door.

Mrs. Henry came at last and helped Susan back into the bed. She brought a flask of hot water wrapped in cloth which she put against Susan's belly to ease the pain. Then she wiped Susan's forehead with a cool cloth.

Penelope came and asked after her, but she was sent away, so she went and fetched John from the greenhouse, which was kind of her, but Susan would not admit him to her sick room either. Mrs. Henry asked if she would have the midwife, but she declined. She knew what was happening. This was not a birth; it was a death.

Sure enough, after a few hours of excruciating pain, a tiny mass of something indescribable swept out of her with copious amounts of blood. Mrs. Henry cleaned her up and removed all of the soiled bed clothes, then bound Susan in rags.

"Your flow this month will be heavier than usual, Mrs. Dean," she said sardonically.

"To make up for the ones I missed in the last few months," Susan responded in kind.

She was beginning to feel infected with the Scottish dourness. What choice did she have? After the ordeal was over, the winter was not, and there were many more months of cold, damp darkness to be endured.

Chapter 4

Ellon Castle, Spring, 1786

John spent the day forming and turfing the ground of the pleasure garden and began trenching the different borders, quarters and clumps in readiness for planting, first marking out the irregular boundaries with stakes. In each clump and border, he left a margin for annual flowers about three to four feet wide. In these margins, roses, jessamines and honeysuckles were placed about six to seven feet apart so that they could intermingle with the annuals. Behind these, short shrubs and evergreens rose progressively taller until the back of the borders, where climbing honeysuckles grew on a mound.

Other clumps had at their centre deciduous trees such as oaks, elms, beech and chestnuts with flowering shrubs mixed among them. These included double-blossomed peach, almond, cherry, arborjuda and tulip trees. On short stakes near the borders, he planted more shrubs such as Portugal laurels, arbutus, striped holly, laurustinus, phillyreas, chinea arborvita, sistus, and several sorts of sumac.

John was tying the new shrubs to stakes when he heard the rustle of a gown behind him on the path. He smiled briefly, remembering that sound from the days long ago when Susan had come to find him in her father's garden, but when he turned expecting to see her face, he was disappointed to see Penelope eying him coyly.

"Good morning, Mr. Dean. It's a lovely day, is it not?"

He could tell she was effecting her most genteel speech for the occasion.

"That it is, madam," John responded.

"It has been such a long trying winter, has it not?"

He thought of the miscarriage that Susan had endured and nodded glumly. What was it about this place that brought about only stillbirths and miscarriages? He looked at Penelope Dering. Oh, yes, he thought. It was her. He went back to his work, unwilling to speak with the woman (his mind supplied other epithets) any longer.

"Why are the Scots such a taciturn people, Mr. Dean? Surely you could take just a few moments of your time to escort me about and tell me the plans you have for the garden this season. Then I shall write to the Earl and relate what excellent work you are doing. It can only be to your benefit."

"I am sorry, madam. If I were not so busy, I would, but you canna tell the Earl I am doing excellent work if I am doing none. Good day to you, madam."

He tipped his hat to her before turning and walking away in the opposite direction towards the greenhouse.

"Another time perhaps, Mr. Dean," she called after him.

Miss Dering returned to the castle. She tapped on the Deans' sitting room door, and then poked her head inside. "Are you busy, Susan?"

Susan was giving Eleanor her morning reading lesson and said as much to Penelope. Now that it was spring and John was busier, Susan had taken up the task of educating her daughter. Johnny immediately dropped out to follow his father out of doors.

"Do you mind if I sit in?" Miss Dering did not wait for an answer, but came and sat in a chair not far from them. "I promise not to disturb you. I shall just watch in silence."

Susan nodded and resumed the lesson with her daughter, trying not to be distracted by the rustling of Miss Dering's silk gown whenever she shifted herself. She could see out of the corner of her eye that Penelope did not half attend to the lesson, but as she was not the student that should not have offended her. However, Eleanor's attention was also diverted, first by Penelope's shifting about and then by her mother's distraction.

Susan finally gave up. "Well, I think that is enough lesson for today. You are doing marvelously well, Ellie. Try to sound out the rest of the story on your own, and you can read it to your father this evening. He will be pleased by your progress."

Eleanor smiled sweetly and, taking her primer under her arm, bowed to the lady before going into her bedroom.

"What is it you want?" Susan asked.

"Are you angry with me?"

"No, of course I am not angry. Only, I have so much work to do. I shall come and find you when I am done and then we can pass some time together."

"What is it you have to do? Perhaps I could help you."

"Well, I must go collect the children's clean clothes from the laundry. Then I must put them all away. I should find the children and ensure that they are all fed and clean, and put Davy down for his nap."

"But surely all of those chores could be managed by the nanny!"

"Yes, of course. But where is the nanny? Bless me if I can find her half the time."

"Really, Susan. It is unacceptable. You should hire a new nanny."

"Yes, I agree, but it is not that simple. Maude was engaged by the Earl. We have spoken to him about the possibility of replacing her, but he is not at all amenable to the idea." Immediately, she regretted that she had let this fact slip. She had promised John she would not mention it to Miss Dering.

"Why did you not tell me this before? I shall speak to the Earl myself. It really is intolerable."

"No, please do not. John would not like you to speak on his behalf."

"Then, let's go and find the silly girl together and I shall talk to her about her duty. He cannot object to that, surely."

Susan followed, doubtful that they would be successful, but willing to attempt anything. Now that Miss Dering knew, perhaps something could be done after all. At any rate, it was not possible to recall the words that had already been spoken. So they went together looking for the wayward nanny. After searching in the servants' quarters, they finally found her, curled up in a big chair in the library reading a novel and eating an apple.

"Here, you! What are you about?" Penelope was enraged at finding her in her own wing of the castle where she had no right to be and reverted to her most common accent. This seemed to have the effect of making Maude even more insolent than usual.

"What business is it of yourn, mistress?"

"You cheeky bit! Who pays your wages, slut?"

"It ain't you, anyway. 'Tis the Earl."

"Get off of that chair and do some'ut to earn your keep."

"Some'ut like you do, perhaps, ma'am?"

Penelope walked over, looking as though she would slap the nanny across the face, and Susan followed in order to restrain her hand if she did so. Much as she would have enjoyed seeing Maude receive a smack, she doubted that it would produce the desired results. So she spoke to Maude more soberly. "Come on. Get up, girl. Go on about your business. The children need clothes and they need to be fed."

Maude looked at her with her usual insolence, but did not respond. Instead, she got up, placed the novel on the table and walked out of the room, with one backward, scathing glance at Penelope.

"Don't think I won't be writing the Earl to tell him of your insolence," Penelope shouted as the nanny slammed the door shut. "How dare she!"

"There is no need to get so angry." Susan tried to calm her. "We have not found it to be a particularly effective method of dealing with the girl."

"I cannot see that your method, whatever it is, has been any more effective."

"She deserves to be dismissed. Perhaps a word from you to the Earl would be the most effective manner of achieving that."

"You can rely on me to write to the Earl immediately." Penelope seemed to recover her composure. "Come, Susan. Let's forget all about this miserable creature and enjoy the rest of the day."

Ellon Castle, Summer, 1786

Penelope informed Susan that she had written the Earl to tell him of Maude's outrageous behavior, but several months passed and she did not revisit the issue. Finally, Susan, beleaguered as usual, brought it up.

"Has the Earl replied to your request regarding Miss Ashcroft, Miss Dering?"

Penelope looked uncomfortable. "No, most strangely, he has not. I have repeated my pleas in every letter I have sent, but he has simply ignored the issue."

Susan considered this very odd but considered it to be a matter between the Earl and his mistress and thus too personal to continue discussing.

"But do not fret, Susan. I have a way to deal with the matter. When the Earl arrives and I appeal to him in person, he will not refuse me."

There was such a defiant look on her face that Susan felt almost confident of a swift resolution.

Soon after this conversation, the Earl arrived, and, a day after his arrival, he most uncharacteristically summoned Susan to tell her in person that Maude Ashcroft had been dismissed. What was even more extraordinary, he asked Susan to convey the news to Miss Dering herself. Susan then went to Penelope's apartment to deliver the Earl's message.

Penelope smiled at the news, and said, "Do you see how well my method worked?"

"But how did you accomplish it!"

"I simply withheld my favours. Would you like me to tell you the details?"

Susan blushed, but her curiosity got the better of her modesty and she nodded, "In broad strokes only, of course."

"Do you promise not to be offended and judge me for my behavior?"

"When have I ever done so?"

Miss Dering glanced at Susan out of the corner of her eye. "Well," she said. "Never directly in so many words, but sometimes your eyes speak volumes."

"I cannot be held accountable for your misreading of my expression. Now tell me how you accomplished it."

"We were in the Earl's bed chamber. Imagine me in my most splendid and exotic French gown, waving my fan and looking all coy, just like them... those ladies I used to see at the ball when I was a serving maid." Penelope stopped speaking to lift up her well-endowed breasts with her hands. "You know," she said, and winked.

Susan could not help but laugh in spite of her embarrassment.

"'Whatcha brought me?' I asked him." She was speaking in a little girl's voice.

"'Let's have a kiss first,' says he. And I purse my lips tight and shake my head like this." Penelope demonstrated. "Then he says, 'Oh, all right. Have it,' and he hands me my gift." Penelope fingered the string of pearls about her neck. "Then he wants his kiss again, but I turn my head at the last second and his kiss lands smack on my cheek. 'What's the matter, Penny? Are you mad at us?' says he. 'Yes, sir, I am, sir,' I say. 'I have sent you lots of letters asking you to dismiss Miss Ashcroft, but you have not even responded to my request.' And I sulk like this." Penelope stuck out her bottom lip.

Susan laughed again, though she was a little ashamed at her own pleasure in the titillating details. John would have been shocked.

"He wants to know what it has got to do with me since she is not even Alexander's nanny, and I tell him how insolent she has been with me. Back and forth it goes, and he tries to steal another kiss, the cunning rascal, but I pull away, till finally he promises me he will dismiss her if I will kiss him. So I let him have a kiss, and he starts to grope about, as men do, and reaches to unbutton my gown. I push him away. 'What is it now, Pretty Penny?' 'No love-making,' says I, 'not till the deed is done.' Oh, then he blusters and says, 'Us has promised to do it; that should be enough for you,' but I am adamant, Susan. I will not give him any more favours, I tell him, not until you come-- I mean you, Susan-- and tell me yourself that Maude is gone. And here you are. What think you of that?"

"Bravo, Miss Dering. I have learned a great lesson today, though I hope I shall never need to employ it. By whatever means you have achieved it, I thank you for your help."

"You are most welcome, Susan. Now run along. The Earl will be coming for his payment soon." Penelope winked at her.

"I am leaving, but pleased be assured that I do not wish to hear the details of the sequel."

Penelope laughed and pushed her out the door.

Ellon Castle, Autumn, 1786

From her vantage point in the upper storey window of the castle, Susan watched flocks of peewits gather and plummet as one body over fields that had recently been stripped of their crops and plowed. Immediately below, she noticed that the sharp colours of the garden had returned after persistent showers. In the intermittent sunlight, the freshly washed leaves of laurels and hollies sparkled amid the strawberry leaves still resplendent with flowers and fruits.

She could see the Earl's carriage approaching when it was still a speck in the distance and wondered if Miss Dering was at her window watching also. The mistress had told her that he was coming and bringing a surprise for Susan as well.

A sharp tug on her gown brought her back to the present room, and she looked down to see Davy frowning at her.

"Mama," he said. "Story." He was three years old already and still her youngest. Since her marriage, she had never been so long without a baby and she missed it strangely.

"Yes," she said, taking his hand. "Where's your brother Will?"

They went together to the sitting room where Eleanor was hunched over her books at the table.

"Have you seen Will?" Susan asked her daughter, who frowned back.

"I am busy doing my lesson," she said in response.

"Davy wants you to read him a story. It will be good practice for you," Susan said. "You can begin while I go and find what mischief Will has managed to get into." Again she ignored her daughter's frown. They had been without a nanny since the summer and Eleanor had been called on to mind the younger children even more often than she had before. There had scarcely been any time for her lessons this fall. Susan was hoping that the surprise Miss Dering had mentioned would be a new nanny, but she did not have time to dwell on her dreams. She had to find Will before he perpetrated some great mischief.

She tried the kitchen first. It was likely that he was there bothering the cook or even Mrs. Henry, whom Susan met coming out of the kitchen door. She smiled at Susan's greeting.

"If you are looking for Will, he is playing with Sandy in the nursery."

"Thank you," Susan said, turning her footsteps in that direction.

"Nanny MacPherson is looking after them, so you needna be concerned." She was Alexander's nanny.

Susan nodded and thanked her again but continued to make her way to Miss Dering's quarters. If nothing else, she wanted to tell her the Earl was arrived. Then she realized that she should have said something to Mrs. Henry as well. She looked back down the hallway where she had been, but the housekeeper was already gone.

Susan knocked on Miss Dering's sitting room door.

"Come in."

She entered and they exchanged greetings.

"Have you seen the Earl's carriage arriving?" Susan asked.

"No," she said, skipping to the window. "I have not such a high vantage point as you have." She looked out. "Why, there it is!" she cried, "just coming in the gate. You will have your surprise soon." She winked at Susan.

"I have also come in search of Will," she said.

"He's with Alexander and his nanny. Just leave them play. He will be all right."

"Are you sure the Earl will not mind Alexander playing with a servant's child."

She laughed giddily. "Of course not. Come along," she said. "Let us go and meet the Earl."

Usually Susan was expected to disappear when the Earl was in residence, but of course, this time he was bringing her new nanny. At least that was her fervent hope, so she followed Miss Dering to the castle porte-cochere.

There, with much embarrassment, she witnessed the incredibly noisy clamour of the greeting between the Earl and his mistress. When he had finished preening himself at her attentions, the Earl finally noticed Susan.

"Madam," he said. "Us has a surprise for you."

He turned back to the coach, offering his hand to its occupant, and out stepped the most sickly, well-dressed little doll Susan had ever seen. She looked as though she would faint from the effort of standing, and she waved a fan weakly in front of her face in order to revive herself.

"May us present Miss Louisa Bantree."

She curtseyed, and Susan wondered what on earth she was to do with such a doll.

"She is to be your new nanny."

Susan managed to say thank you, in spite of the fact that her first inclination had been to ask if he were joking her. Never in her life had she seen a woman less fit to be a nanny. She appeared to be little more than a child herself.

"Take her to her quarters, Mrs. Dean, and introduce her to her charges." The Earl spoke as if Susan were a simpleton, which was what she must have looked like, standing there gawping at the girl.

Finally she offered her hand. "I am Mrs. Dean," she said. Louisa took her hand and Susan did not let go of it; indeed, she was almost afraid the girl would fall if she did so. "Come with me." As they walked up the stairs, Susan asked her about her journey in order to be pleasant.

"Oh, madam!" she exclaimed. "I thought I would die a hundred times! It was such a great distance!"

From the manner of her address, Susan realized that she was another English girl. Was Scotland so devoid of nannies? she wondered.

At last they arrived at the apartment, but the effort of climbing all the stairs had so exhausted the girl that she sat down at the table beside Eleanor, and Susan noticed that she was only a little bit bigger than her eight-year-old daughter.

"Oh, lord!" Nanny Bantree cried, waving the fan in front of her face.

Susan was glad that John was not there to hear her speak in such a manner in front of the children. Eleanor and Davy were both staring at her as if they were wondering what species of creature had landed in their midst.

"Children," Susan said, "This is your new nanny, Miss Bantree. Nanny Bantree, this is my daughter Eleanor."

"Pleased to meet you." The pretty doll dressed in the latest fashion shook the hand of Susan's plainly dressed daughter.

"And my youngest child Davy."

"Hello, Davy." Louisa smiled at the boy who was staring at her. Then, she looked around. "Is that all then?"

"No. There is Will also. He is playing with the Earl's son Alexander at the moment. They are of an age."

"What age is that?"

"Four years. We also have two older boys, James and John, who are both attending school at the moment."

"Only one girl! How sad for you!" She turned to Ellie, who smiled shyly at the attention.

"If you are well enough, Miss Bantree, we could go out to the garden and meet my husband now."

"Oh, lord, no! I could never go back down the stairs and then up again. Do you think I might lie down and start my duties tomorrow? I am so exhausted from the journey."

"Of course, I understand. Let me show you to your room then."

The next day Miss Bantree did not get up from her bed. She had caught a fever, and Susan feared to let the children near her. The already-beleaguered Mrs. Henry was now charged with looking after a patient and there were even fewer people available for child-minding.

~~*

It was drear November, the month when there was little to be done in the garden, and it seemed too early yet to prepare for spring, John thought as he stared at his desk and sighed. He looked out the window of his office and was surprised to see that snow had been falling during the hours of his useless musing, transforming the garden from its lifeless ugliness. Without another wasted thought, he got up and went out to stroll along the garden walk and enjoy its recreation. A lovely dusting of white covered the dark foliage: the upright Swedish juniper at the front of the plantation contrasted with the horizontal yew hedge and behind that, the white peaks of the pencil cedar pointed skyward.

John experienced a restorative healing in the beauty of the snow alone. As he walked back to the house, he realized that these precious moments were worth the chill endured to experience them, and he decided that he would find Susan and invite her to accompany him on a short promenade. They had such few moments alone together, and now that the new nanny was here, she could not use the children as an excuse.

John opened the door to the apartment and found the sitting room empty. He could hear voices coming from one of the bedrooms, however. As he walked toward the sound, a peal of childish laughter greeted him through the half-opened door. He decided to look in and discover what had caused the merriment. Through the doorway, undetected, he espied the children, Eleanor, Will, Alexander and Davy, scattered about the floor where they had fallen in a circle around Nanny Bantree.

"Let's do it again," Will shouted, and the children all jumped up and joined hands, starting to circle their nanny and chanting: "Ring around a rosy, pocketful of posies, Hush-a, hush-a, We all fall down." Whereupon they hurled themselves at her feet, laughing again. At that moment, Miss Bantree turned and saw John at the doorway.

"Sir?" she asked, hesitating.

John smiled at her. "Good morning, Miss Bantree. I did not mean to disturb you. I am looking for Mrs. Dean. Do you know where she is?"

"I believe she is with Miss Dering, sir."

"Thank you. Well, carry on, children. I shall see you later."

The pleasure that he had felt at seeing his children at play dried to bitterness in his mouth. Of course, she would be with the hussy and not with him, and if he wanted her company, he would have to seek her out in Miss Dering's apartment. It was ever thus, and he did not want to go there again. He was weary beyond words of arguing with her about the time she spent with Miss Dering. It did nothing but make her more obdurate in her disobedience to him. He vowed he would say nothing more about the subject with her.

He stopped halfway down the hallway and returned to the family apartment.

"Children," he called as he entered the room. "I have wonderful news. 'Tis snowing! Nanny Bantree, help me put on their overcoats and mittens. We shall go out to play."

The commotion of happiness that ensued banished his bitter apprehension of an argument and strengthened his resolve to ignore his wife's perfidy in future.

Ellon Castle, Winter, 1786

It was February and John was in the greenhouse, planting the seeds that had recently arrived from Edinburgh. He was so happy to have his hands in soil again after another long winter. He heard the door of the greenhouse opening. Still, after all this time, his first thought was that it would be Susan. But of course, it was not. Miss Dering stood there with a parasol umbrella perched prettily on her shoulder, waiting for him to invite her in.

"Come in, madam."

"What are you doing, Mr. Dean?"

"I am planting the flowers for next spring."

"Oh. What kinds of flowers are you planting?"

He told her. She listened to the names blankly as if they were meaningless. He did not mind. He was thinking of Susan and how he used to teach her the names of all the flowers. He wished she would come out to the greenhouse so that he could tell her which flowers did not grow well here in Scotland and which ones thrived. In the old days Susan would have been interested in the exotic garden he had planted behind the castle, and how no amount of his patient tending had sufficed to make it flourish. Every spring the plants had sickened and died. He remembered then, of a sudden, how she had once told him that she hated the cold of winter, and that she wished to live somewhere warm. He felt guilty that he had brought her here to one of the coldest places on earth. No wonder she was not thriving, he thought. Perhaps he ought to take better care of her.

"Mr. Dean."

He heard Miss Dering calling to him as if from miles away. "Aye, madam."

"Where have you been, sir? I was asking you about the soil you are using."

"Aye. Well, I dinna believe it is of very much interest to you even if you pretend that it is." It occurred to him that if Miss Dering was here with him, then, of course, she was not with Susan. "Do you have any idea where my wife is, madam?"

"Why, no, I don't."

"She spends a good deal of time with you, so I thought you might ken where she is now."

"Perhaps she is giving lessons to Eleanor. That is her usual activity at this time of day."

He felt a twinge of guilt that he had never resumed Eleanor's lessons himself, but with the arrival of a new nanny, he had thought Susan would have more time. "I thank you for the information, madam. If you do not mind, I must leave you. I must go find my wife."

John removed his gardening gloves and walked out of the greenhouse, leaving all of his equipment exactly where it lay. Penelope watched him go.

"Extraordinary!" she said, as he closed the door behind him.

~~*

Shortly after, John interrupted his wife and Eleanor at their morning lessons.

"What is it, John?" She truly thought that something bad had happened because it was so unusual for him to leave his work during the day.

"'Tis naught," he said. "Dinna fash."

"Well, but it must be something if you have come here during your workday. I do not think it has happened in all the time we have been here, except perhaps once." She was thinking of her miscarriage, but she did not wish to talk about the incident, and it made her sad to think of it.

"Aye," he said quietly, as if he knew what she was thinking about. "Eleanor," he said to their daughter. "Gang play with your brothers for a wee bit. I maun talk to your mother. I will give you a lesson myself this very evening to make up for the loss of this one. Is that agreeable to you, Ellie?"

"Aye, Papa," she said, getting up from her chair and running off without her book.

"Well, then," Susan said. "What is it you want to speak of?"

He surprised her then, coming towards her, taking her shoulders in his hands and kissing her with such passion and gentleness that it took her breath away.

"Oh," was all she could think to say when he had finished.

"Susan," he said, "My rare exotic flower. How truly sorry I am that I have not taken you some place warm and tropical. How much you have had to suffer in this northern clime. 'Tis no wonder that you lost the baby."

"That was a year ago, John."

"'Tis no matter. It was my fault. I have not tended you as I ought."

"Why did you suddenly think of it?"

"I ken 'tis never far from your thoughts. And you have not gotten pregnant since that time neither. It must be the climate that disagrees with you, do you think?"

"Perhaps," she said.

"We may be able to do something about it now."

His eyes were filled with regret and longing, and she succumbed to his surprising daytime attentions.

~~*

The very next day, the normal routine of the household was restored, and Susan was giving Eleanor her usual lessons. Her student was just putting away her primer and enthusiastically taking out her sewing basket (so unlike Susan at the same age, she thought), when Will burst into the room howling at the top of his lungs. Eleanor made a face at the interruption of her time alone with her Mama, but Susan put her arms out to welcome the wee lad. Nanny Bantree was in her bed, sick again and the children were not allowed to go near her. It was feared that she had the consumption.

"There, there, Sweet William. Why all the tears?"

"Sandy…" he managed to gasp out between sobs.

Susan was a little surprised. Usually it was his little brother Davy who upset him, interrupting his play time with his best friend Alexander.

"And what did Sandy do, Will?"

William's tears began to abate a little under his mother's calming strokes. "He… he broke my soldier!" he managed to lisp before breaking into fresh tears.

"Where is it, Will? Show me. Perhaps Papa can fix it." Susan stood up, lifting him off her lap and taking his hand. "Begin your needlework, Eleanor. I shall be back soon."

Will led her into the hallway, out of the servants' quarters and halfway down the staircase. The landing appeared to be the scene of the aftermath of a fierce battle. Soldiers were strewn hither and yon, pell-mell, as if a giant cannonball had burst in the middle of them.

"Your soldier, is it?" she said, imitating his lisp. "Whose soldiers are these, young man?" she asked, in her most severe tone of voice.

He did not respond so she tugged his arm. "Come on. Whose soldiers?"

"They are my soldiers!" he cried defiantly.

"And?"

"And Sandy's soldiers," he said.

"And?"

"And Johnny's soldiers," he said more quietly.

"And?"

"James's soldiers," he whispered.

"Did you have permission to play with your brothers' soldiers?"

Will did not respond.

"Which one is broken, Will?"

He bent down and picked up one of the little men who evidently had lost his head in the heat of battle.

"Where's his head?"

"'Tis here." Will scrambled among the soldiers to find the errant head.

"Well, my boy. We shall have to go and show this to your father."

Will nodded. "He can fix it."

"And he will come up with a suitable punishment for a boy who plays with his brothers' toys without permission."

Will's eyes widened. "Punishment?"

"You do not expect to go unpunished for such naughty behavior, do you? Is that soldier really one of yours or is it your brother's?" Susan said as they walked to John's office.

"Smine," he said, clutching it to his breast.

"Yours, perhaps, but it could just as easily have been one of your brother's, and how would your brother feel if you broke his soldier?"

They arrived at John's office, knocked and were admitted.

John's smile at seeing them was quickly replaced by the most solemn frown after hearing the news. Susan did not wish to be there for his lecture, nor for the punishment afterward, so she took her leave. Poor little Will was reluctant to let go of her hand, but under his father's stern eye, he did. At the door, she looked back and saw on his face that he wanted to call out after her and it was all she could do to keep herself from returning to comfort him. She tried to give him solace with her eyes as she left, admitting to herself that she was a coward and ought to have stayed.

As she was closing the door, John said to her, "Dinna pick up the soldiers on the stairs, Susan. Our young Will will do that when we are finished here."

She nodded and then escaped to the sitting room where Eleanor and the sewing awaited her.

~~*

John's lecture was short. He did not believe in wasting words on children so young. He took out the switch and slashed it a few times across Will's open palm. Will hollered a little louder than seemed warranted, which would have truly effected his mother had she been there. Fortunately, she was not.

John took Will's other hand and went to the scene of carnage on the landing. There he instructed him to pick up every last soldier and put them back in their proper boxes. There were four boxes there, three plain, rough wooden ones crudely lettered with their boys' names, and one ornately painted.

Seeing the ornate box, John asked, "Do some of these soldiers belong to Alexander?"

"Aye, Papa. They do."

"And were you playing with Alexander when this happened?"

"Aye, Papa. I was."

Then John left him alone to pick up the soldiers and continued down the stairs to Miss Dering's quarters. With his strong sense of justice, he felt it was his duty to ensure that Alexander was punished equally. He knocked on the door to their sitting room.

"Who is it?" Miss Dering called.

"'Tis I, John Dean."

"Enter."

She was sitting in the middle of the room reading a novel. She put her book aside and smiled when he came in. "Would you like a bonbon?" She picked up the box beside her book.

"No, thankee, madam. I have come on a serious matter."

"Oh dear!" she responded to his grim attitude. "What is it then?"

"Is your boy Alexander about?"

"I believe he is in the nursery. What is this regarding?" She stood up as if ready to defend her own.

"Alexander and Will were playing together with Will's brothers' toy soldiers. They have made quite a mess of the landing and broken one of the soldiers."

Penelope smiled, relieved that it was nothing worse.

"I hope you realize it is a serious business, madam," he scolded. "I have whipped Will for it and I suggest you do the same with Alexander."

Penelope looked alarmed. "But he's such a young boy!"

"How old does one have to be to learn right from wrong, madam? If you canna do it, I will do it for you. The boy needs a father to attend to his discipline."

Penelope looked heartily relieved. "You may go to the nursery and discipline him as you see fit. I am sure his father would do the same if he were here. He will be grateful for your assistance in his absence, sir." She moved towards him to touch him then, and John backed away, bowing with formality, and left the room.

"I ought to go with you, sir." She immediately followed. "He must see that I approve of the discipline or he might feel unjustly treated by someone not in authority."

"'Tis a very good thing you are doing, madam. A hard thing, but a good thing."

They found Alexander hiding under his bed. She spoke to him, "Alexander, get up," with sufficient command that he obeyed immediately. "I have just learned that you have been a naughty boy." He stared at the floor and said nothing. "You will receive your punishment from Mr. Dean, and you will take it like a man."

"Do you understand what you did wrong, Alexander?" John asked.

The little boy shook his head.

"Speak up, Alexander," she said.

"No, sir," he mumbled.

"You and Will were playing with his brothers' toy soldiers. It is not right to take the property of others without permission."

"Yes, sir." He looked up then, his eyes shining excitedly. "But we needed a mighty great army. Just like Alexander the Great! Mama told me all about him."

Penelope blushed and looked at John apologetically. He resisted the urge to smile. Although it was a good thing for a mother to teach her son history, it should not be such self-aggrandizing rubbish, he thought.

"And William, the Conq... the ..., what is it , Mama?"

"William, the Conqueror, son," she replied.

In spite of himself, he felt a tinge of pride. She had redeemed herself somewhat in his estimation.

John continued. "I am sure 'twas a mighty great army, but most of the soldiers were not yours. Now, you will put out your hand for your whipping and then join Will to clean up the battlefield."

The boy put out his hand and silently accepted his stinging tribute.

"Alexander, the Great, it is," said John, contrasting in his mind his own son's tears.

"Thankee, sir," Penelope said and shook John's hand. Her eyes shone just a little, and John could not tell if it was with tears or with pride.

Chapter 5

Ellon Castle, Spring, 1787

The weather was growing just a little better, or so Susan tried to console herself every morning. The sun shone a little longer every day. The rains abated and, instead of soaking everything, seemed to hang suspended in the air like a heavy mist. In spite of all her attempts to be optimistic, however, the cold and damp remained solidly and eternally entrenched in the stone walls of the castle. Even in the middle of summer she knew the damp would still be there, providing some relief on those few hot days.

Because of its dank atmosphere, Susan believed that remaining in the castle was particularly unhealthy, and so, one sunny day she went to visit Nanny Bantree in her sick bed to see if she was well enough to take some air. To her surprise, Lavinia Henry was at the nanny's bedside. Of late, a woman from the village had been employed to care for the nanny in order to relieve Mrs. Henry, who had too many duties already.

"Where is the nurse?" Susan asked Mrs. Henry.

"She did not arrive this morning and Louisa is not well enough for me to leave her alone."

Susan followed her gaze to the pale, sweat-drenched nanny, who was breathing in shallow gasps. "I came to see if Louisa could take some air, but evidently, she is too ill," Susan explained. She noticed that Mrs. Henry looked tired and harried. "May I suggest you take advantage of the beautiful spring weather and go outdoors. I shall take your place and sit with Louisa."

Mrs. Henry looked at her doubtfully. "Well, if you dinna mind, Mrs. Dean, I have other duties that I ought to attend to. If you'll stay with Louisa, I shall mind your bairns for you today."

It had not been Susan's intention to pass the whole day with an invalid, but when she looked from the poor beleaguered Mrs. Henry to the sickly Louisa Bantree, she could not see a way in her heart to say no. Besides, Mrs. Henry had offered to mind the children and Susan most certainly was unqualified to do her household chores for her. She was reminded that her position in the house was on a par with the staff, and she felt ashamed for the all the time she squandered with Penelope, pretending to be an idle lady once again.

"Of course, Mrs. Henry. I shall be Louisa's nurse today. Thank you for your offer to mind the children, but perhaps Nanny MacPherson would help you with them if you informed her of the circumstances."

Mrs. Henry smiled wanly, thanked her and returned to the kitchen where she was needed. Susan sat down to watch over Louisa.

She wiped her burning, sweated brow with a cool moist cloth. She gave her sips of water and spoke softly to her. She contemplated the irony of her position waiting on the woman who was intended to be her servant. But she felt no anger towards her for all that. Louisa smiled at her from time to time and Susan wondered where her own mother was who should have been watching over her now.

Mrs. Henry brought a bowl of broth and fed it to the patient while Susan went to take dinner. She did not tarry long over the meal, feeling a strong sense that she was needed at Louisa's bedside. Also, she did not want Mrs. Henry to think she was shirking her duty. So, she quickly ate a cold sandwich and returned.

Mrs. Henry whispered to her that Louisa had taken but one sip of the broth and refused more. Then she shook her head portentously and left the room with the bowl almost as full as when she had arrived.

In spite of Mrs. Henry's grim unspoken conjecture, in the early afternoon Louisa's fever abated. She stopped shivering and lay peacefully in the bed. After an extended period of such calm, she turned to Susan, smiled and said, "It is so good of you, Mum."

Then she closed her eyes and Susan thought she was only sleeping, but there was something about the peacefulness of that sleep—it was so still and she did not seem even to be breathing, she who had been panting just a few hours before—that caused Susan to suspect that Louisa was dead.

For a long while she sat staring at the waxy-faced doll, dreading to touch her to verify if it was true. However, there was no one else and she could not go running through the castle to find someone when she had taken on the duty herself to nurse the nanny. So, she summoned the courage to touch her forehead. It was cold. Susan's finger recoiled from the touch. She sat back and stared another moment, but she did not want to make an announcement nor leave her charge alone until she was certain. She summoned the courage to take up Louisa's hand and feel if the blood still pulsed in her wrist. There was not a throb under the cold flesh. Then Susan placed a feather from the bolster beneath the nanny's nose, but it did not even tremble.

Susan sat back, stunned.

She had never witnessed the spirit pass before. It had been so peaceful as if nothing momentous had even happened. She had expected something more dramatic. This poor little girl who had scarcely lived a life was ever so quietly gone. She thought of the girl's mother and realized that if she were here, she would be wailing and weeping now. Susan should take her place and mourn on her behalf, but she could scarcely squeeze out a single tear.

She hoped that she would never be called upon to nurse the sick again. The nearness of death was too overwhelming. She thought of her own children and prayed that she would never have to sit at any of their deathbeds. She shuddered as a cold draught woke her from her stupour. Then she got up to at last to find Mrs. Henry.

~~*

The children had never before experienced a death. Though Nanny Bantree had not been with them a long time, they had grown fond of the way she had laughed and played with them as if she were one of them. The older ones immediately understood the cryptic message that their nanny "had passed away" and began to cry, and the younger ones, frightened by their siblings' tears, wept even louder.

"Where did Nanny Bantree go, Mama?" Sweet William asked his mother.

She answered as she thought her husband might. "She has gone to be with Jesus."

"Where is Jesus?"

"He is with his Father in Heaven," she said.

"Where is that?" he asked, taxing her ability to answer to the limit.

"Dinna be so daft!" his brother James interrupted.

"Aye! Everyone knows where Heaven is," Johnny added.

Susan was annoyed by the older boys' dismissive attitude and addressed Will. "Perhaps when you go to school like your brothers, you will learn all the answers to your questions. In the meantime, you may ask Papa this evening at devotions."

Every evening, as was the custom among Scots Presbyterians, John assembled the family together for devotions. One of the children would be charged with reading a passage from Holy Scripture, and John would correct his diction. Afterwards, the children would ask questions and he would explain the meaning of the verses.

The devotion always ended with a prayer, usually spoken by John, though as the boys grew older, he sometimes gave them the honour of extemporizing. Susan almost never participated except to listen or to remove the youngest children when they grew too fidgety.

On the evening after Nanny Bantree's death, it was Eleanor's turn to read the Scripture passage that John had chosen: the fifteenth chapter of 1st Corinthians, verses 36 to 55.

Eleanor read too quickly at first because she was self-conscious before her brothers due to her lack of schooling. "Thou fool, that which thou sowest is not quickened, except it die: and that which thou sowest, thou sowest not that the body shall be, but bare grain, it may chance wheat, or some other grain: But God giveth it a body as it hath pleased him, and to every seed his own body."

John interrupted her to draw her attention to the punctuation that she was ignoring. He told her she must slow when she approached a comma and stop altogether at all the other signs. "Elsewise, the words will make no sense, Ellie."

Eleanor blushed, but his reprimand had been gentle, so she resumed, trying to follow his instructions exactly, making long pauses at the punctuation marks and painstakingly sounding out the long words. "So also is the resurrection of the dead. It is sown in corruption; it is raised in incorruption; it is sown in dishonour; it is raised in glory: it is sown in weakness; it is raised in power:"

Johnny sighed deeply and his father scowled at him. Ellie continued.

"It is sown in a natural body; it is raised in a spiritual body. There is a natural body, and there is a spiritual body." Eleanor looked up from the page. "What is a spiritual body, Papa?" she asked.

"Continue reading, dear, and I shall explain afterward if you still do not understand what Paul is saying."

She continued reading until she came to the passage: "Now this I say, brethren, that flesh and blood cannot inherit the kingdom of God; neither doth corruption inherit incorruption. Behold, I shew you a mystery: We shall not all sleep, but we shall be changed, in a moment, in the twinkling of an eye, at the last trump: for the trumpet shall sound, and the dead shall be raised incorruptible, and we shall be changed."

She looked up, her eyes shining. "How shall we be changed, Papa?"

Before he could answer, James interrupted. "We shall be angels," he said. Then realizing his rudeness, he added, "Shan't we, Papa?"

John nodded.

"I want to blow the trumpet. Can I, Papa?" Will interrupted.

"Not if you interrupt the Scripture reading again, Willy. And that goes for your brothers as well," his father admonished, looking at each of them. "Continue, Ellie."

"O death, where is thy sting? O grave, where is thy victory? The sting of death is sin; and the strength of sin is the law. But thanks be to God, which giveth us the victory through our Lord Jesus Christ. Therefore, my beloved brethren, be ye stedfast, unmoveable, always abounding in the work of the Lord, forasmuch as ye know that your labour is not in vain in the Lord." She stopped reading, having come to the end of the chapter her father had assigned.

"Very good, Ellie."

"Thank you, Papa."

"Can anyone tell me what it means?" John asked the children.

James, as usual, answered. "The first part is about a farmer, or a gardener like you, Papa, who plants seeds in the garden, and afterwards, some plants grow up from the seeds."

"Does the gardener know what kind of plants they will be when he sows them?"

"Aye, Papa," Johnny said. "The seeds always arrive in packets from the nursery with their names on them."

John smiled. "You are right, Johnny. But suppose the nurseryman made a mistake and put the wrong seeds in the packet. Would the gardener know then?"

Johnny shook his head vigorously.

"Who would know then?" John asked.

"Only God would know," Eleanor answered solemnly.

"You are right, Ellie. And so it is when we die. Only God knows what we shall become then. I do not know what a spiritual body is. Even Paul does not know: he says it is a mystery. He says we shall all be changed, but we do not know how."

The children, and even Susan, all regarded him with serious attention. "We do not know," he continued, "but we are assured that we shall overcome death and enter the kingdom of God. So," he said to his spell-bound audience. "'We must be steadfast, unmoveable, always abounding in the work of the Lord, forasmuch as we know that our labour is not in vain in the Lord,' just as the Scripture says."

Susan, who had watched and listened quietly to this lesson, considered how much this verse seemed to embody the man who spoke it. His faith was so sure that she almost wished she could climb inside of it and bury her own fear there. She was glad that he was the father of her children and that he knew so well how to gather up their fears unto himself.

"Let us pray," he said. Susan winced at the prospect of his usual long-winded prayer, but this time, all he said was, "Thanks be to God, which giveth us the victory through our Lord Jesus Christ. Amen."

And the children repeated the word, "Amen."

~~*

"Mama!"

Eleanor's voice was loud and insistent, imperious as only a child can be to her mother. It was annoying, but Susan went immediately. Eleanor did not often employ such a summons, and she had never yet taken advantage.

"What is it?"

"'Tis Will. I was working on my letters and he snatched my pencil and scribbled on my book."

"William!" This was indeed behaviour worthy of punishment. "Shall we go and interrupt your father at his work now?"

"No, Mama." The little boy was terrified, and he snatched his hand behind his back as if hiding it from the sting of the switch.

"Then what do you say?"

"I'm sorry, Ellie."

Eleanor glared at him and then forgave him. Even his sister could not stay angry at such a sweet face. Alexander had named him well—William the Conqueror—but he was a conqueror of hearts.

Susan took his hand. "Let's go then."

"Where shall we go, Mama?" He looked at her, still afraid she would take him to his father.

"Away from here and your mischief-making." She was loath to give up her advantage over him.

She knew he was bored. His brother Davy was taking his afternoon nap. "Shall we go find Alexander then?"

William's face lit up. "Aye." John still disapproved of his playing with Alexander because he thought him a bad influence, just as he believed that Penelope was a bad influence on her. But Susan thought it was unfair to blame a child for his parents' sins. At any rate, it was expedient under the circumstances.

They found Penelope seated in the middle of her sitting room with a needle in her hand and a voluminous gown held on the mound of her visibly rotund belly, its silky material billowing about her. She was evidently doing some fine embroidery on the skirt.

Before Susan had time to greet her, William cried, "Where's Sandy?"

A little voice could be heard from under Penelope's skirts: "Here I am!" Then, there was a rustling noise as the fabric began moving. Alexander burst out of his hiding place, laughing.

"Thank heavens, you're here to relieve me," Penelope said. "I must finish this needlework before the Earl arrives tomorrow and Alexander will not give me any peace."

"Where is his nanny?"

"I gave her the day off. She wanted to go into the village for the market today, and, since I will need her even more tomorrow, I permitted it."

"Oh, is it market day today?" Susan asked. It was one of the few diversions to be had in Ellon.

"You know it is."

They had often gone together, but with the Earl's coming, Penelope was too busy.

"Why don't you take the two boys and go yourself?" she suggested.

The temptation was great, but Susan was not sure she could handle the two of them alone. Unfortunately, "little pitchers have large ears" and the boys, who enjoyed a good market as well as the next child, began clamouring to go. Over their heads, she glared at Penelope.

"There's only two of them. One for each hand. I would be ever so grateful if you would take Alexander for me."

"Come along, then," Susan said to the boys, taking one in each hand as Penelope had advised her.

She should have told John, but she knew he would have disapproved, so she informed Eleanor and Mrs. Henry where she was going and then departed, with the two warrior-princes, slaying dragons and defeating enemies, all the way to the market square.

Everyone comes out for a market day in a village-- villagers, farmers and even the inhabitants of other villages from miles around. Although it was on a smaller scale, Susan was reminded of the excitement of going to London when she was a little girl. There was plenty of entertainment. Besides the farmer's produce, all of the artisans and crafters had brought out their wares and the peddlers had opened their packs of used goods. There were jugglers and clowns, puppet shows and mimes. For just a moment Susan was distracted by the pretty baubles on the jewelry table. Out of the corner of her eye, she saw the boys run after the juggler, and by the time she turned around to call them, a multitude of people had come between them.

She followed in the direction they had gone, but they were no longer with the juggler. She searched high and low among the swirling skirts and frolicking fairgoers for two little boys. Her eyes alit on many small boys, but none of them bore the familiar faces of Alexander and William.

The puppeteers were packing up and were heading off. Susan could not see a clown or a mime about any more. It must be getting late and she still had not found them. Her initial worry was growing almost to panic as she searched below the height of the adult faces for the two children. She heard her name spoken through the fog of her anguish.

"Mrs. Dean?"

She looked up.

"What is the matter, madam?"

It was Alexander's nanny, Jean MacPherson. Thank heavens, she thought. Someone to help me. "Have you seen William?" she asked. "He's with Alexander, but they have wandered off."

"Nae, I havena, Mrs. Dean."

There was something oddly reticent about her manner, and then Susan noticed Jean had a companion. It was Maude Ashcroft. It had been months since the nanny had been dismissed, and Susan had assumed she had gone back to England.

She must have been staring rudely, because Jean said, "You know Maude, of course, Mrs. Dean?"

"Yes," Susan said. "I am glad to see you both because you know what the boys look like and you can help me find them."

"Aye, madam," Jean said. "Where did you last see them?"

Susan told her and Jean went immediately to look for the boys, but Maude stood there gawping at her former employer.

"I suppose you're wondering what I am doing here," Maude said.

It was true, but it was not the most important thing on her mind at that moment. She said nothing, but Maude answered her anyway. "I am working for the Earl still," she said smugly. "At Haddo Hall."

Susan doubted that "working" was the word for what she did. "That is nice for you." She had wasted enough time. "Excuse me now while I return to looking for my son and his playmate. I would be most grateful if you would help."

Maude shrugged and Susan left her.

"You may pass the information to Miss Dering, if you will," Maude called after her, but Susan scarcely heard the words. She was intent on her search again and hopeful that Mrs. MacPherson would find the boys.

Another half hour passed, or perhaps an hour. Her path crossed with Mrs. MacPherson's again and, after shaking her head, the nanny suggested that the boys might have gone home.

"Perhaps you are right," Susan said. "Will you continue the search here while I return and look there? If I find them, I shall come back and let you know. I am so sorry to spoil your holiday."

"'Tis nae matter, Mrs. Dean. In the meantime, if I find the bairns here, I shall bring them hame."

"Thank you, Mrs. MacPherson."

All the way home Susan looked about, imagining the boys wandering off into the woods to slay a dragon and being slain themselves by a bear or wolf. Or perhaps trying to cross the stream and being swept away with the fishes in the Ythan River. She looked off in the distance, but could see no boys there dawdling. Oh, how she dreaded raising the alarm at home. John and Penelope would be distraught and would, of course, blame her. She prayed that the two boys would be in the hallway or on the stairs, somewhere that she would find them before she reached the others, so that she would not need to tell anyone.

But of course, her prayer was not answered and she was forced to disturb the harmony of the house with her woeful tale. As she had anticipated, both John and Penelope scolded her, if only with their eyes. John went off to the village in search of the children. As Penelope was pregnant again, she sent Mr. Henry in her stead. Mrs. Henry offered to search the house.

"'Tis possible they returned hame and are just playing in the castle somewhere," Lavinia said, and Susan was grateful for her calm demeanour.

She stood for a moment not sure which way to turn and blaming herself harshly. She wished that John had asked her to go with him. She should go after him to help him, but she could not abide his censure at the moment. First, she went to see that Eleanor and Davy were both still safe.

Eleanor was reading to Davy and smiled at her mother when she peeped in.

"You are such a good girl, Ellie," she said. "Could you watch him a little longer? I must find Will." Davy whimpered and held his hands out to her. She shook her head and began to close the door. She could hear him crying loudly on the other side of it. She could not abide the sound. She opened the door and took him up in her arms. He ceased his tears immediately.

"Eleanor, do you know where Will and Alexander might be playing?"

Ellie got up and took her mother's hand. "Come," she said and led her up the winding castle stairs to the top of the turret. There, in an empty, unused room, they found the boys on the floor, playing with their toy soldiers. Susan did not know whether to weep or to scold.

"Come with me, boys. You must wait in Mr. Dean's office," she said. At first they did not want to follow, but Eleanor let go her mother's hand and took hold of each of them. Susan did not wait to hear how she commanded them. She started to walk down the stairs, sure that they would follow, and they did.

When they arrived at John's office, Susan said, "Eleanor, stay with them a moment. I shall send Mrs. Henry to watch them. Meanwhile, I must fetch your father and Mr. Henry to let them know the boys are found."

Penelope came running into the room at that moment. She wrapped her arms around Alexander so tightly that she almost strangled him. Will looked at his mother as if to ask 'where is my hug?' But Susan was too angry to oblige him. She was angry at Penelope for rewarding her child, who was surely the instigator of the two; she was angry at Penelope and John for blaming her; and she was angry most of all at herself for letting it happen, for almost losing these two precious boys.

She turned away, hoping that Penelope might have enough sense to hug Will as well when she was done smothering Alexander. "I am going to fetch Mr. Dean," she said. "He will know how to deal with scoundrels like you."

Susan handed Davy over to Mrs. Henry and returned to the village market to find the others and tell them that the boys had been discovered. Fortunately, the crowd at the market had diminished and it did not take her as long as she had feared it would. She found Mrs. MacPherson first and apologized again for spoiling her day, especially now that the fair was so nearly over. The nanny said not to worry as she was going to her mother's for supper. Then Susan found Mr. Henry and he immediately set off to the castle. Finally she found John and they walked back together, at first in silence. Susan was greatly relieved, but inevitably, John spoke, his voice too quiet. "What were you thinking, Susan?"

She wanted to say it had been Penelope's idea, but she did not.

"Well, Susan?"

"I thought it would do no harm. The boys were restless and in everyone's way at home."

"Have I not told you that Alexander is a bad influence on Will and they ought not to play together?"

"It is difficult to keep them apart when they live in the same house." She did not mention that it was she who had brought them together.

"Perhaps we ought to seek our own house then, Susan."

Susan said nothing. The thought of all the housework and cooking she would need to do with no servant to help her was overwhelming.

John looked at her for a response. "You are quite pale, Susan. Are you all right?"

Until he asked the question she had not realized how ill she felt. All of the intense emotions of the last few hours, all of the rushing about had left her drained. Her ears began to ring and the world turned white. She stumbled in the path and fainted.

The next thing she was aware of, John was carrying her into the castle. He put her down on the settee in the entranceway.

"Mrs. Henry," he called. She came in an instant.

"The boys are waiting in your office for your punishment," Mrs. Henry said.

"Let them wait. Mrs. Dean is ill."

Lavinia rushed to her side. "What is it, madam?"

Susan smiled wanly. "'Tis only the strain of the last few hours. I shall be fine," she said to reassure her, but the room was spinning and her ears were still ringing. "Just let me lie here for a little while." She knew if she tried to sit up, she would faint again.

"I will look after her, if you wish to see to the boys," Lavinia said.

John left then. Only Susan knew how little he relished punishing his children, but he regarded it as necessary to the foundation of their character, and this trespass of all others merited serious recrimination.

As Lavinia wiped her forehead with a wet towel, Susan could hear Will howling at the top of his lungs, and then a few minutes later, even Alexander "the Great" was screaming. John had done the boys' justice.

Later, when Susan was ensconced in her bed, Sweet William came to her and lisped his apology. Her head was still floating in some kind of fuzzy mist that she was just beginning to recognize. She knew that she was pregnant again.

Ellon Castle, Summer, 1787

It was felicitous that a new nanny arrived shortly after Susan recognized her condition. This time they did not ask the Earl to supply them with a nanny: they engaged their own and requested an incremental raise in salary from the Earl. Even if he did not provide it, they were willing to accept the monetary loss, given their previous experiences with the Earl's choices.

The Henrys had a niece, Elizabeth Henry, who was looking for employment in the neighbourhood. Though she was even younger than Louisa had been, she was a sturdy and sensible country lass, used to caring for her own younger brothers and sisters and not at all given to airs, and Susan was most happy to welcome her into the family. For the first time since leaving London, she could entrust her children to the care of a nanny and not worry. This was important to her because she had already suffered a miscarriage and did not wish to repeat the experience.

The day of her arrival, they were all in the servants' kitchen having dinner. There was a great company around the table—Matthew, Lavinia, Susan, John, James, Johnny, and Eleanor. The new nanny sat at the bairns' table with Mrs. MacPherson, Will, Alexander and Davy. They were halfway through the meal, when Penelope's maid came running into the kitchen in a great flap.

"My mistress has been moaning and weeping and thrashing about all this morning. I think her time has come."

Lavinia got up from her half-finished meal immediately. "Why has she not called for help before this?"

"You ken how many times she has been disappointed. I think she wanted to put it off as long as possible. I maun go for the midwife directly."

"No, stay with her. I shall fetch Mrs. MacGregor," Mrs. Henry said.

"What is wrong with Mama?" Alexander asked.

Mrs. MacPherson took his hand. "'Tis all right, Sandy," she said. "Your mama's going to have a bairn, God willing. A wee brother or sister for you."

"I'm going to have a brother like Will has," he said proudly, looking at the big boys at the next table.

"Or perhaps a sister," said Mrs. MacPherson.

This thought did not appear to please him as well.

Susan got up then. "You have enough to do, Mrs. Henry. I shall go and sit with Miss Dering while the maid goes for the midwife," she said, ignoring John's cross look. She had had enough babies to know that a woman did not want to be left alone at a time like this. Penelope especially would need someone to talk to her and keep her mind off the possible outcome that had become so familiar to her. "The rest of you should pray," she said, and John looked a little more pleased by these words. "Pray that Miss Dering is delivered successfully this time."

"Aye. That we will do," John said, bowing his head and preparing to lead the others. Susan escaped up the stairs to Penelope's bedchamber.

There she found Penelope tossing and turning on the bed, her bedclothes scattered and twisted about her. Penelope looked at her, her eyes wide, Susan suspected more with fear than with pain. She took her hand.

"Do not dwell on bad thoughts, Penelope. Have you felt the baby kicking in the last week?"

"Yes. Many times."

"You see. The baby is alive. Keep that hope in your heart."

"But will the baby be alive at the end of the ordeal? I've lost 'em before in the middle, you know."

"Keep a good thought in your heart for it. Do not be afraid. The baby can sense your fear and lose its will to fight. Give it all the strength you have, Penelope."

She seemed to relax at that for the briefest moment, and then she winced in pain.

"Take a deep breath, and breathe through the pain."

She did as Susan instructed, and her tightened face eased a little. A few moments later, her deep breaths subsided and her body relaxed on the bed again.

"How often are the pains now?"

"Very close."

"You ought to have called for help sooner."

"I do not like the midwife Mrs. MacGregor. She has a sharp tongue and she never fails to tell me it is my fault when the baby dies."

What an evil woman, Susan thought. Perhaps it was her black soul that had caused the deaths of all Penelope's unborn children.

"Will you stay with me, Susan?"

"Of course I will. But the midwife must be here too. She knows more secrets of the art than I do. But I will stay and make sure she casts no evil spells."

Penelope laughed.

By the time the midwife arrived, Susan had imparted all the skills she had acquired through five successful births to Penelope, who was well-prepared to endure this experience.

Mrs. MacGregor wanted to evict Susan, but she would not leave. In spite of the fact that the midwife was as good a god-fearing Presbyterian as was to be found in the village of Ellon, as devout even as Susan's own husband John, Susan considered her to be a witch. There was not an ounce of forgiveness in her soul for Penelope. It was all squeezed out and replaced by condemnation. Such an attitude seemed decidedly unchristian to Susan's way of thinking.

Mrs. Henry came into the room to try to persuade her that she ought to leave this business to the midwife, but Susan was determined to stay there in order to keep Penelope's mind fixed on the goal of delivering a healthy child. She did not want her to be distracted or influenced by Mrs. MacGregor's black condemnation. The midwife may have believed that God wished to punish the innocent unborn for the sins of their parents, but Susan did not. If such was the will of God then Susan would prefer to be a non-believer. Of course, she kept such heretical thoughts to herself.

Susan's will was strong once she had decided that she would not leave her charge. She had witnessed one death already this year and she would not allow another. Her determination must have had a positive effect, because Penelope was delivered of a baby girl at half five in the afternoon. She lay exhausted, her face pale, her hair wet and stringy against the pillow, a naked squalling wrinkled baby in the crook of her arm, her eyes shining with a kind of ecstasy. Susan simply stared, filled with a quiet joy that God had given her this experience to counteract the recent sadness of Louisa's death.

Mrs. MacGregor looked as though she had swallowed a pickle as she went about the unpleasant chore of cleaning up. Susan felt triumphant that they had deprived her of the pleasure she had felt in announcing Penelope's stillbirths to the world. How would she explain now that God had left off punishing the wicked through the deaths of their children?

Susan watched her as she went about her work, and thought, begone Mrs. MacGregor and take the afterbirth with you. Bury it in the backyard and speak your evil incantations over it, if you wish. Or if you are not a witch, then go to the church and pray with all your heart, Mrs. MacGregor, for our little Penny did not die. She is sucking from her mother's breast. She is well and truly born.

~~*

The next day, when Susan went to visit Penelope, the maid would not admit her to Penelope's dressing room. Susan was astonished that she should be thus rebuffed. She could not think what she had done to occasion this displeasure after the previous day's successful labour.

"What! Is your mistress ill?"

"Not at all."

"Then, is she angry with me?"

"No, madam. Miss Dering is only giving suck to her bairn and doesna wish to be disturbed"

Susan was surprised that so much scruple was used on such a common occasion, but then she supposed that it was not so common for Penelope. She resolved to speak to her at the earliest opportunity, and so, returning to the room a little while later, and being admitted, Susan broached the topic.

"Why are you embarrassed to admit me when you are nursing?"

Penelope blushed so deeply that she could not speak for a moment, but Susan persisted in her attempt to elicit a response.

"Well," she said finally. "It is such a common, unladylike activity." She made a face to show her disgust.

"Unladylike! Why, it is an activity indulged in by women of every class and nation."

"Women, yes, but not so much ladies," she said decidedly. "You might find yourself in such reduced circumstances that you must put yourself to wet-nurse, but I am sure your mother did not."

It was Susan's turn to blush then, but not only from the reason that Penelope supposed.

"I am sorry to remind you of your situation. I only mention it as an example," Penelope said.

"You misunderstand my embarrassment. I am rather ashamed that my mother did not have enough care of me to give me her breast."

"What! I did not suckle Alexander and will not this babe either when I find a wet-nurse to do it for me."

"Then you are wrong, Penelope, for it is the very latest fashion among ladies of quality these days. Even were I not in reduced circumstances, I would suckle my own child and still be considered a lady."

She looked at Susan suspiciously then, as if she did not half believe what she was being told.

"'Tis true. If you do not believe me, I shall show you in a book I possess written by an eminent doctor, William Buchan, in which he addresses ladies such as yourself."

Penelope looked rather interested then, so Susan went and fetched her volume of Domestic Medicine. After riffling through the pages, she found the passage she sought, and Penelope, only glancing at it, asked her to read it aloud. Susan suspected that she could not read herself, but did not voice her suspicions so as not to embarrass her.

She read: "If you possibly can, suckle your own child rather than putting it out to wet-nurses who will not look after it."

"That is what the doctor says?" Penelope looked surprised.

"See for yourself." Susan pointed at the passage and put it under Penelope's nose so that she could pretend to read the words and nod.

"All the ladies read this book, you say?"

"Why, it is the most popular book on the topic that there is. I cannot count the number of new editions that have been issued in the ten years or more since it was first published."

"Truly?" Penelope said in some awe. "I could buy a new gown with the money I would save not having to hire a wet-nurse." She looked almost convinced. "But the Earl would not be pleased, I'm sure." She shook her head.

"Well, it need not be more than a year before the baby is weaned, and his lordship will want what is best for his child, will he not?"

"He will wonder how I know what is best."

"Well, then. Keep this book at your bedside, with the page and the passage marked, and if the Earl should question you on the subject, you may show it to him."

Penelope smiled then. "You are a good and clever friend. I thank you for your advice on how to be a lady, and I hope you did not take offence that I remarked on your reduced circumstances."

"Not at all," Susan lied.

"You will always be the paragon of a lady to me."

Susan nodded her appreciation of the remark, but said nothing more.

~~*

The Earl arrived from London as soon as he was able to get away from Parliament. After first greeting his mistress and kissing his new baby Penny, he walked out into the garden to confer with Mr. Dean. He found him pruning the dead blooms of a peony. They walked together in the garden, and the Earl remarked on what he admired and what delighted him in the new plantings. John took careful note. As usual he approved of the bright gaudiness of the garden's colours, but he also praised the heady aromas of the pleasure ground. In the warm breezes of the sweltering heat, the resin of pine, spruce and fir mingled with the heavy perfume of the flowers. The lord of the garden pronounced it good, and so it was good.

"The garden shows more splendidly every year, Mr. Dean."

"Thankee, your lordship. 'Tis an honour to serve one as perspicacious as yourself."

John delighted in the Earl's evident uncertainty about the meaning of the word.

The Earl was obliged to accept the remark as a compliment and invited John to walk with him around the perimeter of the garden. The Earl strolled with his hands behind his back, observing every bush, flower and tree. Beside one shrub he stopped to observe John's two lads engaged in pulling weeds from a flower bed. They both returned his regard—one merely glanced and returned to work, the other stared rudely, his eyes as wide as the center of a daisy.

"And who be these boys, Mr. Dean?" the Earl demanded.

"They are my sons, James and John. They help me in my work when they are able after school."

"What be the name of the gawper?"

"Johnny."

"What be you gawping at, Johnny? Ain't ye never seen an Earl afore?"

"Nae," Johnny said, hopping to his feet to respond after being directly addressed. "My lord." He swept his hat off and bowed in an extravagant manner.

The Earl chuckled. "Are us so strange to look upon?"

"'Tis only I wanted to see why the lads at school call you 'the wicked Earl.' I canna see what is wicked about you."

The Earl laughed heartily. John blushed a deep crimson, and yet he cherished a feeling of pride that his son had spoken the words that he had always been afraid to say. "Away with ye, Johnny. 'Tis not the right manner to speak to your elders," he said, and for form's sake, cuffed him lightly on the side of the head. "Get back to your work now," he commanded.

The Earl continued walking along the path, chuckling to himself. "'Tis a bright lad, that one. He'll go far once he learns to curb his tongue."

"Aye," John said.

"Well, thank you for this amusing stroll in the garden, Mr. Dean. Good day."

John watched the Earl walking back towards the castle and imagined a great tail swishing from under his coat and horns on his head. The wicked Earl, he thought. That was what the village boys called him, and probably their parents also. Now that his own lads were old enough to know that nickname, how soon would it be before they knew the reason why? He was pleased that his son had called the Earl the name to his face and sorry that he had been obliged to punish him for his forthright honesty. The incident had reminded him with stark clarity that this was not a godly place to be raising his children. He would recount the incident to Susan, and perhaps she would finally see the matter as he did.

However, the time never seemed right to leave. Susan was pregnant again. He had so many mouths to feed already. How could he leave an employment now? Then, he should talk to his two oldest sons and explain why the Earl was called wicked, but he so little relished the task that the time did not seem right for that either.

~~*

As he frequently did at sunset, John went out to roll the lawn with a heavy, hollow cast-iron cylinder that flattened the blades of grass, which the weight of the morning dew would hold in position. Early the next day, before the sun dispelled the dew and put the grass into a condition to raise itself again, he would cut the grass down, scything it in a direction contrary to that which it had received from the cylinder's passing over it. It was a back-breaking, exacting chore, and one that he went to more and more slowly as the years passed.

On this particular evening, before he began his work, his attention was drawn to the most glorious sunset he had ever seen. It was so magnificent that he returned to the castle to call all the household out to witness it. Everyone came, including the Earl and his illegitimate family.

All of the sky from one horizon to the other was a pink shade, but in the west, where the sun had just set, there was what looked to be a great stationary flame. From a deep crease of brightest crimson, it spread out in shades of orange growing gradually paler until it reached the zenith of the sky where its peach hues blended into the paler pink that had replaced the sky's usual blue.

They stood in awe, gawping at Nature's extravagant display until the last rose-coloured fingers had faded below the western horizon and the sky had turned dark grey-blue. The others shivered and returned to the castle, but John delayed Susan. He asked her to stay with him a while in the fading twilight. He put his arm around her shoulder. She did not move away. Perhaps the incredible sunset had smoothed away some of her usual prickliness towards him. "Are you cold, Susan?"

"Not at all," she said.

"You have goose-flesh, woman. Dinna lie to me."

"Well, hold me tighter then." She snuggled against him.

He smiled. "This is pleasant. Let us walk in the garden for old time's sake."

"Are you sure there are no wild beasts about?" she asked him.

"There are no more beasties here than there are in England. Is that why you never want to walk in the garden with me? Are you afraid of beasties?"

"Not at all," she said, and her sudden stiffening made him fear that she had become a little cross with his teasing.

"Let us walk," he said, starting out. He was afraid that their moment of grace was about to falter. These moments of quiet happiness were infrequent and they always seemed to vanish as soon as they began to talk. Susan would say that she was too busy and then he would say something else in response, and they would begin to quibble again. So they walked in silence, their old familiar argument lying unspoken between them.

When they had done one complete turn of the garden, John finally dared to broach the topic that was on his mind. "A humorous incident occurred in the garden today. The boys were helping me as they often do, and I was escorting the Earl about. When we came upon the lads, Johnny was staring at the Earl as if he were a creature. Then he asked the Earl why he was called 'wicked.' Apparently, that is what his schoolmates call him. Can you imagine what the Earl's reaction was to that?"

"Oh my. Was he angry with Johnny?"

"No, he was not. The Earl laughed. And I was obliged to punish Johnny for his insolence when all he had done was to speak the truth."

Susan did not say a word for the longest time. "I am sorry for that."

"One of these days I shall be obliged to explain to the boys why the Earl is a wicked man. Do you not think that on that day they will condemn me for my complicity in the situation? Do you not believe that I will be a hypocrite in their eyes? What are we teaching our children by staying here, Susan?"

She did not answer, but said quietly, "You know that we cannot leave now, John."

"Aye, I ken, but I dinna like it."

"When the children are old enough, they will understand. They will learn the truth: that the world is not a perfect place. The Earl is no more wicked than King David or any of the other men in the Bible who had more than one wife."

"Do not equivocate. I want my children to have better morals than that."

"You only want to be in a position to condemn him, but you are not. At any rate, it is a far more Christian attitude to forgive."

"I would forgive him if he were repentant, but the man laughs. He thinks it is humorous that a little boy calls him wicked, and he feels no shame at all to live openly in sin."

"I think it is time to go back in," she said.

He followed her, feeling terribly unsatisfied. He did not think she had understood the gravity of their situation at all. Did she not care a fig for the immortal souls of her children? How little understanding she had of the danger they were in. He would have to take matters into his own hands. As soon as the baby was born, he would begin to make plans for their departure. Where they would go and what they would do he had no idea, but they would leave soon, whether she wanted to or not.

Ellon Castle, Autumn, 1787

It seemed to Susan that they ceased arguing after that one summer evening. Yet, in spite of that, their disagreement continued to grow in secret, nurtured by their silence on the subject. Susan spent a great deal of time with Penelope and her baby namesake, irritating her husband

and making him even less agreeable to be around. Still, he had long ago stopped chastising her on that topic.

In the meantime, Penelope enthusiastically welcomed Susan's company. She seemed grateful for Susan's shared knowledge on child rearing, and she was extremely happy, having brought a baby to full term at last after three miscarriages. Her Penny was a beautiful little girl, whom she could dress like a doll and play with. The house was so full of boys that Susan and Eleanor would often come and sit with Penelope and the baby, pretending they were ladies and sharing the latest fashions from Paris. It was a game that satisfied each of them in different ways. Susan was the only one for whom it was nostalgia rather than a dream, and Penelope was the only one who could ever realize that dream.

"If ever I get my girlish figure back," she said, "I shall have George, pardon me, I mean, the Earl, buy me this gown." She pointed at a picture in the pattern book they were poring over. "It seems such a long time since he was last here, does it not?"

Susan did not think so, but she did not say what she thought. Instead, she said. "I am sure he will be here for Christmas as he always is."

"He was upset last summer to find that I was suckling my child 'like a common animal' he said. Those were his exact words. But I did as you suggested, and showed him the passage in the book. He was astonished. I think he did not know that I could read." She smiled. "He says to me, 'What do you mean by filling your head with nonsense from books?'" Penelope laughed as if the memory were sweet to her. But then she turned serious. "I hope he does not keep away on that account."

"I am sure that he does not," Susan said, not at all sure but not really caring. She was not particularly interested when the conversation turned to talk of the Earl.

His visits only separated her from Penelope, forcing her to spend more time with John, who became even grumpier, if that were possible, when the Earl was in residence.

~~*

It was a Sunday morning and John was at the Presbyterian church of St. Mary. He had taken the two oldest boys with him that morning. As usual, James sat quietly and reverently, while Johnny fidgeted under his father's glare. Even before her pregnancy, Susan had not often attended church with John, claiming the demands of her younger children. John suspected that she could not abide the long sermons and prayers of the Presbyterian service having been raised in the Church of England. To his regret, John had never pressed her to accompany him, though he often thought now that he should have done.

On this particular Sunday, little Johnny's saving angel came in the unusual form of his sister Eleanor, who was sent to the church to inform her father and Mrs. Henry of the imminent birth. All eyes in the church, including the minister's, were turned on the family who began to make their way to the door of the church. Mrs. Henry headed in the opposite direction, tiptoeing to the pew where Mrs. MacGregor was making her prayer. With that action, everyone's curiosity was satisfied as to the meaning of the rude interruption, and their attention returned to the service. Mrs. MacGregor did not seem to mind being disturbed, her usual sour face looking for a moment surprised and then relieved at the news. She stole out of the church after the rest of the family.

Johnny walked ahead of them all, skipping and shuffling and kicking stones. At one point, he walked back beside his sister. "We are going to have another brother," he crowed.

"Maybe not. It could just as well be a girl," Eleanor responded.

"Huh! In our family! You are the only loser girl!" Johnny scoffed.

"That is enough, Johnny. You are not to speak rudely, especially not on the Sabbath day. What you will do instead when we get home, along with all of your brothers and sister, is to pray that your mother is delivered safely of her baby, whether 'tis a boy or a girl. Is that understood?"

"Aye, Papa!" all three of the children chimed in.

~~*

Soon after that Susan heard the sound of her husband and children gathering outside the door in the family sitting room. She could hear John praying and all the children's voices joining in to say 'Amen'. It was the most comforting sound she could imagine. Then she heard Mrs. MacGregor's crisp no-nonsense Scottish burr thrown like cold water into their midst.

"Where's my patient?"

John opened the door of Susan's room and Mrs. MacGregor came in with Lizzie Henry right behind her. She immediately began to order the poor girl about, sending her off to boil water and gather supplies from the kitchen.

"Ain would think she dinna ken a thing, daft lass," Mrs. MacGregor said.

"Have patience. 'Tis her first birth," Susan explained. "But we are old hands." She smiled at her midwife, hoping to soften her.

"That we are, madam. That we are. Now be about your business."

As if heeding her command, the labour pains assailed Susan at once, and she gasped, taking deep breaths to try to assuage the stabbing sensation.

When the pain stopped and she was lying back on the bed panting, Mrs. MacGregor asked, "How far along are we?"

"The pains are very close together. I think it will not be long now."

About a half hour later, the labour ceased and Mrs. MacGregor placed Susan's latest wee bairn upon her breast.

"'Tis a girl, madam!"

Until that moment, Susan did not know that she had been longing for a girl. She had not even let herself believe that it was possible, but when she heard the news, she thought her heart would burst with happiness.

Mrs. MacGregor left Susan to examine the truth of the pronouncement, while she went into the sitting room where everyone was eagerly watching the door since having heard the baby cry. There she made the announcement again: "'Tis a bonny wee lass."

John leapt up from his seat with a great smile on his face and went to Susan's bedside, immediately followed by the children, though Mrs. MacGregor attempted in vain to deny them access.

"You see, Johnny. I told you it would be a girl, and now it is, and I shall have someone on my side for a change," Eleanor said to her brother as they entered the room.

Johnny was quiet at first, looking a little disgruntled by the turn of events, but he finally responded, "We are still the greater number and our side will best your side any day of the week."

"'Tis not a competition, Johnny," his father scolded him. "Let us give a prayer of thanksgiving for the safe deliverance of a child of God."

He took the baby from his wife and pronounced a benediction over her.

Ellon Castle, Winter, 1787

Then followed serene days. Susan lay in bed in the long morning, the warmth of her own body keeping her warm within her bedclothes and the sweet-smelling body of her baby, also named Susan, curled in the crook of her arm. The baby's tiny puckered mouth sucked as she slept.

"Get up, lazy-bones!" John called to Susan before he left.

It was a difficult chore to get out of her cozy nest: the air outside of the bed was the usual damp winter chill that emanated from the castle's stone walls in every season. A castle might be romantic in theory, but in reality she knew from long experience, it was bitter, bitter hard.

Susan slipped a foot out from under the cover. The cold threatened to snap her toes off. She shuddered and pulled it back in. She promised herself that she would lie there only a few more minutes. She could hear the children on the other side of the door. James and Johnny would be off to school soon. There was no need to get out of bed for them; they were almost as independent as their father now.

Susie squirmed beside her, but her eyes were still shut tight. There truly was nothing on earth as beautiful as a sleeping baby, she thought.

Will and Davy were making such a racket that Susan was afraid they would wake the baby, but she dared not call out to scold them as that surely would have. In a few minutes Lizzie would surely come and take them to the kitchen. She waited, and soon enough it was quiet once again outside her door, and there was no reason to get up at all. Why should she feel guilty? She must have woken three times in the night to feed the baby. She dozed off.

Next thing she knew the door opened slowly and Eleanor came to the side of her bed.

"Good morning, Mama."

Susan shook herself awake. "Good morning, Ellie." She looked at her daughter, wondering what she wanted.

"Will we have a lesson this morning, Mama?"

It had been several weeks since their last lesson, before the baby was born, and Susan could see that Ellie missed them. When Susan was her age, she would arise and dress and run outside before the governess was up, and the governess would have to find her for her lesson. Susan's father's estate was large and parts of it were very wild (though not as wild as here in Scotland, of course) and many times the governess could not find her, and she would escape her lessons and play outside in the wilderness until she was hungry enough to go inside. Of course, the governess had whipped her for it then, but she never regretted those carefree days of exploring.

Susan almost pitied the pale earnest girl beside her who came searching for her lessons. "Well," she said, pulling herself up on her elbow. "Let me get dressed and we shall have your lesson before Susie wakes up and disturbs our peace."

Eleanor smiled and jumped up. She ran from the bed chamber, and Susan got out of the bed in one swift movement. In spite of her best effort not to disturb the baby, the sudden shock of cold air she felt when the blanket was removed woke her, and she began to cry.

As Susan stroked her face to comfort her, the baby's lips sought her finger to suck on it, and Susan gave it to her for a moment. She thought she heard Eleanor utter a mild curse on the other side of the door.

It made her smile. The serious little scholar had a little fire in her after all.

Susan started to get dressed, determined to give Ellie a lesson anyway. Behind her on the big empty bed, the abandoned baby started squirming, whimpering, and then, flailing and wailing.

Susan continued tying herself up, even more awkwardly than usual in her haste. Although it had been a long time since she had had someone else to dress her, she had never learned to do it artfully. Sometimes when they were together, Penelope corrected her gown for her. It was a telling act of the strange reversal of their fortunes— Penelope, a former maid, now mistress, and Susan, a former mistress, now, the wife of a servant.

Eleanor knocked at her door.

"Come in, dear."

She entered. "Shall I take the bairn for you, Mama?"

Though she was dressed now, and could have taken her herself, she said, "Yes. Will you take her while I get some breakfast?"

Eleanor picked up the baby and said, "Mama, I think Susie needs a clean napkin. I shall change her while you eat."

"Thank you, Ellie." In the parlour, there was a plate with bread and butter on the table, which John must have left for her. Susan ate it hungrily, picking up every crumb with her moistened finger. She placed a leftover lump of cold, hard butter in her mouth and felt it slip soothingly down her throat as it melted. Some tea would be good to warm her, she thought.

As she was finishing, Eleanor came out with the baby, still crying even in her clean clothes.

"I think perhaps she is hungry, Mama."

"Perchance," Susan said, meaning most likely. The baby had a prodigious appetite. Susan sat down and started to unbutton her bodice. "All right," she said, "give the wee wretch to me."

Eleanor handed her mother the baby, sat down at the table and sighed.

"Do you have your primer, dear?" Susan asked. "We may as well start a lesson while the baby is nursing."

Ellie's response was a radiant smile. Poor little girl who loved learning so much. How cruel were the fates to make her a female, and worst of all, to give her such a tutor as me.

When the baby was sated and the young girl had had a brief lesson, they went in search of their usual company. Susan instructed Eleanor to bring her reader so that she could amuse the babies by reading to them.

Ellie objected that they were too young to understand.

"No," her mother said. "Not so. For even the youngest newborn loves the sounds of words."

Eleanor was pleased by this assurance and brought her book.

Penelope had tea ready for them which Susan was still craving. There was more bread and butter and strawberry preserves, her favourite! The flavours carried her back on the wings of memory home to the south on a warm spring day. She closed her eyes and the castle walls disappeared, replaced by sunshine trickling through the trees on her face and birds singing. Then a cool breeze stirred her hair. It was naught but a castle draught. She shivered and pulled her wrap tighter.

All morning the three of them, Penelope, Eleanor and Susan, played dolls with their living babies. It was not the kind of lesson Eleanor wanted, but it was the kind of lesson that would most truly prepare her for the life she was to lead. Their morning revelry was scarcely ever disturbed by the boisterous boys now that they had excellent nannies to attend to them. So the winter of 1787-8 passed.

~~*

It was Christmas and the Earl had come. Susan, Eleanor and the baby were banished from Penelope's private quarters and forced to spend their time in the servants' quarters. John had returned to Scottish custom and worked on Christmas day, ignoring the holiday

altogether. The boys attended school as usual. Nanny Henry
and her aunt and uncle Henry, being Scots as well, did not
consider it important to celebrate Christmas either. And
Susan, because the Earl was there, was cut off from the
only Englishwoman on the estate who had any notion of
what a Christmas celebration was. She sat down with
Eleanor and tried to devise an appropriate festivity for the
holiday.

"We should have sweets," Eleanor stated
emphatically.

"By all means," her mother conceded, "if you can
coax from your father the pennies to buy them."

"Hmmph," Ellie responded, knowing full well the
difficulty of such an endeavour, even for her. "Well, we
may have pudding at any rate."

"I believe that Mrs. Henry will be amenable to such
an idea. Should we go to see her about it?"

"Shall we be obliged to make it for her, do you
think?"

"Perhaps she will request our assistance at least.
'Twould be a good thing for you, Ellie, if you learned to
make a pudding."

"I should like that."

"What else shall we have?"

"Gifts. I think we cannot have Christmas without
gifts, Mama."

"Never fear, Ellie. I have been sewing while you have
been sleeping, and so you shall have a gift. But I will not
say what it is until the boys are home, so that everyone may
be surprised at once."

Eleanor smiled. "And Papa has a present for you,
Mama, but I will not say what neither."

It was usually a potted plant that he had miraculously
coaxed into bloom in the greenhouse, which was,

nonetheless, a welcome gift in the depths of winter, and Susan would act suitably surprised.

"I have an idea, Eleanor. Go and persuade Papa to take you out in the snow to cut some holly, and mistletoe, if you can find it. Then we shall decorate the sitting room so that it looks quite jolly."

So Ellie scampered off happily to find her father and Susan tended to Susie who was still voraciously hungry and growing at a prodigious rate.

Christmas passed quietly, with a special pudding for dessert, in which Lavinia had hidden pennies, and an exchange of gifts—new clothes for the children, drawings from the children and, of course, her potted plant from John. It was a geranium, not her favourite flower by any means, but one that was bright and cheery on these gray days.

~~*

The Earl braved the December cold to walk in the garden with Dean.

"The garden in winter is not totally devoid of beauty, my lord." Dean's words escaped from his mouth accompanied by puffs of white fog.

"Aye," the Earl grudgingly acknowledged. "There is yet some greenery."

A rook cawed from the top of a spruce tree as if in confirmation.

The Earl paused before a garden clump in the center of which was a sickly brown shrub. He shook his head and tsked. "Mr. Dean, is that not our Rhododendron maximum?"

"It is, my lord."

"And is not the rhododendron an evergreen shrub?"

"Aye."

"This specimen has turned quite brown. Why is that, Mr. Dean?"

John was no more pleased than the Earl. He hated to admit his failure, but the Earl had insisted on having this shrub with its stupendous flowers of pink and white in his garden, and Dean had never tended one before. "Perhaps we are too far north for this particular shrub, my lord," he gave as his explanation.

"Our gardener at Haddo House just ten miles from here has had great success with our rhododendron there."

"I must confess that I know very little about this particular shrub, my lord."

"Dinna fash, Dean. 'Tis but a short trip to Haddo House. If you like, us will send our carriage to take you there next month where you may confer with your colleague Mr. Malcolm on the care and grooming of the rhododendron in the northern clime of Scotland. Perhaps the plant may yet be saved. Would that be amenable to you?"

"You are most kind, my lord."

"Let us go back to the castle, Dean. 'Tis not only the rhododendron that finds this climate too cold." The Earl laughed, and John was greatly relieved that their promenade was ended.

~~*

Two days after Christmas, while Eleanor was reading her lessons to her, Susan received an unexpected visit from Penelope.

In her surprise, she asked rather impertinently, "Where is the Earl? Has he left already?"

Penelope nodded, looking distressed in spite of an evident effort to hide her emotions. "Yes, he has gone back to Haddo House to spend Hogmanay with his family."

Susan imagined she heard John saying 'As he ought.'

"Oh," she said, not sure whether to commiserate with her or not. "'Tis a shame for you and the children. Did you pass a good Christmas?"

"Yes," Penelope responded, trying to put on her best face. She recounted all the gifts that her children had received and the wondrous turkey feast (which the servants were fortunate to have the remains of the next day, though Susan did not mention this). Susan's had been a very dull Christmas by comparison, which assurance seemed to bolster Penelope's morale somewhat.

"And," Susan added. "You may now celebrate Hogmanay with the rest of us. Never fear. The Scots know how to throw a party when they want to."

Susan immediately regretted her invitation. John would be most unhappy about the addition of Penelope to their party on New Years' Eve.

Chapter 6

Ellon Castle, spring, 1788

It was more than two months before the proposed visit to Haddo House actually took place, and by that time the Earl had returned to England. Early in March, a carriage was sent for Dean so that he could go and discuss the Rhododendron maximum with his colleague at Haddo House. It was only a distance of ten miles or so, a comfortable round-trip for a day's outing, so John suggested to Susan that she go with him. It had been a long time since the two of them had spent any time alone together, and now that there was a competent nanny, they could leave the children without compunction. Susan had never been so excited about a trip in all her life. She needed a respite from her duties as a mother. Even with a nanny, six children were a great deal of work.

Susan perceived that Penelope was jealous when she told her the news. She implored Susan to be her spy and tell her everything she could about Haddo House, its disposition, number of servants, garden, and, most especially, principal occupants. Susan was a little embarrassed to be asked to perform such a task. However, she reluctantly agreed that she would recount everything that she saw but that she would make no exceptional forays into the family's private territory unless she was expressly invited to do so.

They set off on a lovely March morning. The sky was a little overcast but the clouds were so distant that they did not portend rain. The swaying motion of the carriage reminded Susan of her first coach ride to Scotland that had occurred precisely ten years before.

"Do you recall our first voyage, John, when we traveled from London to Dundee? I sat alone in the carriage and you were riding outside on the coach."

He took her hand in his. "Aye. How much more pleasant it is to sit side by side." Their shared memory made the ten-mile voyage seem so brief as to be but a moment.

Mr. Malcolm, the head gardener of Haddo House, greeted them upon their arrival at the estate. There seemed to be an immediate fraternity of feeling between the two men, as if they had always known each other. Since Susan knew this not to be the case, she assumed it to be their common interests that drew them so close on first acquaintance.

Even though she had long since become accustomed to the Scottish brogue, Susan soon found herself unable to understand the language that they spoke together with its floral terms in Latin, detailed description of soil conditions and climate considerations. Regardless, she followed them on their tour, blissfully ignorant of their conversation and simply enjoying the sensations of the garden.

She became lost in a reverie where colour confronted her eyes, sweet aromas assailed her nose, and the gentle twitter of birds provided a musical background. Still, she half-attended their conversation, and her ears pricked when she heard them mention the "wicked Earl."

"Aye. I understand the delicacy of your position and your repugnance of it, Mr. Dean. We all have to overlook a great deal of indiscretion in our employment with the Earl. Fortunately, he is seldom in residence here, so it is not very difficult."

Susan wondered at this statement, since he did not spend a lot of time at Ellon Castle either. Perhaps he spent most of the year in England. In that, she envied him a little.

"I for one am weary of it. Do you know of any gardening positions available in the vicinity, Mr.

Malcolm?" She was surprised to hear her husband ask this question. Evidently, he did not know that she was listening, so she turned her head as if she were looking at a distant tree, but listened even more intently.

"I canna say that I do. Not in the general vicinity, at any rate. I can tell you that Scottish gardeners are much in demand in Ireland, though. Have you thought of relocating across the water?"

"I have thought of emigration of course, but to America. I have two brothers in New England whom I have not seen in many years."

With this remark, Susan could not help but stare at him, and he returned her look.

Malcolm too became aware of her presence. "Perhaps Mrs. Dean would like to see the house now?" he suggested.

"Yes," she said. "I would. You have a lovely garden here, sir. Thank you for the tour."

Mr. Malcolm showed them to the servants' quarters which they reached directly through a back entrance. Penelope would be most disappointed that Susan did not have the opportunity to walk through the family quarters in order to spy on her rival's territory, but Susan was relieved that she would be spared the embarrassment of describing it to her.

In the kitchen the housekeeper made a great fuss over them. The cook had prepared a dinner so that they would be refreshed for their return journey. As they sat and enjoyed the feast, other servants came in one by one to be introduced and to sit and chat. When their former nanny Maude walked in and sat across from them in her usual insolent manner, John was evidently surprised.

"Miss Ashcroft! I thought you had returned to England!"

"Mrs. Dean! You did not tell your husband that I was here at Haddo House?"

"No," Susan said. "I told no one. In truth, I had forgotten about it."

"I am astonished! I thought you would have told your husband at the very least."

John looked rather cross to Susan, so she did her best to explain it for his sake. "It was that day about a year ago when I went to the market in Ellon with Will and Alexander. You remember that I lost the boys and was so distraught. We were all so busy with finding them again and so relieved when we did find them that it slipped out of my memory. That is why I did not tell you that I had seen Maude in the village."

"Well, I hope that you will remember me to my friends at Ellon Castle this time, Mrs. Dean."

Susan nodded half-heartedly.

As they ate their dinner, they answered Maude's enquiries after the other servants at Ellon, and, most indiscreetly, after the mistress of the castle. Susan could tell that some of the servants were a little embarrassed at her indiscretion, but all of them listened attentively to hear any gossip they could about the wicked Earl's mistress. Susan said as little as she could.

Susan was so uncomfortable under the circumstances that it was a relief to finish the meal and escape to the garden once again. She left John with Mr. Malcolm at the greenhouse discussing business and set off to explore on her own. She had scarcely begun to embark on the labyrinthine pathways, when she was hallooed by a most unwelcome visitor. Maude arrived beside her a little out of breath.

"Mrs. Dean, I hope you don't mind if I join you." She did not stop to hear a response. "I have some news to impart that will interest you, something which I could not speak of in front of the other servants."

She was positively radiant with happiness—quite a different person from the sour-faced young girl who had traveled all the way from London with them.

"You will never guess what news I have."

"No, I am quite sure I will never guess unless you tell me."

"Where shall I begin?"

"I do not know."

"I am to have a baby."

Susan could not apprehend the joy in this particular piece of news, considering Maude's position.

As if reading her mind, Maude added, "And my situation is to be entirely changed."

"So, the father of the child will marry you?" Susan asked, assuming this to be the source of her joy.

She laughed, a silly, haughty little laugh. "No. The father of the child is the Earl himself."

Susan stopped, in shock. "And this is your joyful news?"

"I am to have my own castle," she stated triumphantly. "The Earl is, even now, looking for a suitable estate. What do you think of that, Mrs. Dean?" Fortunately she did not wait for a reply. "You will pass the information on to Miss Dering, will you not? She will be most interested to know my news, I should think."

Susan was sure she would be crushed.

"Promise me you will tell her."

"I shall not promise you that."

"Then I shall tell your husband. I am quite sure he will convey the news."

She was very good at reading people, the evil little witch. "All right. I shall promise." Susan kept her fingers crossed behind her back. How could she tell her best friend that the Earl was cheating on her, and not with his wife, either?

Susan was glad when John had finished all his business and they were in the carriage again with Haddo House fading in the distance behind them.

After some time had passed in silence, John asked her what she was thinking. As Maude had correctly deduced, she did not want to share with him the news about the pregnancy. It would only confirm his poor opinion of the Earl and add more fuel to the fire he had begun to tend, his desire to leave the Earl's employment. This reminded her of what he had said to Mr. Malcolm about emigration, which would serve as the weighty topic now occupying her thoughts. "You did not tell me that you were still considering emigration to America."

"'Tis something that has been on my mind for a very long time. You know that, even before I met you, I was considering emigration. But then the rebellion and our marriage interrupted my plans."

"After the war ended, when we discussed it, I told you that I did not wish to leave my homeland. What has changed that you are considering it again?"

"Do you need to ask me that? You know I am unhappy in the Earl's employment."

"But you did not tell me you were considering it so seriously."

"I was afraid that you might not have changed your mind about emigration."

"Then why did you not ask me?"

"I am asking you now."

"Then I shall tell you. I am still fervently opposed. I have already moved far from my own country to be with you. I do not wish to be transported farther still to the ends of the earth, to some place even more primitive than this."

John looked crushed. The rest of the trip passed as it had begun—in silence.

Ellon Castle, Summer 1788

Dinner was being cleared from the servants' table and Susan had gone to take the youngest children to their room for their afternoon nap, and still John sat at the table. Mrs. Henry was beginning to look at him oddly. He would need to screw up the courage to ask his question soon.

Miss Dering's maid entered the kitchen. "My poor mistress is locked up in her room with a headache. Do you have some remedy about, Mrs. Henry?" she asked.

"Aye. Ask the cook for some. Miss Dering has been feeling poorly quite often these days."

"Aye. I expect she misses the Earl," the maid laughed and John could not help but blush.

Mr. Henry, who was placidly smoking his after-dinner pipe, removed it from between his teeth, and said, "Aye. The master is usually here this time of year. What is he about?"

Mrs. Henry scolded her husband. "I told you that the Earl wrote to say that he has bought the estate of Formartine for his son and heir and that he is busy helping the young man establish his family there."

"Oh, aye. I do recollect now, madam."

"The Formartine estate?" Miss Dering's maid questioned. "Isn't that where the Byrons live? Poor Mrs. Byron having her home picked over by that vulture the Earl. And he is her cousin no less."

"Tsk, tsk. Loose lips sink ships." Mrs. Henry said to the maid.

Mr. Henry removed his pipe again. "Mrs. Byron and her husband are the authors of their own misfortunes. 'Tis not the Earl that put them into debt."

"I still pity any woman that the Earl meets," the maid said and then shrugged, before leaving the room with a tray for her mistress.

"Who is the Earl's son?" John asked Mrs. Henry.

"Did you not meet any of the family at Haddo House?"

John shook his head.

"He is another George Gordon, a young man like yourself with a rather large family considering his youth."

"And how did the Byrons get into debt?"

"Gambling," Mr. Henry replied.

"But, Mr. Dean, I am sure you did not stay behind this afternoon in order to gossip with the servants," Mrs. Henry interrupted. "What is on your mind, sir?"

"You are right. I should come to my business. I know that you have a large acquaintance abroad, and I was wondering if I might have the addresses of any of your friends in Ireland."

"For what purpose, if you dinna mind me asking?"

"Not at all. I am considering moving my family and I wished to enquire about the possibility of employment."

"What does Mrs. Dean think of the plan?" Mrs. Henry asked.

"I havena yet told her madam," he murmured, a little embarrassed by her brusque tone.

"Well, surely she should be the first to know!" Mrs. Henry cried.

The door opened and Susan entered. "I could not help overhearing," she said. "What is it that I ought to be informed of?"

John was too embarrassed to reply, but with Mrs. Henry and Susan both glaring at him, he had no choice. "I was just telling the Henrys of my intention to move as soon as I find a suitable position elsewhere."

Susan did not speak at first. He could almost see her emotions beneath the surface, but she controlled them. Her voice was restrained when she said to the Henrys, "Mr. Dean did mention the possibility of emigration to me." Then she addressed John. "Has there been some new development that I do not know of?"

"I was just asking the Henrys for the addresses of some of their acquaintances in Ireland. I know that you dinna wish to go so far frae hame as the New World."

Susan nodded.

"Well, I have chattered idly for too long. I maun go back to work now."

John stood up and walked to the door. As he passed his wife, she said, "We shall discuss this further this evening, sir."

"Aye," he replied. "Good day to you all," he called to the Henrys.

~~*

Later that afternoon, Penelope knocked on the sitting room door and entered before a response was given. Susan wiped the tears from her eyes and hoped that her friend had not noticed, but Penelope moved swiftly to her side, took her hand and said, "What is it, dear? Why are you crying?"

Susan attempted to smile. "Nothing at all."

"Come now. I know something is amiss. You are always so jolly. What is it?"

Susan was unwilling to reveal her marital secrets. It would not be appropriate to break the news before John found another position elsewhere, which God forbid he did. "Nothing," she repeated.

Five-year-old Will opened the door from his bed-chamber where he was supposed to have been sleeping with Davy. "What Papa said made her cry. He says we are to move to Ireland. But I willna go and leave my friend Sandy."

"Hush, Will," Susan said, wishing she had not confided to the child when he had asked her earlier. "This is a private family matter and you are not to talk about it before others. Do you understand?"

"Ah ha." Penelope seemed jubilant at having discovered the cause of Susan's grief. "But how can you consider leaving Ellon Castle? We are all so happy here. Tell me. Why does he want to go?"

"I cannot tell you that, Penelope. I cannot confide our private family affairs to you."

"How often have I told you intimate details of my bedroom?"

"Hush, Penelope." Susan inclined her head to indicate that Will was still in the room. The quiet young lad had already overheard enough.

As if thinking that very thought, Penelope asked him, "Do you know why your papa wants to leave Ellon Castle?"

Before he could answer, Susan said, "Will, go to your room."

Familiar with that particular tone of his mother's voice, he quickly turned and ran back to his bedroom.

Susan said to Penelope, "Be a dear friend and do not mention this again."

Penelope pursed her lips tightly, nodded and left the apartment.

~~*

In the garden that very afternoon, John was trimming the dead blossoms from the rose bush when he heard the voice of Miss Dering. "Good afternoon, sir." He looked up as the head of another rose tumbled from the bush, its petals scattering like bits of red paper on the lawn.

"Good afternoon," he said to be polite. Her eyes were looking down at the roses.

"Do you think I might have those petals, sir? They would make a splendid pot-pourri for my wardrobe."

"Certainly, madam. You may gather them up if you wish." He would not stoop to do her bidding even though she was his mistress and even though he pitied her.

She coloured at the slight he had done her.

"Susan has informed me that you are seeking to leave our employ. She does not give me any reason. May I ask the cause of your dissatisfaction?"

"You may ask, madam. But I may not feel obliged to respond."

"Your manner is quite churlish. Have I done something to offend you, sir?"

"Your manner of living is what gives me offence, madam."

She looked confused. "I do not understand you, Mr. Dean. You have been in my employ for four years and I have not altered my manner of living in that time. What has changed that you now so suddenly consider it to be offensive?"

"It has always been offensive to me, madam. I would have left at any time in the last four years, if I had been by myself, or if I had had the independent means to support my family, or if my wife had not been with child. Any number of circumstances has prevented me from following the wishes of my own heart."

"I am sorry, sir..." Penelope did not seem to know how to respond.

"Aye," John said. "You are a sorrowful creature, and not a fit companion for my wife. I regret that she took up with the likes of you."

Penelope continued standing, seeming too shocked to move. "But since your wife is my friend, sir, I have come to you to beg on her behalf that you consider her happiness first. She is miserable at the thought of leaving Ellon Castle."

John snorted in derision. "I shall thank you to mind your own affairs."

She blushed deep crimson, the colour of the fallen petals, turned and began to walk back to the castle.

"You dinna want the rose petals, madam?" he called after her.

She did not respond.

~~*

Penelope found Susan at her apartment just preparing to go out with her two little boys.

"We are going to visit Papa, are we not?" she said to Will and Davy.

"Aye," they both hollered, jumping up and down excitedly. Susan had thought it prudent to tell John of her discussion with Penelope in the sitting room, and so when the boys woke up, she dressed them for the outing.

"Perhaps you will reconsider when I tell you that I have already spoken to Mr. Dean," Penelope said.

"You did what? I asked you not to mention it again."

"I would not have mentioned it to you again."

"You are equivocating. You know it is a private matter. You had no right to speak of it with my husband either." Susan was angrier than she had ever been with her friend, so angry that she was sorely tempted to tell her about Maude and the wicked Earl.

"I am sorry, Susan."

"I must go to him. He will be angry, and I promised the boys." In spite of her words, Susan stood there, uncertain whether she should take the boys and expose them to his anger, or if perhaps their presence would mitigate it. It would be better to go alone so that she could explain to him.

"You ought not to go now. I would not expose the boys to his anger if I were you."

"But I promised them."

"Perhaps they will come with me and Alexander. We will go on an outing to the village. Would you like that, boys?" Penelope bent down to their level. It was rare that she interacted with them at all, and the novelty of an outing with the mistress seemed of interest to them.

"Aye," they clamoured excitedly.

"All right," Susan agreed to it. "But you will be on your best behaviour. I do not want to hear from Miss Dering that you have misbehaved."

The boys assured her they would be good.

"Why don't you come too, Susan?" Penelope asked.

"No. I must speak to John and try to untangle this mess you have made."

So Penelope took the two boys to her son's nursery to find the rest of their party.

Susan stood alone, ready to go out but reluctant to confront her husband. Why ever had Penelope intruded in their private concern? She shook her head. Well, it had to be faced. Away she went into the garden.

Even from behind, she could tell that he was angry. He had just amassed all of the weeds and dead blossoms, the garden waste of his day's labour, into a great heap and was standing stock still before it ready to set it alight with his flintlock. The scratching of the stone on stone concealed the rustle of Susan's gown as she approached him. She arrived at his side just as the flame caught and the dry kindling quickly began to smoke and then crackle into tiny flames.

John jumped at the suddenness of his wife's appearance. "Susan, you startled me."

"I am sorry, John. I understand you have had an unpleasant encounter with Miss Dering." There was no point beating about the bush; the issue must be approached head on.

"Aye. The whore came to tell me of your unhappiness with my decision."

Susan was struck not only by his language but also by the bitterness in his voice.

"How could you have betrayed my confidence, Susan?" He turned and looked straight in her eyes.

She returned his direct look. "How could you believe that I would, John?" It was her intention to fight fire with fire.

"She said that you did."

"And you believe a woman that you call a 'whore', without first speaking to your wife?"

He looked away.

She was glad that she had countered him, but she did not wish to betray her friend either. "I did not tell her. It was Will. He must have overheard our conversation in the kitchen." She was a little ashamed at her dissembling, but she did not wish to increase his anger by admitting that she had told him herself.

John looked back at her, his face resuming its stolid expression of anger. "You dare to bring a little boy into the middle of this? And where are the children now?"

"Miss Dering has taken the boys with Alexander on an outing so that I could talk with you in private."

"Aye. I know that you think a bastard is a fit playfellow for your sons."

"It is not the boy's fault." Susan could never understand the social scorn heaped on children on account of their parents' indiscretion.

The fire was fully engaged now and Susan could feel the hot flames on her face. She took a step back from it.

His eyes followed her, his anger as intense as the conflagration in front of him. "I have no wish to stand here talking nonsense. You have had your way long enough,

Susan. Too long." He turned back to the flames that seemed almost invisible in the brightness of the day.

Susan was concerned that a spark would leap out and set him ablaze. "Come away from the heat, John."

"No, Susan. You step forward and feel it." Then he took hold of her arm and pulled her forcefully to stand beside him. She was terrified that he had lost his senses. "Do you feel the heat, Susan?"

She nodded, saying nothing, fearful to incite him.

"That is a tiny fraction of the heat that awaits you in Hell."

She quivered at the dark look in his eyes. No Presbyterian preacher had ever preached fire and brimstone as effectively as John was doing at that moment.

"I may not be able to save you, Susan, but I will be damned myself if I let you suffer my children to lose their eternal souls." She could feel the intense heat searing her cheek and closed her eyes in anticipation of imminent pain. He let go of her.

The moment she felt his grip loosen, she pulled away from him and stepped back. She was panting with relief at being released from the terror she had felt at being held so close to the fire. She could not stand to look at him, still so near to danger himself, but she knew that he was beyond heeding her. She turned and walked back to the house, ignoring her deep desire to run, and trying to ignore the new fear that thundered louder than the flames in her head—the fear that the love they had shared was gone.

~~*

That evening John retained a taciturn demeanor and said nothing to her beyond what was strictly necessary. In bed, he kept his back to her and she lay there looking at it, wondering if life would ever be the same again. The silence in the room made her breathing so audible that she was afraid he would comment on it.

She would just have to wait. These things took time. She had never seen him this angry before, so it would probably take longer than usual for his rage to subside, but one day it would, and he would smile at her again. She had only to be patient.

She sighed. Patience had never been her strong suit.

In the meantime, she had learned one certain thing about him: he was in earnest about his religious beliefs.

He had indulged her for a long time, and she had mistaken this indulgence for a moral ambiguity not unlike her own. But no longer. He had demonstrated to her, in no uncertain terms, that he would not allow his children to become as morally stagnant as he believed her to be. From John's point of view, she was on a direct road to Hell. For herself, she had never seriously believed in Hell. Her God was too kind and just to send any of his creatures to eternal damnation. She could not believe that her own husband would think she merited such a fate. Everyone died, and no one knew what happened after death, no one except John, of course, who was certain that she was damned.

Staring at his back she began to feel that, if there were a Hell, it would be like this banishment from love. John was a just man, she knew that, and yet he had reached the limits of his compassion. Even though her God's compassion was limitless, she had to live in this world with John. So what could she do about it? She would have to circumscribe the boundaries of her belief to match the littler circle of his belief. That was the only way to have peace in her home, and perhaps, peace in her heart.

Tomorrow she would have to say good-bye to the dearest friend she had ever known.

~~*

It seemed a regular day. After breakfast, John took his two oldest sons with him and went out to the garden. Susan gave some chores to Eleanor and left the two youngest boys in the care of their nanny. She took her baby Susie and went as usual to Penelope's apartment. She was dreading the conversation that would be their last as bosom companions.

As usual, Penelope had tea prepared for them. Susie began to fuss and Susan nursed her, glad of the short respite it gave her before the emotional scene she imagined was soon to take place.

A little while later, she was placing the pacified and sleeping baby in Penny's crib, when there was a knock at the door.

Penelope opened it. It was Mr. Henry.

"Begging your pardon, madam. You have a visitor…"

Before he could announce the name, Maude pushed him aside and entered the room. "Ain't you happy to see me, Miss Dering?" she said aggressively.

"What is the meaning of this intrusion?" Penelope asked. As she was still holding the door open and facing Henry, he assumed the words were directed at him.

"I am sorry, madam. She wouldna take nae for an answer."

"That's all right, Henry. Thank you." Penelope shut the door.

In the meantime, Maude had seen Susan at the crib. "Well, well. If it ain't my former mistress, Mrs. Dean. Good morning to you."

Susan nodded, uncertainly.

"Why have you not conveyed my messages to Miss Dering?"

"I did not wish to do so."

"So you have forced me to come and tell her myself."
Maude turned to face Penelope, who looked as nervous as
Susan felt.

"What is it you feel you must tell me, Maude?"

"You may not address me as Maude any longer. I
hold a position now that is equal to your own." The young
woman's usual contemptuous expression returned to her
face. "You must call me 'Miss Ashcroft'."

"All right, Miss Ashcroft. What has occasioned your
rise in position, if I might ask?"

"You might. In fact, it is the very news that I have
come to communicate to you." Maude's voice positively
crowed with pleasure, so that she could not refrain from
turning to Susan and saying, "I must thank you, Mrs. Dean,
for not telling her. It is such a great joy for me to do it
myself."

Penelope was standing there looking so vulnerable
that Susan wished she could spare her somehow.

"You will be delighted to learn that I am moving at
this very moment (my carriage is without) to my new
home—the fortress of Cairnbulg. Perhaps you have heard
of it? 'Tis a castle equally as grand as this one. I daresay,
grander." Maude glowed.

Penelope demurred. "How pleasant for you. Who is
to be your employer?"

Maude laughed, a haughty, grating sound. "No
employer. I am to be the mistress of the fortress, just as you
are mistress here."

Susan saw that Penelope's face had turned quite pale.

"You may, if you wish, congratulate me. I am to have
a baby soon."

Neither of the listeners took up the invitation.

"And the father, as Mrs. Dean already knows, is the
great Earl himself, George Gordon, Lord Haddo, Third Earl
of Aberdeen." She clapped her gloved hands together. "Are
you not happy for me, Miss Dering?"

Susan moved swiftly to her friend's side, catching her as she faltered and leading her to a chair. Then she turned to Maude. "There. I think you have finished what you came for. I am sure you can find your own way out."

Maude pranced out the door that she had entered, leaving enough devastation behind to satisfy her.

Susan turned to Penelope, whose pale face was still expressionless. There were no words, no tears, no recriminations. Her silence was even more frightening. What did one do for someone in such a state? Slap her face? Throw cold water on her? Smelling salts? The latter seemed the least violent, and Susan went to the sideboard searching through drawers until she found some. She held them under Penelope's nose till she sneezed loudly, waking the baby.

Susan did not know whom to attend first, but she stayed at Penelope's side while she came around.

"See to the baby. I am fine," Penelope said at last.

Susan did as she was bid, picking up Susie and comforting her till she stopped crying. Then she placed her on the floor, where she was now able to creep about, and went to her friend sitting unmoved on the chair.

"Are you all right, Penelope?"

Penelope shook herself a little and stood up, perhaps a little too quickly. She stumbled, almost falling back into the seat. Susan reached out to catch her, but she shook her head. "I'm fine." There was a kind of steely anger in her voice that Susan understood immediately. She did not wish to be pitied.

Susan had no wish to hurt her pride. There was no way that she could tell Penelope today that they could no longer be friends.

"You knew and you did not tell me." Penelope's voice was hard.

"I could not hurt you."

"You call yourself my friend."

Susan recognized immediately the repressed anger in her voice. She sensed hostility even here. Perhaps it would not be such a bad day for a break-up after all. She picked up her baby and walked towards the door. There, she turned and said, "I have always considered myself to be your friend, and I wished to spare your feelings. However, if you think that was unfriendly of me, then perhaps we are no longer friends." She walked out, closing the door behind her.

There, that was done. It had not been so bad after all. But as Susan walked away, she felt as if the pieces of her heart were crumbling to dust inside of her.

~~*

The news spread quickly through the servants' quarters, the more so since Miss Ashcroft was not at all reticent about sharing it with everyone she met. The kitchen was buzzing with it when John came into dinner.

"Mr. Dean, have you heard the news?" Mrs. Henry asked him as she put a plate of food in front of him.

"What news is that, madam?"

"Maude Ashcroft, your former nanny, is with child, and the Earl is the father. She is to have her own castle just like Miss Dering. The fortress of Cairnbulg, as I understand it."

"Your news has quite taken away my appetite, Mrs. Henry." He pushed his plate aside.

"Why do you let it bother you?" Mr. Henry asked. "In for a penny, in for a pound."

"Do you mean to say that you think one sin heaped atop another does not worsen the situation?"

Henry shrugged. "I mean to say that I think you are too sensitive about another man's sins, Dean."

"Come, you must eat." Mrs. Henry passed him the bread.

"I willna."

Susan entered the kitchen with Eleanor.

"Here, Mrs. Dean. Your husband willna eat."

"He has heard the news, then?"

"'Tis disgusting. You had best take the children to the apartment to eat their lunch there, so they willna be exposed to the servants' gossip today."

"Yes, John. You may imagine how poor Miss Dering feels about it," Susan said.

"Perhaps it will cause her to reflect on her immortal soul."

"One can only pray," Mrs. Henry said.

"Dinna pray too heartily, my dear. If she repents, she may abandon the castle and go back to England. Then we may all find ourselves without employment." Henry sniggered over his flummery.

John stood up, unable to stomach the company any longer. "Let me help you take some food to the apartment for the children, Susan," he said, gathering up his plate and walking to the door, where he said, "Good day to you all."

~~*

The afternoon sunlight filtered through the trees leaving stripes of brightness on the dark green of the lawn. The interplay of light and shadow added even more variety of shades of green to the garden. A light breeze gently lifted the leaves so that they sparkled and shimmered, wafting the sweet scent of vegetation to the gardener's senses. The stresses of the morning seemed to have evaporated and he felt a profound sense of peace such as he had often felt before in the garden. A church was a fine place, he thought, but a church soon filled with a preacher's bombastic sermon, drowning out the quiet that was needed to truly feel the gentle touch of God.

Beyond the quiet twittering of birds, John heard another sound—soft, intermittent, unidentifiable, like the mewing of a kitten perhaps, or a wounded animal. He began to follow the sound into the wood. At first, he did not see her; wearing a light green silk gown with a dark velvet cloak, she was perfectly disguised in this forest. But he recognized her shuddering form leaning on a bench at the same moment she became aware of him. She started up, wiping the tears from her eyes with the back of her hand.

He knew it was not Susan; he had just left her behind in the castle; but the first yearning of his heart was that it be her.

Penelope said, "I must look a fright."

She did, too, her eyes all red, her hair disheveled, a gloriously beautiful, vulnerable fright. John swallowed hard. The things the devil sends to tempt us, he thought. He should turn around right now and leave her, and yet it seemed to him as if it would be stomping on a wounded bird to do so. She was one of God's creatures after all. In the Good Book, Jesus had often spoken to fallen women to show them the error of their ways. Am I joking? he thought, I am not Jesus. But he stood there, firmly rooted to the spot like a stolid tree.

"Mr. Dean. You are speechless in the face of my shame."

"I hope, madam," he said, trying to find the words that Jesus might say, "that you have realized the error of your ways."

"'Vanity of vanities, saith the preacher; all is vanity,'" she responded, and then laughed, a gentle self-reproving laugh.

He was dismayed. What is this? She quotes scripture to me?

"I see I have startled you. You thought me a poor uneducated girl. I am sorry to disabuse you, but you may spare me your sermons, for I have heard enough of them already. You see, my father is a dissenting preacher in Sussex."

"Really! Well, then, you may go back to him with your bairns, and he will receive you with much rejoicing."

"Is that what you think would happen?"

"Aye, just like the prodigal son."

She laughed again, this time sounding truly amused. "That's a nice story, Mr. Dean, but there's a reason the main character was a prodigal son and not a prodigal daughter. I should think another Bible story would be a more likely scenario—the stoning of the woman taken in sin."

"But Jesus stayed the stoning when he said, 'He that is without sin among you, let him first cast a stone at her."

"Well then, that would be my father, the one who is without sin. He will certainly cast the first stone and the second one, and the last one too, for that matter."

"But surely that is blasphemy, madam. No man is without sin."

"No man but my father. A most extraordinary man. No, I will not go back to him. I would sooner rot in Hell."

More blasphemy! He ought to turn around and leave her now. She was not a wounded bird, unless that bird was a fighting cock. "Well, madam, I shall leave you now to the contemplation of your myriad sins. I must be about my work."

"Mr. Dean," she seemed to want to grasp him desperately with her voice before he turned away. "Tell me one thing before you go."

"What is it, madam?"

"Do I still have it?"

"Have what?" He coloured, knowing precisely what she meant before the words were out of his mouth.

"The power to seduce, you silly man."

He wanted to run, but he steeled himself, turning stiffly and walking away slowly.

"Never mind. You have already answered me. I saw your eyes when you first discovered me. Go ahead and run, but you have your own sins to contemplate." Her derisive laughter followed him down the path. He was embarrassed by how much he was blushing. He was ashamed of his own shame. To think he had thought he could save her when he was the one in need of saving. He prayed that God would forgive his momentary lapse into the sin of pride.

It was time to leave this place. It seemed a veritable Eden on the surface, but it was a place upheld by the wages of sin. A man could not serve a wicked master long and not become wicked. Even if he resisted temptation himself, he could not expect the same strength from his wife and his bairns. This was the sin that he was committing—allowing his family to be led astray, and for what? A roof over their heads and food in their bellies. There were other roofs and other gardens that grew healthier food, and if he were the sort of man he ought to be, he would find the one they ought to be living in. It was not here, in this fool's paradise.

Ellon Castle, Autumn, 1788

Miss Dering sent for Mr. Dean before he commenced his work, and he entered her apartment, cap in hand. He could see that she had been crying and it unnerved him. He stared at a spot just above her head. "You wanted to see me, madam."

"I am at my wit's end, Mr. Dean, and I believe you are the cause of it."

"How is that, madam?"

"I understand that you have forbidden your boys to play with my Alexander?" She paused.

"Aye." He was relieved to know that Susan was finally obeying his strictures.

"You have no idea how that has broken his heart. You have four sons and it is little matter to them, but Alexander does not know what to do with himself, and he does not understand why he is being punished in this manner. He wails and weeps and breaks things. Poor Miss MacPherson and I don't know what to do about the boy."

John felt a momentary twinge of guilt, but the lad had to learn that life was hard sooner or later.

"You have no remedy for me, Mr. Dean? And you are the one that has put me in this predicament."

"The lad is a bright boy. Why do you not engage a tutor for him?"

"I do not think the Earl would approve of such an expense at this time, I am afraid."

"Then send him to the Tollbooth School. The fees would be no burden to your pocket book. And the lad would receive sufficient occupation to overcome his boredom, I assure you."

"That is an excellent idea, Mr. Dean. Would your sons, James and Johnny, accompany him on the first day?"

John was mortified again. He thought immediately of redoubling his efforts to find employment in Ireland. "Well, perhaps for the first day, but I am sure Alexander will soon find the way himself."

"Thank you and good day, sir."

He left, feeling relieved by this reassurance that Susan no longer visited the mistress nor allowed their sons to play with hers.

~~*

James and Johnny were sent home from school early, their clothes all tattered and their faces scratched and bruised. They looked very proud of themselves when their mother fussed over their condition.

"Have you been beaten? Who has done this to you? Why are you home so early?"

"We have not been beaten, Mama," Johnny answered indignantly.

"Nae. Ye ought to see the state of the boys we beat on."

"Shame on you, James!" Nanny Henry hooted.

James seemed a little more chastened by her words. "Here's the letter to explain why we are hame early, Mama." He handed it to Susan.

"James and John Dean, having been engaged in an altercation with their schoolmates, have been sent home to be dealt with as deemed appropriate by their parents," she read. "This tells me nothing but that you have been fighting, and that I can see with my own eyes," Susan said. "Explain the particulars to me."

"It was on account of the other boys calling poor Sandy rude names. He was crying and James told them to stop, but they wouldna." Johnny's words spilled out pell-mell, and Susan, as usual, turned to his brother to clarify them.

"The older boys were teasing Alexander because he is the son of the wicked Earl, and a bastard." He looked at his mother. "Pardon me, but that was the word used."

She nodded at him to continue.

"I told them to leave off because he was crying so piteously, but they wouldna, as Johnny said. Since he is such a little boy and our friend, we thought it our place to protect him."

"So you started a fight…"

"Nae, Mama. We didna start it. We merely finished it," Johnny shouted.

"Did you get a whipping from the schoolmaster?" Nanny Henry asked.

"Aye, but it caused no great pain at all in comparison to what we endured in the battle we had fought to defend Alexander the Great," James crowed.

"You will not be so proud of yourselves when your Papa has heard of this," Susan said.

The boys were suddenly quiet.

"Nanny Henry, you watch the bairns and I shall take the boys to their father to receive their just punishment."

"Aye, Mrs. Dean."

Then Susan led James and Johnny, now more contrite and quiet, to see their father, who was pulling dead plants from the shrubbery.

"Why are you lads home in the middle of the day?" he asked as they approached.

"I have brought you two miscreants, sir, who have been fighting in the schoolyard." She handed her husband the letter.

John read it quietly, and then looked at the boys to hear their case.

James repeated the particulars, and adding, "You taught us that we ought always to defend those who are weaker than ourselves, Papa."

"That I did, James, but I must chastise you for your method of defense. Would it not have been enough to inform the schoolmaster of the other boys' offences, and let him deal with them? Then you would have been innocent of all blame."

"But we couldna leave him to be beaten by the other boys!" Johnny said stoutly.

"Aye, but look at this paper, Johnny." John showed the letter to his son. "Look what it says here: 'John Dean, having been engaged in an altercation with schoolmates...' That's my name there. Imagine my shock at seeing my ain name condemned for such behavior." John turned to the older boy. "And you, James, as the oldest, I would have expected you to show your brother the wisest way to behave in such a situation, and not rush in like a ruffian yourself."

John broke off the dried stem of a shrub and stripped it of its leaves. "As you behaved like ruffians, so shall you be punished like ruffians. Hold out your hand, James."

James did so and accepted the slashing of the cane without flinching. Susan averted her eyes as the cane drew blood.

John stopped and turned to Johnny.

"Master John," he said. "Your turn."

Johnny followed his older brother's example, though with the difference that the tears started in his eyes as the blood flowed from his cuts.

"Now, go back with your mother and behave yourselves for the rest of the day."

"Perhaps they should be put to work to help you in the garden, John," Susan suggested. She did not know how to keep two such boys from further mischief, and she had enough to do to contain their younger brothers, even with the nanny's help.

"'Tis a good suggestion, and I will devise some chores for them to do later, but first I want them put to paper to write out seven hundred times each, I will not fight in the schoolyard. Is that understood, lads?"

"Aye, Papa," they both said, following their mother back to the castle even more quietly and contritely than they had gone out.

~~*

Later, when they were alone, John spoke to his wife.

"Do you see now why I wish to remove my family from this household?" John looked at Susan with the same stern demeanour she had become used to lately.

She did not like his expression and sought the words to conciliate. "You are proud of the boys for the way they protected young Alexander. I know you are. I saw it in your eyes."

"I am not proud that they were put in the situation of having to defend a bastard."

Susan made a face. "That is daft, and you know it." She started to walk away from him, disgusted by what she considered his misplaced piety.

"Do not walk away when I am talking to you, madam."

He was being altogether too high-handed and suffocating these days, but she had vowed to herself to act the obedient wife, and so she stopped and faced him, making sure to show him her displeasure at the necessity.

He looked at her for a long time as she waited for his next words. "I have had enough of talking where I am not heeded," he said at last. "Go your own way, woman."

She turned and went to her room, her heart a heavy burden within.

He slept with his back to her again, the silent mountain of his enmity. She wished that she could touch it so that he would melt away into soft flesh again and become her lover. But her anger had turned her heart to stone as well, though she did not know that stone could ache. She fell asleep staring at that mountain, wondering how she could scale it.

She awoke to the sound of a child crying out, screaming in terror. In two seconds she was on her feet and running to her boys' room, so fast that she did not feel the cold floor beneath her. She looked in, but all was still and silent. She had recognized that it was a boy's cry, but she went to the girls' room anyway to check that Eleanor and Susan were all right. Then she heard the cry again. It was coming from a distance—another part of the castle. It was not one of her children, so she returned to her room, expecting to receive her husband's admonitions, but when she crawled back into bed, she noticed that he was gone. She had not seen him leave.

Her feeling of oppression was replaced by a tight sense of fear. She lay shivering in the darkness until weariness at last overtook her, and she slept.

In the morning, his side of the bed was still empty. Where had he gone? Perhaps he had come back during the night and then left again early without waking her. Perhaps he had not come back. The cold white sheet revealed nothing.

~~*

During the night when Susan had been startled into flight, John had awoken and recognized Alexander's cry. Immediately, he got up and followed Susan out the door. When she turned into her sons' room, he had gone out the sitting room door.

Halfway to Penelope's apartment, his mind awoke and asked him what he was doing. The boy needs a father tonight, he answered. 'Tis none of your affair: the boy is not yours, his mind answered.

John almost turned back at the logic of his mind, but his legs kept moving him in the direction of the wee lad's cry. He recalled Alexander's brave eyes looking up at him when he had been strapped a few years before. He had fallen in love with the fatherless child then, but he had not realized it until this moment.

He knocked on the door to Penelope's apartment. In a moment she opened it, looking disheveled and frightened. He glanced at her chemise, and her hand reached up and clutched his robe. "Mr. Dean!" she cried. "Can you help me? It's Alexander. He has had a nightmare."

"No doubt," John replied. "The lad has had a frightening day at school."

"Really? I did not know."

"Of course. He would not tell you because he was embarrassed by it. I was remiss in not informing you earlier. Perhaps I may compensate now by giving the lad some comfort."

"Please, come in." Penelope released his robe and stepped aside to admit him. Brushing so close to her, he caught a whiff of her scent. Some flower he could not identify. It unnerved him.

"Sir," she said. "I am most grateful for your assistance. What is it that happened at school?"

"Alexander was teased by the other boys because of his parentage." Here, he stopped and fixed his eye on her, hoping it would serve as a sermon for the moment, until he had comforted the boy. "My sons, James and Johnny, came to his rescue and were sent home for fighting. I regret that I did not inform you of this incident earlier, madam, so that you would have been better prepared to deal with his fears."

"I would be so grateful to you if you would speak to him now."

"Aye, madam."

She directed him to Alexander's room. He saw Alexander sitting bolt upright in his bed among the disarray of sheets. His eyes were wide, shining in the light of a candle that cast dark, flickering shadows into the corners of the room.

Alexander's eyes grew wider still as John entered.

"Dinna fear, master Alexander. I havena come to punish ye tonight. May I sit on your bed, lad."

Alexander sobbed, unable to speak, but he nodded.

"You have had a terrible dream, lad."

The little boy nodded.

"We call that a nightmare, but 'tis not real. You needna fear any longer. You are awake and the dream is over."

Alexander's big brown eyes looked up at him. "But I dinna want to go to school anymore," he said quickly.

"Some of the lads were cruel to you," John stated.

"Aye."

"But James and Johnny put them in their place, did they not?"

Alexander smiled through his tears and nodded.

"So now you maun go to school tomorrow. You maun show those bullies that you dinna care a fig for their words. They'll not assault you again, for if they do, they will have to answer to James and Johnny, and bullies are really great cowards underneath."

"Are they?" the boy asked.

"Aye, that they are. They willna touch you again, you may be sure."

"When I get bigger I shall beat them myself. One day when I am Alexander the Great."

"That you will, lad. That you will. Go to sleep now, and dream about the day when you will be a great man."

"Aye, Papa," the child let slip. John was strangely touched. Neither of the adults corrected him.

He lay down on the bed again and his mother did her best to arrange the blankets about him comfortably. "I shall just go and see Mr. Dean out now. Sleep well, my son," she said. Then she kissed him and walked out the door that John was holding for her.

As she brushed by him he smelled her perfume again. This time he recognized it as lily of the valley, that tiny shy white flower that hides beneath great green leaves in the springtime. He followed her to the sitting room.

She turned to him, her eyes over-brimming pools sparkling in the half-light. "I cannot thank you enough, Mr. Dean." She kissed him. Suddenly. Lightly. A mere gesture of thanks, he presumed. But something about the sweetness of the gesture, the scent of the perfume, the darkness, the aching of his own heart, made him respond. Deeply, passionately. He put his arms around her to hold her in place while he kissed her and he felt her body become liquid in his grasp. He knew he had only to take and she would be his.

He felt his face flush and the heat only inflamed him more. But his mind recognized the blush as shame and began to speak to him. You cannot do this. You must not do this.

He was angry at the interference of his meddling mind. He knew he would need to heed it—either now or later. And he knew it would be much worse later.

But his body kept saying, just a little more and I will stop. Just a little more sweetness.

His anger at himself made his actions swift and brutal.

He pushed her back against the wall, lifted her thin chemise and found the crease between her legs, already moist and welcoming. Swift and brutal and far too easy. A distant sense of annoyance with himself.

He withdrew abruptly and threw her aside.

He could not go back to his wife's bed, so he walked to a distant room of the castle where he sat staring out the window at his garden, wishing it were warmer so he could go out.

He hated this castle. It was cold and full of ancient ghosts. Even the children had grown tired of playing in it, he thought. He had to redouble his efforts to get out of here.

He wished with all his heart he could have this night back again.

All the fears he had had for the immortal souls of his wife and children, and he was the one who had gone and thrown his own away.

~~*

In the morning, Susan arose and left the empty bed behind her. She went to wake her sons so that they could get ready for school.

"Quietly now," she said. "Do not wake Will and Davy."

She returned to her room to dress herself. A few moments later there was a knock at the door. She answered it still in her shift, praying that it would be John, but knowing that he would not have knocked. Still, perhaps there was news of him.

When she opened it, Penelope was standing there, looking fresh and well-dressed. "Oh." Susan had not expected her.

"May I come in to speak to your two sons? I want to thank them for their protection of Alexander. May I see them before they leave for school?"

"If you do not mind waiting in the sitting room while they dress, I shall let them know you are here."

Susan went into her sons' room again and told them Miss Dering was there waiting to see them so they should dress before coming out. Then she went back to her own room to continue her toilette, excusing herself to Penelope for leaving her alone.

A few minutes later, while tying up her bodice, Susan heard voices on the other side of the door. At first she thought the boys had come out to talk to Penelope, but the voices were whispering, which seemed rather strange. She went to the door of her room and put her ear against it. It was John's voice, whispering to Penelope, though he sounded angry. She had not heard him come in. Maddeningly, she could not make out any of his words. Why did he need to whisper?

She went back to the looking glass to check her hair, sweeping up the untidy strands and pinning them in a sort of temporary order. Then she went to the door and opened it.

They stopped whispering and looked at her. Susan was startled by the guilt she recognized in her husband's eyes. Never in all their marriage had she once suspected he would be capable of infidelity to her.

The silence continued, awkward and terrifying, like another presence in the room.

Finally, the door to her sons' room opened and the boys came out, loud and full of life.

"Good morning, Miss Dering," James said.

"Good morning, James. Good morning, Johnny." Penelope recovered her aplomb. "I wanted to tell you how proud I am that you defended my little Alexander yesterday. May I have leave to reward each of you with a kiss?"

Before Susan could say no, the two boys blushed and nodded. Penelope stepped forward and kissed each of them on the forehead. It felt to Susan as if Penelope were assaulting their innocence. She could see that John was uncomfortable also, but like her, he stood still and said nothing.

Then Penelope stepped back and addressed the boys again. "I came to ask if you would accompany Alexander to school today and look after him again if it is necessary."

"We will certainly, madam," James assured her. Susan felt her heart tighten. He spoke like a young man instead of a boy.

"But, madam, you ought not to place my sons in jeopardy again. They have already been expelled from school over this matter, and their education might be compromised if they are expelled again," John said.

"Of course, you are right, sir. I would not wish the boys to get into any trouble. I only hope they will do whatever they can to protect my son. As you said yourself to Alexander last night, it is most unlikely that the other boys will attack again."

Susan looked at her husband. So, he had been in Penelope's apartment last night. He did not return her gaze.

"Well, I must go to breakfast now." Penelope bustled out of their apartment.

"The boys will fetch young Alexander before they leave, madam," John said as she departed. Then John and the boys left to go to the kitchen, but Susan held back.

"Aren't you coming, Mama?" Johnny asked.

"No. I shall stay and see to the other children, in case they should waken. I shall have breakfast when Nanny Henry comes to relieve me. Have a good day at school, boys, and do not get into any more trouble, no matter what Miss Dering asks of you. You will speak to them, John?"

He looked at her finally, his eyes sincere. "I shall," he said.

They would talk about this later, she thought. Or perhaps they would not. Would he tell her what he had done? She doubted it, and anyway, it would be easier for her not to know. She would not be required to forgive if she did not know. Forgiveness was merely another kind of cheating. You said you forgave, but your heart could not. The anger that she felt was too much like grief; only time could assuage it.

She finally understood that they must leave this place. It was clear to her now that from the beginning John had been fighting for their marriage. She wished to have back all the times that she had defied him. This was her punishment for being willful. She hoped with all her heart that he would still want to leave, that he was not under Penelope's spell. They had to go at once. Their marriage would be forever ruptured if they did not. It was a broken marriage now, but it could still be mended.

If they talked later, she knew it would be about going away. She began to plan what she would say.

~~*

All that day, and the many days that followed, John tried to come to terms with this new creature that he had become—a sinner.

Of course, he had committed sins before, but for the most part, they were unimportant, the sins of everyday life, of inescapable human nature-- anger, impatience, little white lies. In fact, he had been rather proud of his greatest sin, the prideful sense that he had been better than almost everyone else.

All that was gone now, and he felt as if he were being tossed in a storm at sea, running from one side of the ship and then back to the other. None of the arguments his mind dredged up was able to provide him with solace, but he could not stop his thoughts from tumbling up, all willy-nilly, each one uglier than the next.

"It was her fault, the wicked seductive temptress Penelope. How could you have fallen for her tricks?" he asked himself

His mind fleeted to that brief encounter and his senses were drunk again with the colours in the soft candlelight, the perfume, the sweet temptation of her lips. Then his lewd wanton rapid grasping. He was angry with himself. "You should have taken your time and enjoyed it more. If you have to suffer the stings of conscience now, at least you could have savoured the stolen moment of sin more deeply."

Though this evil thought passed through his head faster than the time it took to read the words, it only added to the burden of guilt that he was feeling. He prayed for forgiveness for having thought it, prayed it would not return.

"Your actions are your own fault, no one else's."

"But if only Susan had been a more obedient wife in the last few years. If only she had listened to me when I wanted to move, none of this would have happened."

"It isn't her fault," he told himself.

"Not exactly, but…" He could not help feeling that her willfulness mitigated his action in some way. His conscience sought some refuge in this justification.

"You know that two wrongs do not make a right. You know that her behaviour does not justify your sin." There was no refuge there.

"But if only I'd never met her, I would be far away from this place now, in North America." He let his mind wander to any idyllic Eden in the New World. "I have been lost from the moment I met her. She manipulated me into this marriage against my will."

"You are lying to yourself. It has never been against your will. You have always wanted her, always loved her. How could you have betrayed that love?" It was inconceivable to him that he had done it, and for something as worthless as that moment of sin.

He would scourge himself of it somehow.

"Should I tell her?"

His heart sank. "How can I tell her? What purpose would it serve except to hurt her more?"

"But will my penitence be complete if I do not tell her?"

He did not wish for its completion. He wanted to hold it constantly in his bare hand—a live cinder—so that he could remember, and never sin in such a way again.

He was angry with the devil who had taken up residence in his head, but for the longest time, in spite of all his prayers, he could not seem to shake him loose.

~~*

Susan watched John now, day and night, but especially night. She stayed awake night after night in case he left her and then she was cranky all day long. He never left her bed, so she started to sleep again, the kind of sleep a new mother has, near the surface and ready to wake at the smallest sounds. It was not much more restful than no sleep, and her day-time humour continued to suffer.

She watched him in the daytime, too. Myriad times in the morning her eyes of their own volition would seek the window and she would go to it and find him in the garden. She would watch him at work, anxious that no one should come to visit him. If the weather was bad and he worked indoors, she would walk by his office, listening at the door for voices.

The strain was becoming too much to bear. She could not bring herself to speak to him about it and end the suspense, though. She began to see that he was sorry and that he would not resume any affair that he may have briefly entertained with Penelope. Gladly she would forgive him, if he told her, but he would have to tell her. She would not beg the truth from him.

Gradually she almost began to believe that she had imagined the whole incident. Nothing had happened. But there was another way to know for certain, a way she dreaded to take but knew she must. All of her vigilance would count for nothing if Penelope decided to move in on her husband. If he had succumbed to her once, he could fall again. There was no doubt that Penelope was skillful enough to succeed if she willed it. And Susan had no doubt but that Penelope would tell her the truth. With her it would not be a matter of confession but rather a badge of pride.

Against her own will, but desperate for a kind of resolution and an outlet for her repressed rage, Susan prepared herself to face her opponent and former friend.

Penelope greeted her with surprise and welcomed her in to the sitting room with her accustomed warmth. "Come in. It has been a long time since your last visit. What brings you here now?"

Susan entered, her face set in a grim expression. "We have to talk," she said.

Penelope turned to the nanny. "Jean, would you take Penny for a walk. 'Tis a lovely day for it."

The nanny nodded and carried Penny from the apartment.

"Now, Susan. Would you like some tea?"

Susan would not be seduced by warm drinks and words. "No, thank you."

"What brings you here then, if it is not to resume our friendship?"

"Do not pretend to be my friend. I have come to ask a very personal question, one which a friend need never ask another friend. Have you had carnal relations with my husband?"

"Oh, dear. We are blunt, ain't we?"

"Do not speak to me as though you were the Earl. Answer my question."

"You ought to ask your own husband that. Has he not confessed? One would have thought such a Christian man would have confessed."

"That is none of your affair. I am asking you." Susan had steeled herself now. She was ready for any response.

"Well, though you were not friend enough to me to tell me when the Earl had cheated on me, I shall tell you. You are as impatient as your husband was. You go straight to the point of the matter. No dallying or banter, just thrust and jab like a schoolboy. Cannot say as I am interested in another go round with the man. You may rest assured he is safe from me."

Susan felt her cheeks redden through this speech and her heart sank down to her slippers. Cheap. She was such a common strumpet and she cheapened everything. How could Susan have sat with her day after day, bantering and blithering, when she could have been spending her time with the worthy gentleman she had married. And how could she blame him for one brief dalliance? But she did.

"How dare you speak of my husband in such coarse and unkind words! He is an honourable man and his pinky is worth more than the whole of you."

"Believe what you want to believe, but I have seen another side of him."

Susan wanted to scream in frustration. It was not so much that Penelope had had an affair with her husband, but that she was so willing to cast him aside as if he were rubbish. Penelope had robbed her of the opportunity to warn her away. She wanted to choke the insolent whore.

"Stay away from my husband," Susan hissed.

"You can be assured…"

Susan interrupted her. "And stay away from my children." Susan got up and walked to the door where she turned. "And stay away from me."

Susan went out and slammed the door behind her. She simmered as she walked back to her apartment, not allowing herself to think any more because her thoughts fueled her anger and she needed to calm down.

She went to their family room and found the nanny with the children.

"Miss Henry, I have a headache and am going to lie down for a while."

"Aye, madam. You look unwell. May I get you anything?"

"No, thank you. Just mind the children for me."

"Aye. I will."

Susan went into her room and washed her face trying to put out the fire that burned within. Then she went to her bed, lay down and promptly fell into the kind of deep sleep she had so long been lacking.

~~*

That evening at supper in the servants' kitchen, Susan addressed her husband across the table.

"Have you received any news in response to your enquiries for employment in Ireland?" She continued to eat her potatoes as if his response was of little consequence.

John looked up anxiously. She had never shown the slightest interest in his enquiries before. Cold fear gripped his heart. "I have not, I am afraid," he said.

"How many enquiries have you sent out?" she asked with a continued attempt at nonchalance that did not fool him.

"Four," he said, "or perhaps five," trying to sound as offhand as she.

"You are not sure?" She looked up from her plate at him, accusingly, he thought.

"I am not sure if I have sent out the fifth one. It may be on my desk at the moment."

"Do you mind if I read it after supper? You are generally a better gardener than you are a pen man, and I want to be sure that you do yourself justice in the crafting of the letter. I may be able to suggest some improvements in the wording."

As the extent of her solicitude grew so did his fear. She knew. What other possible reason would she have for her sudden unprecedented desire to see him succeed in his pursuit of an Irish career? "Of course I would not mind. I appreciate your interest in my affairs."

"They are my affairs too," she said, and the way she said it, as if his remark was an insult to her, made his heart quake even more. "Your affairs are my affairs and the affairs of the children. We are a family."

He was embarrassed and looked around the table to see if anyone else had noticed her accusatory tone.

Ellon Castle, Winter, 1788

At eight o'clock in the morning it was raining. John wanted to go out and check his plans for next season's garden. He ate breakfast and waited. At nine o'clock it was still raining and showed no signs of abating; the sky was uniformly dull flat grey from one horizon to the other.

His intention to go out had not changed either. So he resigned himself to the necessity of getting cold and wet. Arming himself as well as he could against the inclement weather, John set out into the garden. He did not take his plans with him as he had proposed to do. They would have been ruined in this sodden rain.

He would do his best to place the flowers and shrubs from memory on the canvas of the true garden. After all, it was no longer a mystery to him. He had worked here almost five years now, and it was become like a child to him. As much as he wanted to leave Ellon Castle, it would be hard to leave this garden behind. He would miss it.

His eyes misted with tears so that he could scarcely see the naked boughs, the rotting foliage, the sorrow and abandonment of the garden in winter. It echoed his heart's pain.

He had almost come to terms with his sin now. His soul had reached some form of equilibrium at least. Every private prayer had become a confession and every moment spent in the garden was an absolution. The moral debate over whether to tell Susan had ended in his decision not to say a word. She had seemed to know, but she had not pressed him. They had both chosen silence as the easiest way to deal with it.

He knew full well that there was a sin in that choice. He was too proud to be brought down low before her. He could not bear to make her his confessor. Better to leave the sin unspoken. Still, he behaved as a penitent toward her, perhaps even more than he would have if he had told her the truth because there was this additional compounding sin. He added it to his daily confession. The garden was a good place to pray.

He arrived at the usual bench where he sat for this purpose. It was soggy with water, and, though for a second he balked at the idea of sitting there, his penitential soul demanded the sacrifice. He sat and began to pray.

Behind him, he heard the soft swish of a skirt. God, she was hounding him again. He was sick to death of her and he was going to finally tell the bloody whore. He turned around to address her. "Would you please…"

It was Susan.

After all this time, waiting for her to come, and she had finally come when it was too late. But he smiled in spite of that, for she had come and it meant something to him. She was not to know that it was too late.

"Would I please what?" she asked, advancing toward him.

He saw the girl she had been inside the woman she was now. Time had only made her more beautiful in his eyes, adding layers that deepened and softened her beauty and taking away none of that fresh young girl, at least not from his mind's eye. There she was eternally young.

"I am sorry, Susan. I thought you were someone else."

"To whom would you speak in such a rude manner? Mr. Henry or one of the garden workers? Certainly not one of the children? Or Miss Dering." She added that name after a pause and without a question so that he would clearly understand that she knew, he thought.

He did not respond at first. Emerging from a prayer, it was impossible for him to lie at that moment. At any rate, he did not want to lie to her. There was no point. She already knew.

"Aye," he said finally. "I thought from the sound of your skirt that it was Miss Dering. I wanted to ask her to leave off following me to the garden."

Susan smiled a weak sort of smile. "Does she often do that?"

"Not as often as she used to."John returned the same smile. "I did not expect you, Susan, or I would have been more welcoming. You do not usually come out to the garden."

She shivered. She had a woolen plaid shawl over her shoulders that she pulled a little tighter against the cold as if in explanation. "I have a particular reason for venturing into this unpleasant clime to find you. A letter has just arrived from Ireland. Perhaps it is the news we have been waiting for."

"Let us go and find out." He put his arm around her and escorted her back to the castle. They both walked in the silence of their thoughts, and each step felt like a quagmire. They would continue walking on this insecure ground until they reached a surer footing one day. Neither felt the need for a dramatic confession and forgiveness. Silence and a slow forgetting would be enough.

They arrived at the porte-cochere and John removed his great coat and shook it before entering the castle walls. Inside, Susan removed her shawl and hung it up. Then they went into the kitchen to warm their hands before the fire.

Susan picked up the envelope from the table where she had left it. "Here it is." She handed it to him.

With hands still stiff from the cold, he tore it open and read the contents to himself. His face erupted in a great smile so that it was not necessary for him to read aloud for her to know.

"I have been accepted on an estate in Ireland."

He restrained himself from taking hold of her and dancing around the room as he had done five years before.

Instead he looked at her and asked with great solemnity, "Will you come with me, Susan?"

"Intreat me not to leave thee, or to return from following after thee: for whither thou goest I will go; and where thou lodgest, I will lodge: thy people shall be my people, and thy God my God." She spoke these words to him as if she had been memorizing them for this very purpose. John's heart was full and he wanted to cry, but instead he kissed her. He kept his eyes open so that he could see her face and know that it was she that he kissed— the woman that he still loved, the mother of his children, the one who would go with him into the next chapter of his life.

~~*

In all the excitement of preparing herself and all the children for their move to a new country across the Irish Sea, Susan had quite forgotten about Penelope, who had obeyed her demands and avoided her. So, she was surprised when Penelope appeared at her apartment door one morning in February.

"May I come in, Susan?" she asked, as bold as brass.

Susan hesitated a moment.

"I have only come to say good-bye," Penelope explained.

What did it matter now? They were leaving soon. "All right, then. Come in."

She entered, her skirts all a-rustle, and planted herself in the largest armchair, looking about the sitting room. "So, 'tis true. You are leaving."

"You know it is."

"Well, as I said, I wanted to say good-bye and to wish you well. Though I also wanted to assure you that such a move is unnecessary."

"I beg to disagree," Susan said, primly certain of the rightness of her position.

"'Tis not necessary to quibble either." Penelope crossed her hands in her lap and stared at them.

"Is there anything else?"

"Yes. I want to tell you that I have come to regret my action and also the manner in which I revealed it to you. Most of all I regret the loss of our friendship."

"I am sure that you do." Susan could not help but enjoy Penelope's discomfort. "As I am sure you will continue to regret it when we are gone."

"That is true and it is the very matter I wished to discuss with you. I hope that you will write to me, Susan. Will you write to me?"

"How can you ask such a thing? I have no interest in continuing our relationship."

"But perhaps you will one day when you come to forgive me, or at least look more kindly on me."

"I cannot imagine such a day ever occurring."

"But Susan, think what power I have given you."

"I beg your pardon?"

"I have given you knowledge, and such knowledge, if it is used correctly, is power."

"You have given me nothing but heartache and unhappiness."

"You think that now, but one day you may come to think differently. Let me explain."

Susan wished she could throw her out, but she was curious to hear this explanation and nodded.

"I was devastated at first when I learned that the Earl had been unfaithful to me with that hussy Maude. But when I recovered myself, I realized I could use that knowledge to get what I wanted. You know that the Earl did not come at Christmas this year. He passed that holiday with his new family at the Fortress of Cairnbulg. But the Earl has been persuaded to repay me and my children handsomely for his neglect of us."

Susan stood up. "I do not wish to hear any more."

"No, wait. I know the Earl has very little compunction about his peccadilloes. He seems to think he has a god-given right to stomp on people's hearts. But even in a man as cruel as that, one can find a whiff of a conscience if one searches hard enough. Enough of a sense of duty, at any rate, to raise a few bobs' worth of jewels." Penelope fingered a string of pearls around her neck. "Imagine, dear, what you could wring from Mr. Dean. Anything your heart desires, Susan, provided of course, that it is within his means to give it to you. I hope that his new employment will be lucrative."

Susan felt herself blushing. Penelope was sordidly mercenary to the end. "That is none of your affair. And at any rate, I want nothing from my husband but his steadfast heart, which I have already." Susan walked to the door. "So good day to you, madam."

"Will you write to me, do you think?"

"Good bye, Miss Dering."

Penelope stood up and smoothed the back of her gown. "Well, I am sure you will one day when you know what power you have."

Then she swept out of the room, and Susan slammed the door after her, angry with herself, in spite of her best effort not to be, for having listened.

Chapter 7

En route to Ireland, Spring, 1789

The gentle lapping of water on the sides of the ship was a muted background to the snapping of the sheets filling with wind, the squeaking ropes and the clanking metal. The icy wind carried the scent of spring flowers on the fresh air.

They were on a ship bound for Ireland, having left the port of Aberdeen earlier that morning. Behind them was their castle home, their good friends the Henrys, the beautiful mistress of the castle who had torn the fabric of their marriage, and her children, Alexander, the one who would be great but whose heart had almost shattered at their going, and the little girl named Penny after her mother.

For a large part of their voyage they traveled through a new canal that sliced its way from the Firth of Forth to the Firth of Clyde, cutting Scotland in half and reducing the distance that had to be traveled on the rough and open sea.

Susan knew that John was delighted to be so long within sight of land, watching its natural vegetation, identifying plants and observing the contrasts of the colours—the dusky purple and the deep green of heather, the bright flashes of yellow on the green broom, the tan fields of waving grasses. He did not relish the dark unnaturally coloured waves of the dangerous sea.

Nor did Susan. For her the reason was more physical, that her stomach was not disturbed and upset. The ship did not heave beneath her feet and she could watch and listen to her children. Oh, what contentment there was in watching tehm. They were infinitely interesting, each an individual, each different, filled with energy, always interacting, inventing, imagining.

She heard their delighted voices, not above the sailors' cries, but in the middle somehow, woven within. The older boys James and Johnny were standing discreetly by the sailors, asking questions. John had a tight hold on the younger boys Will and Davy, who wanted to jump in and get in the way.

John was wary of sailors. It stemmed from his experience of being impressed. He stayed close to Susan as if she could save him again if he got in trouble. And the girls stayed close to their mother too—Eleanor because it was her nature, and Susie because she was a baby still and her mother would not let it be any other way. There was an invisible cord that held them together, and Susan hung on to it, aware of the dangers—of falling overboard, of being abducted, of being trampled on, of running and running until you became one with the wind, of leaving the earth, of flying away.

To think that she and John had peopled this part of the earth and now were moving their family to another part, to a new adventure, to a new home.

Susan was more glad of that than she had ever thought possible. She looked at John and smiled. Then his face was transformed. Clearly, clearly, she could see its expression change, relax and become like the face that he wore at the end of a church service on Sunday.

It was as if he had received her benediction.

End Notes

In the genealogical search of our great-great-great-great-grandparents Susan Kirke and John Dean, my cousin Noreen Dean found this transcription in the Old Parochial Records of Scotland: Susan Kirk Dean born 11/11/1787, christened 18/11/1787, father John Dean, gardener at Ellon Castle, mother Susan Kirk, witnesses Matthew and Lavinia Henry.

In 2000, I visited Ellon Castle near Aberdeen. The garden is still there after more than 200 years, and it is part of the Scottish National Trust. A photo of the ruins of the castle and part of the garden graces the cover of this novel. While in Ellon, I visited the local library and found an article on the history of the castle. At the time Dean was the gardener there, it was owned by the "wicked" Earl of Aberdeen who had set up his mistress there with her children. The book *Scotland's Castles and Great Houses* by Magnus Magnusson describes what a strange and fascinating individual George Gordon, Earl of Aberdeen was. So, the idea for *The Gardener's Wife* was born.

Since the novel was completed, the website Scotland's People has released the actual handwritten entry of Susan Dean's baptism from its Parochial Records, and it reads: witnesses Matthew and his son Louis Henry. Out of a poor transcription, Lavinia Henry was born, but as this is my fanciful recreation of a time long past, I know you will not mind.

Another error I have recently discovered relates to the fourth book of the series *A Garden in the Wilderness*. In it, Daniel and Alexander Henry, who live in Upper Musquodoboit, Nova Scotia where the Deans settle, are the sons of Matthew and Lavinia. Further research has proven that they came with their father James from Caithness County, Scotland (coincidentally where my Malcolm ancestors also come from). That does not preclude the possibility that they may have been related to the Ellon Henrys.

At this distance in time it is difficult to learn everything, and so, in a very real sense, historical fiction is speculative fiction also.

About the Author

Edeana Malcolm discovered the story of Susan Kirke and John Dean while researching the genealogy of her maternal grandfather Everett Dean and his family in Nova Scotia. The couple's scandalous love story and subsequent journey to Nova Scotia inspired her not only to write this romance novel, but also to continue the series about their later life together in Scotland, Ireland and Nova Scotia. The final book in the series *A Garden in the Wilderness* is available through Borealis Press at http://www.borealispress.com

Edeana has previously published six short stories and is an active member of Victoria Writers' Society. She lives in Victoria, BC with her husband David Bray. Visit her website at http://www.edeana.com

Sample Chapter of Book 3

Letters from the Gardener

CHAPTER 1

Belfast, May, 1789
My dearest Matthew and Lavinia,
We approached the shores of the City of our Destination with trepidation. Our new land seemed to me an inferno as smoke billowed from fires on the beaches. Poor Mrs. Dean was nauseated from the reek that emanated from them. She almost tossed her collywobbles, as they say.

A deckhand informed us that this smoke was the result of seaweed being burned to produce the barilla used to bleach the white linen for which Belfast is so famous. I was apprehensive that our new home would be such a hellish place, but, on leaving the ship and penetrating further into the City beyond the shore, I was delighted at its aspect. Belfast has a nice, neat English appearance and most of its houses are made of brick.

My new employer Mr. Henry Joy met us at the dock and conveyed us to our new house on the western extremity of the town, far from the smoky beach and busy city, on the banks of the Farset River. I can scarcely describe the pleasure I feel at being master of my own cottage, though Mrs. Dean complains it is small for such a large family as ours and looks the same as the dozens of others among which it is situated. I know that the children will miss the abundant woodlands of bonny Ellon, and our good friends in Scotland, you both chief among them.

As you know, Mr. Joy is a wealthy and influential man whose family owns the paper mill, but I have since learned that they own the newspaper as well, such felicitously complementary enterprises. I will be keeping the garden at his country residence as his town house is on the High Street, and the garden that once appertained to it is now replaced with new businesses and buildings. I do not often see Mr. Joy as his time is much taken up by his financial affairs in the city, although the rest of his family, his wife and young children, are more often in residence.

Mrs. Dean has recovered from the effects of our brief sea voyage, which did not much agree with her. Like an exotic, she does not well tolerate being transplanted. Her bruised and torn roots take a long while to acclimatize to unfamiliar soil. She requires the gardener's especial attention and care. Mrs. Dean sends her warmest regards to you and all the occupants of Ellon Castle, which, adjoined with my own, I hope that you will be so kind as to share with others of our acquaintance there.

Yours most sincerely,
John Dean

"I am not a shrub, John," Susan said as she squinted at her husband over the letter he had given her to read for her approval. It had given her a headache to decipher his handwritten flourishes and she was in a foul mood. "What I require are servants."

He scowled. "Dinna fash. Mr. Joy has placed an advertisement for a housekeeper in the News-Letter. What I wanted to know is if you would like to add a post scriptum to the letter?"

"You have already expressed my regards," she said as she deposited the letter on the table between them. "Besides, I have no time to write. I am worked off my feet. I am glad we shall have a housekeeper soon, but I cannot manage with just one servant."

"You managed with one at Ellon Castle," he said, picking up the letter. "I shall post it then."

"Yes, but at Ellon Castle we had our meals provided and our laundry and housekeeping done. All that I required was a nurse for the babies."

"The bairns are grown so you have no more need of a nurse."

"How can you say that? Susie is only two years old." Her voice was getting shriller with frustration.

"I havena the means to pay for more than one servant," he said firmly, standing up to leave the room.

Susan knew there would be no more discussion.

"'Tis time to put this bairn to bed," John said as he almost collided with wee Susie who was coming through the doorway.

Susan got up and went to her youngest child, who looked as exhausted as her mother felt. "Come, dear. Let's find your bed."

As she was singing a lullaby to settle Susie, her two youngest boys came into the bedroom. "We want you to tell us a story before bed, Mama," six-year-old Will said.

"Yes, Mama. Tell us a story," his younger brother Davy agreed.

"Hush. I'm trying to calm your sister."

Susie sat up in bed, her eyes wide with anticipation, and said, "Story."

"All right," Susan acquiesced.

The boys sat on the edge of their sister's bed and looked at her.

They were attentive no matter how many times she repeated the same story, and she was just as eager to repeat the tale. "When I was a little girl, I lived in a fine big mansion in England. Three-- no maybe four -- houses the size of this cottage would have fit in it. I was the only child; I had no brothers and sisters. But the house was filled with servants, upstairs and downstairs, and every which way. We had a garden... Oh, let me tell you about that garden. The whole town of Belfast could have fit into that garden.

There were serpentine paths and shrubberies, a wilderness and arbors. There was even a temple and statues. While I was a little girl growing up, the garden was growing too. Every year something new was added, and whenever I played in the garden, I would make new discoveries."

"Tell us about the best discovery you ever made in the garden, Mama," Will asked.

"That was much later, when I was nearly grown up. I want to tell you about when I was a little girl."

"No, tell us about the best discovery, Mama," Davy pleaded.

They tolerated only a little variation in the way she told the tale. "Indeed," she said. "One day, I found the gardener standing in the early morning dew, scything the long grass. He was the most handsome man that I had ever seen." Susan halted her story for a moment while she savoured the memory of that sight.

"Who was he, Mama?" Davy asked.

"He was Papa." Will stole his mother's surprise ending, and both the boys giggled. Susie clapped her hands.

"Was Papa a handsome man then?" Will asked.

"What do you mean? Your papa is still a handsome man. Do you not agree with me, Susie?" The little girl nodded her head in agreement.

Susan remembered their first meeting in the garden and their long conversations along its serpentine path. Their lives had followed an equally sinuous route since then. The thirteen years of their marriage had not seemed to alter her husband, but they had greatly altered her. She gave her three youngest children a weak smile before continuing the arduous task of settling them for the night.

***

Susan glanced at the row of neat brick houses as she walked by. Each house was an unadorned box so like their own that she feared she would not be able to distinguish it on her return. Fortunately, her four boys who were with her assured her they could identify it. As she walked into town, she noticed a smoky haze obscured the sky so that she could not tell whether the sun was shining or the sky was grey. She thought of the clean crisp air far away in Scotland and the grey heron that used to stand on the shore of the Ythan River waiting for a fish to flash by.

"Shit!"

Her son's curse yanked her back to the present. She saw that Will had indeed stepped in something unpleasant in the roadway. The other boys had erupted in giggles.

"Mind your tongue, Will!" Susan struggled to suppress a smile. "Wipe your shoe on the cobblestone and we shall clean it better when we get home. Now, all of you, mind where you tread." She wondered where the boy had learned such language.

Susan smelled the stench, not only from Will's shoe, but also hanging in the greasy, smoky air. She stepped carefully over the refuse scattered about the unclean streets as they made their way through the ever-increasing human traffic near the centre of town.

Having left young Susie sleeping in the care of her ten-year-old sister Eleanor, Susan had set out with her four restless boys to provide them amusement and exercise and to buy some washing soap because John needed clean working clothes for the morrow. The reason that they must be clean at the start of each day eluded her. It was certain that they would be soiled again within the first half hour of digging and mucking in the garden.

Though this was their first venture into town, they had no difficulty finding the market, which consisted of a great many well-stocked stalls aligning the High Street. Susan examined the smiling faces of the women vendors chattering to each other behind the tables spread with their wares. Finally, she addressed the stout woman at the closest table. "Have you any washing soap?"

"What'd you say, missus?' The woman squinted at her.

"I asked if you might have some washing soap."

The women's next-door neighbour elbowed her. "Ain't she a fine English lady, then?" The two crones started to laugh.

Susan could feel her face redden at their rudeness. She stood there looking at them, waiting for them to recover from their hilarity.

James her eldest came to her rescue. He jutted his chin and declared, "Our mother is a fine English lady. So, answer her question, do you have any washing soap or not?"

The stout woman took a deep breath and regained control of herself. "Oh, I have not had such a good chuckle in a long time." Then she produced a bar of yellow soap and handed it to James.

"Dinna mind our mother. She is fra' England," Johnny said to the two women.

"Aye, that she is. And how does she come for to have such bonny Scotch lads?" the neighbour lady asked him.

Perhaps she married a Scotchman, Susan thought but did not say. She could not bring herself to speak another word to these women lest they should laugh at her accent again. So, she put down a ha'penny and turned away without bothering to explore the rest of the market. The boys reluctantly followed her.

By counting the number from the end of the street, they found their house.

"Eleanor, we have returned. Is everything all right?"

"Aye, Mama. Susie is still sleeping. Have you got the washing soap?"

"Yes," she replied, a little annoyed.

Susan put a large kettle of water on the fire. She struggled with the vat, trying to pull it into the centre of the kitchen. Then she sat back.

"What shall we do while we wait for the water to boil?"

"We could prepare dinner while we wait."

"Prepare dinner! Already? It seems as though we just ate breakfast."

"What did you buy at the market?"

Susan blushed. She should have thought of that. "Nothing," she admitted.

"Well, then, we shall make parritch again. You can go back to the market again this afternoon."

Susan thought of the embarrassment she had suffered there. She did not want to go again, but parritch for supper would be too much and then there would be none left for breakfast the next day. Perhaps she would send James.

When the water was finally boiling, Susan poured it into the vat, refilled the kettle and put it back on the fire. Then she took the bar of soap so newly purchased, and with a knife, peeled the yellow curls, dropping them into the vat.

"You must make sure that the soap is well dissolved or it will leave a residue on the clothes," Eleanor informed her mother.

"How did you get to be such a know-it-all?" Susan asked.

"I used to watch the washer-woman at Ellon Castle."

Susan was grateful that Eleanor had been so astute. She had never bothered to observe anyone washing clothes before. When the vat was full of hot water from the kettle, she put John's clothes into the soapy water to soak.

After a dinner of parritch, Susan scrubbed the clothes on a washboard one item at a time, and lifted them into a second vat where she rinsed them. When it came time to wring out the excess water from the clothes, Susan wished she had not sent the boys to the market to buy potatoes. She could have used their strength as she twisted the garments as hard as she could whilst poor little Eleanor held the other end. Then Susan hung them on a line in the garden, still heavy and dripping with moisture despite their best efforts.

At the end of it, Susan was exhausted, her arms ached, and she felt she could not do another chore, but there were still potatoes to peel and Susie was scattering clothes from a box that had not yet been unpacked.

When John arrived home from his garden, she was not in a cheerful mood. When he came to give her a kiss on the cheek, she sighed.

"What ails you, Susan?"

"Eleanor and I have washed your clothes today."

"Aye?" he asked, as if it were nothing at all.

"I have never washed clothes before. It is a great deal more work than it looks to be, John. Have you ever washed clothes?"

"I do women's work?" John laughed.

"Then you have no idea how difficult it is, so you ought not to make light of it. We must hire a washerwoman, John. I am not equal to the task."

The smile vanished from John's face. "Do you imagine me to be a wealthy man like your father? I have income to provide you with one servant, and one servant only, so consider well which it is to be—a cook, a nurse, a washerwoman or a housekeeper. I am only surprised you do not ask for a lady's maid as well."

"I have lived without a lady's maid for a long time as you well know and you do me wrong to even mention it."

"I am sorry, my dear. I admit you are an excellent mother, so you have no need of a nurse, and you and Eleanor together managed to wash my clothes today, so you know that can be done. You may even learn to cook one day," he said smiling.

Susan groaned.

"Is that the worst of your day then, a little hard work?"

"No, it is not. I went with the boys to the market to buy the washing soap."

"Aye?"

"The women there mocked my English accent."

"They didna."

"They did indeed. You may ask the boys."

"Well, and if I had a penny for all the Englishmen who mocked my Scottish burr, I might be able to buy you more servants. You might learn as I did, to emulate the accent of the people around you so they take no notice of you," he said, putting on his best English accent.

She had not heard him speak like that in many years, and she smiled in spite of herself.

The next day, when his gardening clothes still hung damp on the clothes line, John relented enough to give Susan permission to hire a part-time washing woman.

***

The young woman at the door looked as hale and hearty as any Susan had ever seen. She introduced herself, but Susan found the name so foreign to her ears that she asked her to repeat it.

"Meghan Byrne," she said.

Susan smiled. "Come in and have a seat, missus."

"I have come about the advertisement for a housekeeper that I saw in the Belfast News-Letter," she said once comfortably seated. She looked about her. Every one of Susan's six was peering in from the kitchen doorway. "Are those all yours, madam?"

"Yes," Susan responded. "Aye." She was thinking of John's remark of the night before but she did not know which of the two words was the correct response in Belfast.

The young woman waited politely for Susan to speak again, but when no question was forthcoming, she asked, "What will I be expected for to do, madam?"

"Well," Susan looked at her hands. "Keep house, of course." In for a penny in for a pound, she thought, and continued. "And cook and do the laundry."

The woman looked aghast. "I am not a washerwoman, madam. If I was to do the washing for a family this size, I should have no time to clean house."

"But you can cook?" Susan asked hopefully.

"Yes, but if I have to cook, I am afraid my house-cleaning chores will suffer."

"Never mind that. We can make do with a dirty house, but we must eat."

"If you say so, madam, but I cannot do breakfast. I cannot arrive so early in the morning. 'Tis a good long walk from my home to here."

Susan had imagined that their servant would live with them, but there was no room to lodge a servant in this little box. "Of course not. I am sure I can manage to make the parritch," she said. "I did it this morning." The burnt smell still lingered in the air. John had hurried out the door claiming to be late, and the children had done their best to eat it, but most of it had been thrown out.

"When can you start?" Susan asked, her growling stomach urging her to hire the woman.

"What will you pay me?"

Susan named the amount that John had said she might spend.

"I think if I am expected for to do the cooking as well, I should receive more than that."

"'Tis all I have, missus. Take it or leave it."

"I shall take it. Do you want I start now?"

"Yes. Can you begin by making dinner? The children are hungry."

As if on cue, they burst through the door to confirm their mother's assessment.

"Quiet, children. One at a time," Susan admonished them. She wanted to introduce the new servant to them but could not. "Can you repeat your name to them, missus?"

"I am Meghan Byrne."

As earnestly as she listened, Susan could only barely make out the first syllable. "May I call you Meg?" she asked.

"If you must, and what shall I call you?"

"Mrs. Dean," Susan responded. "Let me show you the kitchen."

That afternoon, true to her oath of the night before, Susan asked her new housekeeper if she knew of a washerwoman. Meg named her aunt, who accompanied her the next morning. She turned out to be a big, beefy woman by the name of Mrs. Connor with arms as broad as Susan's neck and a ready smile on her red face. Susan could barely understand her, but she repeated everything with a good humour until she was understood. She said she would come twice a week to do the washing. When their bargain was struck, Susan was so happy that she wanted to hug the dear woman, but she hugged Susie instead.

***

Susan sat at the table in the sitting room fanning herself against the heat that still lingered in their box on this sweltering August evening. John sat down beside her and opened the post that had arrived for him that morning. Susan watched him. The letter had aroused her curiosity. It was from Ellon Castle but was addressed only to John and not to her, which she found rather strange. In spite of her inquisitiveness, she had not opened it. There appeared to be a second letter inside the first. John put the first aside after only a brief glimpse and began to read the interior epistle. His face grew solemn and she worried it might be from Penelope.

"Who is that letter from?"

"You will never imagine."

"Tell me."

He did not respond but held his hand out to silence her until he had read to the bottom of the page. Then he looked at her with such a look of pity that she could scarcely abide it.

"Tell me," she said, with restrained anger.

"Do you remember Herbert Fitzwilliam?"

Her anger vanished. "I am not likely to forget him, am I?" He was a cousin of her mother's to whom she had been betrothed long ago when she ran away to marry John. Even when her parents disowned her, the strange Mr. Fitzwilliam proved to be their friend by aiding them in their elopement. She never understood why he had agreed to marry her in the first place nor why, in spite of his agreement, he had helped her to escape with another man.

"He writes with news of your father."

Susan felt the blood seep from her face and she grasped the edge of the table.

"Calm yourself, Mrs. Dean," her husband said.

The formality of his address warned her that what she feared was a certainty.

"He writes to inform us that your father is dead." John spoke so softly that she could scarcely hear him. She felt her heart cease to beat for a moment and then resume.

"Let me read the letter."

John handed it to her.

London, February, 1789
Dear Mr. Dean,

I address this letter to you and not your wife as I wish you to convey its contents to her as you see fittest. They are, I am sorry to relate, not news of a happy nature. Mrs. Dean's father, James Kirke, after a long illness, nothing to you, so I will not mention it. We have as yet not been blessed with progeny, though at our advancing years, it is little to be looked for. At any rate, Mrs. Fitzwilliam has two sons from her previous marriage and this is enough of a challenge for me.

I am sorry that I have no word of sympathy for Mrs. Dean from her mother, but please extend my deepest sympathies to your lovely wife as a poor substitute.

I remain, your affectionate and devoted friend,
Herbert Fitzwilliam, MP

Susan put down the letter and felt the tears come. Her father had been dead for several months already without her knowledge. Why did she weep for him now?

After her marriage to John, he had cut her off without a penny, leaving her family to live on John's income alone. Then he had done all he could to thwart John's efforts to make a decent salary. Her father's blacklisting of her husband was the reason that they wandered all over Britain looking for a home and why they were in this wretched town now. He was the reason that they were impoverished and why she had to bargain with her husband to have more than one servant. Why should she weep for him?

Susie tugged at Susan's long skirt, whimpering to be picked up. Before she could attend to her, her four wild boys came running through the parlour, and little Susie let go her mother's skirt and toddled out to join her brothers where she was promptly knocked down. From her seat on the floor, she howled her outraged indignation. Eleanor put down the book she had been reading and went to pick her up.

John threw up his hands and cried out, "Can we not have peace in our ain hame? Your mother has just received some sad news and needs some quiet now. Be off to your rooms."

The two oldest boys and Eleanor left immediately with Susie, but Will and Davy stared at their mother.

"I sent you to bed. Why are you standing there?" John asked.

The youngest one, Davy, said, "We want Mama to put us to bed."

"Off with you now," their father commanded.

"'Tis all right. I shall take them up."

She went up the stairs with the pair of them, feeling weary with the weight of her news. While she tucked them in, she wept quietly. Will seemed embarrassed by her tears, but Davy asked, "Why are you weeping, Mama?"

"My papa has died."

Davy's eyes opened wide with fear.

"Papa didna die. He is just downstairs," Will said.

"Not your papa, dear. My papa," Susan said.

"Do you have a papa?" Davy asked.

William explained to him that everyone has a papa.

"Do you have a mama, too?" Davy looked incredulous. Susan could see that he had never considered this a possibility. Little wonder. The children had grown up without knowing their grandparents. The family had stopped at Dundee on the way from Ellon to Belfast and visited John's mother, and the children had loved her immediately. She reminded them of Lavinia, who was like a grandmother to them.

How could Susan tell them of her own mother? She would not.

"No," she replied, contradicting Will, who had just said that everyone has a mama.

"You do not?" he asked her.

"No."

"Are you crying for her?" Will said.

I am not. Nor ever shall. She had wept for the lack of a mother's love when she was the age that Will was now. Her mother's heart was pinched as tight as a penny in the hand of a miser. It was not surprising that she had shown no pity for the willful young woman that Susan had become, the one who had run away with the gardener; she had never shown any pity for the little girl who had tried so hard to please her.

When she was a child, Susan used to follow her mother about, just as her own little namesake did now. She remembered her mother's shrill voice as she had called for the nurse. "Come and take this child away, will you? I cannot abide her whimpering."

Susan kissed the boys and then went to give a good-night kiss to Susie. She remembered when she had been called Susie too, a little girl waiting at the edge of the garden for her father. They were going to walk and he was going to show her the garden's latest fantasy. The sky was unusually cloudless and it was a perfect day for such an outing.

As she waited, the sun beat down on her, causing her to squint, and she realized that she ought to have put on a bonnet. Her mother would be cross with her. She hoped her father would come out soon.

Where was he? He ought to have been there by now? Soon her pale skin would redden and her mother would know that she had not worn her bonnet. Perhaps she ought to go back inside and send the maid to fetch it.

This ten-year-old Susie pressed the great iron latch on the front door and stepped back into the cool, dark foyer. She heard a great commotion. It was her mother and father shouting at each other. She cringed.

She wished that she had run into the woods where the trees would have protected her from the sunlight and where she would not have been seen. She could hear her parents moving about in the very next room. Her mother was hurling objects as well as words at her father. At any moment, her mother might come through that door, and then she would have words to fling at her too.

Susie wondered if she would be able to run across the foyer to the stairs before her mother appeared. Perhaps it would be better to turn around and go back outside. But the sound of the door opening had alerted her mother already. Susie saw her mother's anger-distorted face at the parlour door.

"Here is your little wench!" Her mother screeched. "And what have you been doing?" She turned the full brunt of her anger on the child, whose heart plummeted. "Look at your face-- burned and blistered by the sun. How dare you run wild like a gypsy! What will the neighbours say? Where is your nursemaid? She will rue the day she let you run wild. Get to your chamber, child. Someone will be there soon to administer a suitable punishment, I promise you, and not that miserable milquetoast of a father either!"

It was the butler who administered the whipping in the end-- the only person in the world she grew to hate more than her mother.

Her father did not always protect her, but he did what he could. He was her only comfort and the one who taught her what it was to love, so that she could love her own children. In fact, they had comforted each other, and when Susan left, her father must have died slowly, as a once-vigorous plant is killed by a weed that wraps itself around and slowly sucks the life from it.

That was the father whom she wept for, the one who had come to her, when he could, and taken her hand and walked with her in the garden, giving her childhood its only joys.

While Susan was upstairs, John perused the letter from Matthew and Lavinia that had come with Fitzwilliam's unhappy tidings.

Ellon, July, 1789
Dear John and Susan,

The enclosed letter came for you this morning and, as it seems to bear important news, I am forwarding it forthwith. I hope the news contained therein is good. I cannot post it without including a short missive in response to your letter, for which I give you thanks.

God be praised that ye made it to Belfast safe and sound! I am writing because Matthew cannot. Although he learned his letters in school, he has used them so infrequently that he has no patience to form them now. More is the pity as he is by far the better story-teller of the pair of us. So, you must content yourselves with my banter. However, Matthew sends his best regards and, I am sure, will instruct me to include some interesting tidbits that I may have left out.

How we miss your wee'uns! The castle is so quiet without you all. It is some consolation to us that we still have the company of Alexander and Penny, though you can scarce imagine how they miss your children also. We shall never know the pleasure of grandchildren since our sons are so far away in Nova Scotia. I hope that your letters will not be as infrequent as those that come to us from that far-flung colony. My heart so rejoices when the post arrives.

Ellon is little changed since you left it, although everything is more somber without your bonny presence. I pray this brief letter finds you all in good health.

Your very good friend,
Lavinia Henry

Postscriptum: Matthew is sorry to inform you that the rhododendron has died without your excellent care, but that all other plants are thriving in the shrubbery. A new gardener is expected any day now.

There was one more letter in the bundle that had arrived from Scotland. It was addressed to Susan. John knew that it came from her friend Penelope, the mistress of

Ellon Castle. He did not want to give it to his wife to read in her present condition, so he thought he might put it aside for her to read later. Then he thought perhaps he ought to read it himself first to make sure there was nothing in it to upset Susan. He told himself that he wanted to protect her, but he knew that it was more than that. He felt an intense curiosity to know what the whore had said about him.

He had never confessed to his wife that he had cheated on her with Penelope, but she had known. It was the unspoken chasm that had come between them and the reason that they had so suddenly uprooted themselves from Scotland. John felt his guilt keenly. He also felt that to break the seal of Penelope's letter and read it would be like committing the same indiscretion all over again. He knew that if he read it, he would need to destroy it immediately so that Susan would not know that he had read it. That was not so terrible. What could the whore say that was of any consequence to either of them anymore? It was an effrontery to them that she had even written.

He tore open the seal in one swift angry motion, and read.

Ellon, August, 1789
My dear Susan,

Lavinia kindly related to me your warmest regards and gave me your address in Belfast so that I might write and thank you for your good wishes. I remember our times together with great fondness. Ellon Castle is even colder and lonelier without you and your family here to provide cheer.

Alexander has had such a terrible time without your eldest sons James and John to protect him at the school. After one particularly nasty beating, we decided to withdraw him. He is now being tutored at home by a young gentleman that the Earl has engaged. The tutor is almost as handsome as your good husband, though I know I ought not to make so bold as to say that.

Penny is as distressed as her mother with the loss of her playmate Susie. We are all in suspense awaiting a letter from you to ease our heartsickness. Please write with news of all your children. I hope that Mr. Dean is well also and that he has come, as I have, to a greater understanding of the worth of his good wife.

You remain in my heart, as I hope that I remain in yours,

Your friend,
Penelope Dering

With disappointment and guilt, John tossed the missive into the fireplace.

Made in the USA
Lexington, KY
10 December 2017